War of the l

An Achim Jeffers

War of the Heart

An Achim Jeffers Novel

By

Josiah Jay Starr

Spirit of 1811 Publishing
New Orleans, Louisiana
www.spiritof1811publishing.com

Spirit of 1811 Publishing

New Orleans, Louisiana

www.spiritof1811publishing.com

Library of Congress Control Number 2020910833

Paperback ISBN: 978-1-953-10200-3

Hardback ISBN: 978-1-953-10201-0

eBook ISBN: 978-1-953-10202-7

Audiobook ISBN: 978-1-953-10203-4

Editors: Kimberly Rose

Interior Design: Daiana Marchesi

Cover Design: Luísa Dias - https://www.luisadias.com/

Dedicated to Mildred Heard
and the loving memories of:
Doris (Dot) Johnson
John L. Drew
Jeffery Buggs
Aaron Mackey

Chapter One

This was not one of those overpriced hotel rooms in downtown New Orleans. In a place like this, there would be no cheap pillowcases, shaggy bath towels or vomit stained carpets. This wasn't exactly the room that drunken tourists would use to recover from a long night of binge drinking out on Bourbon Street. This was an exclusive Presidential Suite. The very top floor of a five-star luxury hotel. With its cool marble floors and breathtaking paintings, poor black men like me, are not supposed to be able to afford such luxury or even be allowed to come up here.

Attempting to fight away the nervous butterflies in my stomach, I once again adjusted my cheap powder blue tie before popping several peppermints into my mouth to cool my hot breath. This was indeed a foreign environment for me, and I could literally feel the heavy weight of the ambience of eloquence that surrounded me. The room's plush furniture, rare artwork and exclusive décor overwhelmed my limited existence. Unable to quail my silent discomfort, I rose from my seat and aimlessly paced the room before it's panoramic view of New Orleans caused me to stop and ponder. Looking down from behind the large panel windows, I took in the magnificent view of the Mississippi River as it stretched out towards the light blue horizon. The river seemed to churn like an angry brown mass of life from my high perch in the heavens. I noticed that several small tugboats struggled to transit the river's mighty current as I watched the swirling brown water toss them around like plastic toys. Being a black man, I could relate to the unique plight and challenges opposing the besieged tugboats. In a world where I was surrounded by such godly beauty and elegance, my every effort to fight my way forward in this world had been filled with the ugly realities of progress.

Even as a young child, I always knew that I would grow up to become a pastor, and after years of prayer and dedication, that is exactly what I had become. Yet, despite my own selfish plans for my life, God saw fit to alter my path and guided me to work for Robert Charles. At Robert Charles, I found myself fighting a war that many black men had chosen to ignore or fearfully neglect. Living this new life as a Counter-Racist hitman, I spied out White Supremacists and waited for the perfect moment to visit the vengeance of the Lord upon them. In this business, perfection and precision are paramount. I patiently counted the days until Robert Charles would order me to reap the cold law of justice from the soil of this hate-filled earth. Unlike packed Sunday services, combatting White Supremacy is an unpopular task that is too often shunned and ridiculed within black society. Due to this, I often find myself alone and detached from the very people I'm fighting to save.

Yet, from the embarrassment of luxury within this Presidential Suite, it felt like the world of chaos that I had come from was somehow fake or intangible. In this hotel room, I found myself detached from my own black reality. Inside of this privileged little bubble, I was immune from it all. While I watched the world beneath where I was at that moment, one thought dominated my mind. There is no way I could afford to stay alone in a room like this, not even for one selfish night of pure self-indulgence. Even if this unrealistic peace was all just a momentary gift. Even if this room was just a short reprieve from my dangerous reality, I decided it was best to soak it in as much as possible, while never forgetting what was truly important to me.

The only thing I was missing in this moment was her. Her presence would have made this throne a perfect one as we would both stare down at this kingdom from our perch in the heavens. I would do anything to share this moment with that beautiful black woman. To see the look in her eyes as she viewed the world

I had set before her feet. Besides, it's little things like love that motivate men to greatness or in some unfortunate cases, infamy. Before I walked through the hotel's ice-cold lobby, I had called her, but there was no response from her end. My heart hoped that she might be eager to hear from me, but instead, I felt that same ole disappointment as her phone continued to ring without her answering. Instead of hearing the sweet sound of her voice, all I heard was the robotic tone of her depressing voice mail. Once again, I was left to debate if chasing after this beautiful black woman was truly worth my efforts.

The sudden sound of a door opening and footsteps tapping on the cold marble floor broke my inner quandary. On instinct, I jerked my eyes away from the window and looked over my shoulder. It was my boss, Mr. Darryl. As our eyes met, I noticed the faint look of exhaustion on my mentor's face. His pace was slow and delicate as he walked towards me. Mr. Darryl was a short black man with a noticeable limp in his stride. His gold-plated walking cane glistened as he leaned against it with each deliberate step. He appeared stylish as his three-piece suit was perfectly tailored. The sweet fragrance of his cheap cologne reminded me of the dutiful church elders I would see at worship services as a young child. The wrinkles on his brown skin conveyed the wisdom gained from experiencing decades of life's unique plight. I could see small beads of sweat forming on his forehead, just below his fading grey hairline. This was the old wise man that had taught me everything that I knew about this business. Mr.

Darryl cultivated me from my old life as a pastor, and into my new calling as a hitman. For me, he was the earthly father of this reborn life I had chosen.

"Let's have one last look at the damn evidence before I make the final call son," Mr. Darryl explained as he pointed his cane towards the dining room set.

I grabbed my briefcase and rushed over towards the thick glass table. Out of respect, I pulled out his chair and helped ease him into his seat. After seating myself, I opened my briefcase and removed its contents. It took several minutes to arrange the evidence on the table in front of my boss as he quietly watched like a curious father, inspecting what I was doing.

"Thank you for being so patient with this old man," Mr. Darryl offered with a bright smile. "When you get my age, son, bathroom breaks tend to get a little more exciting."

"No problem Mr. Darryl," I replied with a chuckle.

He picked up a stack of photos and began thumbing through them, pausing only briefly to peer down at each one with a focused squint through his thick set of bifocals. I steadied myself for the inevitable follow-up questions I knew were surely coming. I was certain he had questions about what I had been able to find out. If he didn't have questions, our big bosses at Robert Charles would certainly have a few questions to ask me themselves.

"Young man, can you do me a favor?" Mr. Darryl asked without even bothering to look up at me. "In the refrigerator, on the bottom drawer to the left, there is a bottle of natural apple juice sitting next to a small fifth of Jack. Make me a drink please."

"Yes sir!" I murmured on my way to the kitchen.

"Just a splash of that Jack now. I just need a little taste, so don't go crazy," he explained as he picked up another stack of photos to examine.

I made it to the kitchen and carefully mixed Mr. Darryl's drink before bringing it to the dining room. "Here you go sir," I said while placing the drink in front of him. Without hesitation, he grabbed the drink and took a big sip while glaring at me with an intense stare.

"Tastes about right", he said with a surprised expression. Mr. Darryl took several more sips while scanning a photo with a curious grin. I could feel the questions coming, and I braced myself to provide him the right answers.

"You like my hotel suite, son?" He asked with a wide smile.

"Yes sir," I eagerly replied.

"Do you…want this suite for yourself one day, son?" he asked.

"Well…yes sir. I guess I would like to be up here one day."

Mr. Darryl laughed at me and turned his eyes back to the photo. "Yeah, this is really nice isn't it? For over forty years, Robert Charles has been good to me," he explained.

"Robert Charles saw it fit to hire me in the late 70's back when I was kneecapping these damn bastards up in Memphis. They moved me down to Baton Rouge to put in a little work and I've just stayed down here ever since."

"When I first moved to New Orleans, I lived with a beautiful black woman named Gwendolyn. I met her at a Church over in

New Orleans East. She was a fine little thang with brown skin and beautiful brown eyes. She was everything a black man want in a Black woman. She always kept the house clean and made sure that there was good food to eat at all times."

"She adored me, and I was in love with her, but it didn't work out though," Mr. Darryl declared with regret in his eyes.

"Young man, our occupation will absolutely kill your love life. No black woman will support what we must do here. Remember that and prepare yourself for it. You must be willing to deny yourself for all of this to work out."

"Since you're about to retire," I jokingly interjected. "You should think about giving Gwendolyn a call and see if ya'll could give it one last go. Maybe the Lord will bless both of you this time around. You never can tell what God's plan is until you exercise some faith."

"I wish I could Achim," he dismissively responded with dejection in his spirit. "If I had it to do all over again, I would choose a life with Gwendolyn over this damned Presidential Suite any day of the week. A big part of me still loves that woman a whole lot. I guess it's the notion of it all that still has me captured these days."

"Thank God this black man only has one life to give because if I had another crack at it, I wouldn't have the strength to give my life away so easily. Especially, if I knew what I know now. I'd choose me instead of this lonely life working with Robert Charles. I'd choose to be selfish son." He explained, now having blood-shot eyes.

Mr. Darryl's words touched me as I saw him wipe away a tear with his balled fist. I never knew how he truly felt about this job. The magnitude of the concern in his voice made me think about my own plight. It was then that I began to realize how much he must have sacrificed to be here. Here he was a man well into retirement age; an old man reviewing mind-numbing evidence about a band of thugs instead of reviewing the cocktail menu onboard an exclusive cruise ship. Mr. Darryl reached down towards the table and pulled two photos out of a stack. After taking the final gulp of his drink, he laid out the first photo on the table in front of me so I could see it.

"Achim, is she OK?" he cautiously asked as he pointed at the black woman in the photo?

I wanted to lie to him. I wanted to be the black man that seemed to have all the easy answers, but I could not bring myself to mislead him. He was a good man and a father figure to me. When White Supremacy and the randomness of life had combined to turn my picture-perfect black life upside down, Mr. Darryl and Robert Charles gave me a new direction and renewed purpose. Neither Mr. Darryl nor Robert Charles deserved to be lied to, so I had no choice but to tell him the truth. An extremely complicated truth. A truth that made our future decisions murky and much less definitive.

"Mr. Darryl," I began. "I don't know sir…I'm not sure about Jessica Baker," I replied while looking him directly in his eyes.

He remained still as we stared at each other. The hotel room grew eerily quiet as we examined one another, looking for any signs of mistrust or manipulation between us. Mr. Darryl may be old, but I could tell his mind was sharp. He still had his street senses about him, those deep internal gut feelings that readily tell you when something was off or not quite right. I began to wonder if he knew that I cared about Jessica. Could Mr. Darryl have somehow found out that my business with her was more than just professional? My heart had crossed the line regarding my dealings with this woman. Even worse, my love for her was making this whole case harder.

"Alright then," Mr. Darryl finally declared, breaking our silence.

"How about this damn fella here?" he asked while placing the last photo in front of me.

"I've been following Kevin for a year now sir," I began. "I know this guy's daily routine better than mine. The evidence we have on Kevin speaks for itself."

"Kevin Longstreet is not OK. He is a damn problem because he knows way too much about FOWL's operation, and he has personally invested in it himself. I have even seen Kevin at Andy's Tavern, drinking and partying with members of FOWL."

"If we want to deliver the Davis family the justice they paid for, then Kevin has to go. We can't just move forward with our plans and hope this guy somehow stays out of our way. Kevin can spoil everything for us. He must be eliminated."

"That's why I'm here today Mr. Darryl. I need to know how far Robert Charles is willing to push this to get justice for the Davis family. I don't want to go off on my own script on this one," I further explained.

"You guys gotta make the call. Do Kevin Longstreet and Jessica Baker, live or die?"

I watched as Mr. Darryl began to nod his head in approval of my sentiments. The look on his face was deep and intense. This was indeed a big decision because it involved the lives of two black people. There is a code of conduct for these sorts of situations and I was intent on following it to the letter. Mr. Darryl grabbed another small stack of photos from the table and quickly flipped through them until he stopped and gazed upon one.

"So, we have all the evidence we need on these four bastards, right?" he pointedly asked me.

"Yes sir. I have two years' worth of photos and video evidence on each of these FOWL members. I was able to get inside their secret storage unit and I have inventoried every single item locked away inside. I have fingerprints of all the FOWL members, and I've compared those prints with all the evidence collected from the Eric Davis murder trial. I even went through these guys' trash bins to find old bank statements and receipts tracking their spending habits. We have all we need to expose these four guys, Mr. Darryl," I calmly explained. "All I need is the final word from Robert Charles to start the operation and we will certainly eliminate all of them."

Mr. Darryl threw the photos down on the table and grabbed his walking cane. As he began to lean forward to elevate himself from his seat, I jumped up to assist him.

"I am not a damn cripple," he loudly barked, waving me away with his hand. "You've done enough work, son. There is no need for you to kiss my old ass anymore. You're probably going to have my job here soon enough anyway. So, don't worry yourself about helping me anymore. My time is about done."

In defiance, Mr. Darryl slowly rose from his seat and pulled his cellphone out of his jacket pocket. "I have to make a few phone calls now. You give me a few minutes and I'll have your answer," he said.

I watched as Mr. Darryl disappeared behind a large bedroom door. It felt like the entire room shook as he slammed the heavy door behind him. This was it for me, as my years of painstaking work was now to be considered by Robert Charles. For me, this was a referendum on my professional standing. My reputation as a field operator was at stake. For the Davis family, this was their last chance at obtaining justice and freeing a loved one from an unrighteous conviction. For the both of us, I needed to get this right. Failure was not a choice.

After waiting for about ten minutes, I heard something strange stirring from within the bedroom door. I focused my attention towards the commotion, realizing that it was the faint yet undistinguishable voice of Mr. Darryl.

Seconds later, the bedroom door slowly swung open. The small limping figure of Mr. Darryl creeped out towards the dining area. I once again pulled out his seat, but this time, he limped right by me and walked towards the large window panel. He put his wrinkled hand up against the glass and leaned forward. As he braced himself against the panel, tears began to flow down his face as he silently gazed out over the mighty Mississippi River's brown water. I felt puzzled and didn't know what to say as he stood there in complete silence. I was almost afraid to ask him, but I knew it was relevant that I did. Whatever the decision, I knew it had been a hard one to make.

"Sir…. what's the word?" I cautiously asked.

"You know why I recruited you to Robert Charles, Achim?" Mr. Darryl interrupted. "Because I see my young self in you."

"I was once like you, Achim. In fact, part of me is still you."

"But along this path to justice, the struggle can change you from a young roaring lion into an old used up toothless reject."

"We have reached the point where there are certain things, I am no longer willing to do, and there are certain things that still must be done," Mr. Darryl lamented as he wiped away tears from his face.

"Robert Charles has decided to give you the discretion to do what you believe is required in order to obtain justice for the Davis family."

"But Mr. Darryl," I interrupted. "What do I do about this black woman?" I timidly asked.

"If you happen to encounter any loose ends along the way, take care of them without prejudice," Mr. Darryl said, fighting to hold in the tears. "If you determine that they are not on our side, then they are on the wrong side. Therefore, they must be eliminated."

"But remember what I told you earlier son. Once you give all yourself to this, there is no turning back from this lonely road of life."

I was stunned. Mr. Darryl's answer shocked me. I would be allowed to eliminate my own people. Eliminating the adversary was one thing but killing your own was completely another. I stood there motionless as the thoughts of what I had to do soaked into my consciousness. Mr. Darryl turned from the window and walked over to the front door of his hotel room. "You didn't lie to me today, Achim. You came straight up the middle. You're a good young man and I respect the hell out of that. I believe that you will make the right decisions for us and Robert Charles. Whatever that decision happens to be, just know that I support you."

"On a separate note, Robert Charles asked me if you were ready to replace me and assume my responsibilities."

"I told them that you are ready. In fact, I told them you will do a better job than I've ever done in my forty years in this business," a now smiling Mr. Darryl explained while unlocking the front door.

This was my cue to leave, and I hastily began to pack away my evidence into my worn brown briefcase. "Thank you, Mr. Darryl," I replied as a grateful feeling pulsed through my soul. "I've learned a lot from you sir, and I want to thank you for your endorsement."

"The job is not yours yet, Achim," he further explained. "Robert Charles has decided that you can't assume the position until you clean this Eric Davis mess up first. When you do, then my job will be yours and I can retire in peace."

"Don't forget to validate your parking at the front desk or these greedy bastards will charge your black ass that $35 parking rate," He ordered.

He opened the front door and stepped aside. We exchanged a long handshake and I walked in the hallway outside of his hotel room. I looked back inside of the room as he held the door open, gazing up at me with a strange and curious expression. In an instant, he shut the door and that was it for us. There were no sentimental goodbyes in this business, just orders given, and orders followed.

I took the long elevator ride down to the ground floor and made my way to the reception desk. As I handed my parking ticket over to the young light-skinned black lady working behind the counter, my thoughts were a mix of excitement and dread. This was my opportunity; a God-given opportunity to rise up the ranks while doing something I genuinely cared about. Yet, I had reservations about what I might be required to do to earn this promotion. Fighting our enemy was business as usual but killing one of my own was something totally different. Internally, it's going to be something I will ponder on since it will be my first time. Although I was certain I would have no issues killing the loathsome black male, having to kill the woman was a bridge I wasn't sure I was ready to cross.

As the receptionist punched my parking ticket, she cracked a gracious but phony smile, and quickly handed the ticket back to me. "Thank you, sir. Have a nice day," she said in a core New Orleans accent. I took my ticket and returned a forced smile. We both were in a hurry and had other things to accomplish. We both had jobs that needed to be done. Now, it was time to prepare myself for what I knew had to be done and leave this busy lady to continue with her own priorities.

My drive home across the Mississippi River Bridge was a lonely one. Far gone memories of my old life crept into my mind and replaced my innermost worries as I zoomed past traffic in the fast lane. The dreadful sight of my empty driveway hammered home my painful disposition. Opening my front door and walking into my empty three-bedroom apartment only worsened my ordeal. There was no wife to come home to anymore and I would no longer hold and feed my infant son. My reality was just a void of nothingness. The murderer of my family had himself opened a front door, walking through it into the most painful day of my life. Cruel fate would have the white gunmen drive into our middle-class neighborhood and arrive at the front door of my church. The authorities said the gunman had boasted online about wanting to shoot up a black church and kill a bunch of Dindu's. It was his barbarous way of teaching us black folks a lesson for promoting the Black Lives Matter movement. Within a single second, the white gunmen had collected his aim and pulled the trigger, changing my life forever in that instant. One cowardly act of white supremacist terrorism had erased all the happiness in my life, while wounding me in the arm and killing scores of my congregation, including my wife and infant son.

No one cared if I didn't arrive back home from work or if I stayed home all day long. No one cared if I left the toilet seat up or if my dirty white socks littered the hallway. To the world, the bloody massacre at my church was just another gun control issue to use as a political football, for insincere political campaigns. The hell with that lie, I knew better then to believe that weak excuse. All that I cared for had been taken from me in an act the white media would simply label as unfortunate, and not the White Supremacist terrorist act that it truly was. I had been robbed of the precious things in my life. All I had left was a few bar stools, a sofa bed, and a big flat screen TV. This empty apartment, which was once a home, had become the theme of my black existence. For me, this was a new life of extreme passion and painfully lonely ambition. Even though my empty home was a far cry from the excesses of Mr. Darryl's Presidential Suite, I could see the correlation between these two vastly different environments. Was this promotion worth giving my life up for Robert Charles's purpose? Could I ultimately find happiness with this type of lifestyle? A lifestyle that only took me further away from rebuilding the life I once had.

I walked over to my refrigerator and pulled out a bottle of grape juice. After guzzling it down to half a bottle in a mere four gulps, I reconsidered saving the rest of the juice for later. "Fuck it," I blurted out to myself. "I didn't come this far to quit." I took a deep breath and then finished the entire bottle before throwing the empty vessel into the trash bin. The empty bottle was useless to me now. Like my past, all its beautifully created contents were forever gone, so it had no further purpose for me.

In a spare bedroom, my gear bag was hidden away in the back of a small closet. After looking down at my watch I knew it was time to prepare myself for tonight's mission. I picked up a barstool and walked into the spare bedroom. It took several minutes of digging around before I found my gear bag buried underneath several cardboard boxes of old college textbooks and my handwritten copies of old sermons. With one powerful jerk, I pulled the bag out of its discrete space and placed it next to the stool. After emptying the bag of its contents, I arranged my gear around the stool. My guns, bullets, knives, gloves, a prepaid cellphone, and a laptop all neatly compiled on the carpet underneath me. They were beautiful. As a hitman, these were my tools of warfare now. Gone were the days when I would preach about the importance of voting, while imploring the virtues of turning the other cheek to a deadly adversary. I had learned the hard way that the childish hope of bringing morality to the immoral was a scam doomed for failure. If the struggles of Black Americans were to one day end, we would have to exercise our faith. We could no longer pretend with our words. Our faith needed to be put into deadly action.

I picked up a knife and a blade sharpener. The silver metal blade reflected a mirror-like image of me as I began to sharpen its edge. I could clearly see the image of my freshly shaven face and focused brown eyes staring back at me. I had to get myself mentally ready for the realities of this part of the mission. In silence, I closed my eyes for a moment and offered a silent prayer to the Lord, asking Him for strength to face all these challenges.

It was only a matter of time before Kevin Longstreet would call me begging for a hookup. He would no doubt invoke some fake ideal of black male brotherhood between us to score cheap drugs from me. It was my job to play along with his crooked scheme, so I always knew I had to ignore his disingenuous intentions. I had worked hard to make Kevin comfortable with me in this whole process. For me, investigating Kevin was akin to fishing. All I needed to do was wiggle the bait and like clockwork, he would most certainly come calling. The man is a weak ass coward. Weak ass cowards like Kevin did not deserve to live among decent black people, especially when black people are in a war for their future. Kevin is dead weight that the black community desperately needs to throw overboard. Today, his burdensome weight would sink to the bottom of the ocean.

Almost on cue, I felt my prepaid cellphone vibrate on the floor. I put down the knife and grabbed the vibrating phone from the carpet. When I saw the number, it was just as I had assumed. Kevin had just sent me a text, so I opened it and read the content of his message.

"WAT UP NIGGA! IT'S THA DAY AGAIN". I carefully typed a coded reply and pushed down on the green send button.

"U Already know bruh. We good," was the content of my reply. After two minutes, my phone buzzed again.

"COME FUCK WITH YA BOI THAN," he replied.

"Fa sho. I will get at u. I gotcha," I quickly replied.

Kevin wanted to buy some drugs from me, and I knew it was time to end our conversation. There was no way I would allow him to specifically discuss drug transactions with me on a cellphone. He was the kind of person that might have the wrong people around listening to whatever we say. I turned the prepaid cellphone off and connected it to its charger. It had been just over a year since I first started spying on Kevin. He was a remorseless drug addict with a sick penchant for misusing single mothers and sexually abusing their young daughters. No one with any street morals in the hood associated with him or even sold him dope. Only desperate low-level dealers would do business with such a person, which is why I had to pose as one. During my investigation, I found that Kevin was not only an NOPD informant, but also an informant for the DEA. I grew to personally despised this treasonous bastard. Instinctively,

I knew I had to move carefully when I was around this black traitor. Time after time, I watched as Kevin ratted out each of his previous drug suppliers. He would cleverly set up black men for a fall, thereby landing each of them in prison.

The decision to start selling drugs to Kevin was a calculated risk. Mr. Darryl and I had discussed it at length before he finally relented to my request and blessed my idea. I always felt a bit of uneasiness churning inside me every time I sold drugs to Kevin. There was nothing this turncoat wouldn't do to avoid the prison time he so richly deserved. Unlike Jessica Baker, there was no doubt in my mind that Kevin had helped FOWL set up Eric Davis. In fact, Kevin was just as bad as those bastards in many ways. He walked among the black community, yet deep inside, he was a cannibalistic monster that fed off of the plight of the black community.

Unlike Mr. Darryl, I did not have a drop of self-condemnation for wanting to kill this black tool. Although he was black like me, I didn't see him as one. Jessica Baker, on the other hand, confused me. I wasn't quite sure where she fell in all this mess, but deep inside, I held on to the belief that she wasn't the monster Kevin Longstreet was.

Lifting the screen on my Laptop computer, I pressed the power button and logged in. Within seconds, my computer linked up with the camera I had planted inside the storage garage. The video feed from inside the bastard's storage unit displayed nothing but a pitch-black image. Kevin hadn't arrived at the storage unit yet, but I was certain he would show up. Plus, there was no use in arranging a drug deal with Kevin until I was sure that broke loser would be with money.

I walked to the closet and carefully picked out the best clothes to wear for tonight's operation. After considerable deliberation, I decided it was best to wear a thin sports hoody and a pair of dark blue jeans for tonight's duties. I took the clothes and threw them into the washing machine with bleach and water. After pouring the bleach into the washing machine, an ingenious idea popped into my head. I walked into the kitchen and retrieved the empty juice bottle from the trash bin. After washing and cleaning out the bottle, I poured bleach into it and screwed on the top.

Suddenly, I heard a loud beeping noise from the spare bedroom. Racing back to the room to ascertain what the problem was, I quickly noticed that the video of the inside of the storage unit had changed. I sat on the stool and put the computer on my lap and began to watch the clear images, studying them for potential clues. The storage space became filled with light as a shadowy figure slowly rose the garage door. The figure walked into the storage unit and turned towards the wall. Suddenly, an explosion of light ensued as the lights inside the space were turned on. At this point, I recognized the shadowy figure as Kevin Longstreet. Kevin lowered the garage door behind him and began to look around inside. He jolted from box to box, opening their tops and peering down inside. Finally, he opened a box and reached in to pull out a handful of jewelry before stuffing the loot away in his pants pocket. He then reached into the box a second time, pulling out a large fur coat and a brown Chanel purse before opening a trash bag and dumping the items inside. He walked towards the garage door and opened it before tossing the trash bag outside of the storage unit and turning off the lights. Seconds later, Kevin walked out of the storage unit and closed the garage door. Within minutes after Kevin's arrival, my camera feed once again returned to its original state of pitch blackness.

I had seen this before, and I knew the score. This negro was going behind his partner's back to steal from them. There was absolutely no honor amongst this evil den of thieves. It only showcased the typical low life of criminals and how they operated. You could never trust them under any circumstances. They would always find a way to try and screw each other over. Yet, my investigation owed a lot to Kevin's reckless actions. Without him being a complete idiot, it would have taken me forever to locate this storage unit filled with loot. Not long after I began to follow Kevin, I noticed he would frequently come to the storage unit before buying drugs or embarking upon a weekend of partying. So, I decided I needed to find a way into the storage unit to look around for myself. With a little help from a strategically placed friend, I was able to find a key that would let me in. What I found inside the storage unit amazed me. It held hundreds of thousands of dollars; worth of stolen furniture, clothes, electronics, and jewelry. All of which was hidden away inside this inconspicuous storage garage tucked away in the redneck haven of Harvey, Louisiana.

After planting my motion-activated camera in the ceiling, I had a video of the whole gang of bastards visiting the storage unit each month. Each one of them would take old items out and replace those old items with goods they had recently stolen. Seeing all of that convinced me that I needed to get closer to Kevin. Kevin was the bastard's eyes and ears on the streets. He gave FOWL information they needed to rob black people, hold them to ransom, or set them up for a fall. The act of selling Kevin dope was risky, but it was a risk we needed to take to send the right message to our adversaries. Kevin was the key to this whole effort to free Eric Davis. He was FOWL's main source for street intel and there means of operating in the black enclaves of New Orleans. If we eliminate him, we will surely hinder their ability to operate as freely as they had been.

It wouldn't take Kevin long to hit up his favorite pawn shop and cash in his stolen goods. Once he had his money, he would most certainly reach out to me for drugs. My prices were dirt cheap and my product was strong as hell. Kevin had no idea what was awaiting him today, but it would soon be revealed to him. I turned off the laptop and reached down to the floor. My hands found an extra-large pair of latex gloves and I put them on. Walking back to the closet, I opened a secret compartment and pulled out several Ziploc baggies of dope. After examining the product, I placed the small baggies next to my sharpened blade. Suddenly, the sound of a ringtone exploded from my nearly empty living room. My personal cellphone was ringing, and the ringtone was Jessica Baker's.

I walked into the living room to answer Jessica's call. After pressing the answer button, I paused to gather my thoughts. "Hello," I answered pretending to sound a bit confused.

"Hey Achim, how are you," she asked with a bit of spunk in her voice. I took a deep breath to calm down, trying to remind myself that this was all just business.

"I'm good Jessica," I replied. "How about you?"

"I'm good, just enjoying a nice day off from work," she explained.

"I just hope that I hit the lottery tonight, so I can retire early and avoid going back to work tomorrow," she teased.

"Hell yeah," I replied. "If I hit the damn lottery, I'd quit Uber that same day. Working for other people is too damn stressful for us."

"Damn Skippy," Jessica retorted. "Let me mess up and hit the lottery. NOPD won't have to worry about this sister anymore," she added with a chuckle.

"What about me?" I asked in a fake tone of disappointment. "If you hit the lottery, will I ever have to worry about you anymore?"

"I don't know. We shall see," Jessica explained in flirty laughter.

"How about we discuss what you are going to do with your lottery money over dinner tonight?" I asked.

"Sure," Jessica shot back.

"But we will also discuss how you will be giving me half of your winnings if your black behind wins the lottery," she teased.

"You can have it all as long as I can be with you, beautiful," I retorted.

There was a long pause. I could tell from her silence that my frank words had surprised her. Jessica's tone had been one of playfulness, while my last statement was clearly serious in manner and delivery. As the long seconds slowly rolled by, my mind began to wander and caused me to worry. Was Jessica's surprise at my seriousness a good sign or a troubling one? I didn't know how she felt about me. Did I move too fast for her? Did I make her uncomfortable with my frank admission? As our long pause continued to draw out, I knew I would soon receive my feedback.

"Well, you can be with me tonight for free," she answered. "I feel like eating seafood, how about you?"

To my relief, she was with it and didn't have any issue about the things I said to her. I knew then that Jessica did have some sort of interest in me. The thought of Jessica having feelings for me boosted my courage, so I decided to take the risk and double down on my passes at her.

"Jessica wants seafood, then I'm going to make sure she gets seafood," I answered confidently.

"I know the perfect place for us. I will be your dark and handsome lottery ticket to some great grub tonight. Don't worry about a thing, just come hungry and I will make you happy."

"You better," she jokingly replied. "Because if this seafood isn't any good, you will hear from me about it."

We made plans to meet in the Bywater later in the evening and ended our phone call. Looking at my watch, I suddenly realized it was time to get moving. After changing into my work clothes, I grabbed my knife, the bleach, the prepaid cellphone, and loaded them into my truck. While wearing latex gloves, I took the Ziploc baggies of drugs and hid them inside my pocket. I looked through my briefcase and took out the photo I needed for this mission. After folding the photo in half, I placed it in my pocket with the drugs. Everything I needed for tonight's business was ready to go. After all the spying and investigating I had done for this case, Eric Davis's moment of vindication had finally arrived. All the days I spent digging through trash cans to find any form of evidence. All the hours I spent following these people around the city, trying to unearth their connections to the false conviction of Eric Davis. After all the work I have done, this would be the beginning of their much-deserved downfall.

I drove myself to the low end of Algiers and parked my truck in the parking lot of an abandoned strip mall. Before Hurricane Katrina, this strip mall was a hot spot and it boomed with business. Nowadays, people rarely bothered to stop here. The molding insides of the shopping centers are covered by sad deteriorating storefronts, all of which made this commercial property hard to sell. The renovation costs alone required a small fortune. Only exhausted truckers looking for a roomy and free place to park their rigs dared to enter the parking lot. Tonight however, I found myself all alone at this abandoned strip mall.

After parking, I just sat inside my truck for half an hour watching the traffic pass by. A handful of cars had driven by me and nobody bothered to notice me sitting there.

Grabbing the prepaid cellphone, I pushed the power button and watched as it came to life and began searching for service. Seconds later, the text messages from Kevin came rolling in. I had already missed five of them. From the tone of his text messages, I knew he was in a hurry and wanted his shit as soon as possible. My delay was probably ruining his big plans for the night and I could tell with each subsequent text message that he was getting more upset. His last text message read:

"HOLLA @ UR BOI? LEMME KNOW WHEN U BOUT TO SLIDE THRU FAM."

I couldn't drag this act out any further, not without putting myself or the mission at risk. Kevin was a dope head with police connections. He wasn't someone you wanted to upset or disappoint. The drugs inside my car would get me hard prison time, but the evidence stored in my briefcase would certainly get me killed. I typed out a coded response and pushed the send button. It was time to end all of this now.

"I can't come your way dawg. Sorry, bruh. I will be posting up at the mall across the river. I will see u their fam if you come thru", I texted Kevin.

My coded message was just clear enough for only Kevin to understand it. I needed to keep him off balance and have him come to me instead of vice versa. There was no telling what Law

Enforcement agency Kevin could be working with. On the flip side, he could just as easily be setting me up to get robbed, so I needed to have a homecourt advantage.

"AIGHT BET FAM," he texted.

Twenty minutes passed and Kevin was a no show. My mind raced and my palms became sweaty. What if he didn't show? What if he's watching me with the police right now? At that moment, I knew I had to get on the move. As I exited the truck, I grabbed my phone, the bottle of bleach, and my knife. After making sure I hid the knife away underneath my hoodie, I walked several blocks away from the strip mall. The urge to get as much distance between myself and my truck overwhelmed me.

Suddenly, I saw the headlights of a car driving down the road. It was a dark blue sedan. As it got closer to me, I noticed the out of state license plate. I immediately knew it had to be a rental car. The car slowed to a stop in front of me and I recognized the driver and his voice.

"Nigga, where you goin looking like you homeless?" A curious-looking Kevin asked from a half-lowered window.

The rental car looked as if it had been freshly washed and waxed. Kevin's dark brown skin looked freshly moisturized. His hair was trimmed and neat. His clothes were ironed and crisp. Even from outside the car, I could smell the lingering scent of his favorite breath mints, mixed with new car air freshener. Instantly, I knew Kevin had big plans for tonight. Renting a car and cleaning himself up was his way of doing it big.

"Bruh, I'm walking back to my lady's apartment to finish washing my clothes. My damn washing machine broke down and I had to go borrow some bleach," I stated while raising my bottle of bleach so Kevin could see it.

"Man, you shoulda hollered at me earlier bruh. You could've used my place to wash your clothes."

Immediately, I knew Kevin was lying to me. He didn't have his own home or apartment, let alone a washing machine or dryer. Kevin could give a damn about helping me. Like all dope fiends, he was just looking for an angle to get a discount.

"I ain't trying to worry nobody dawg. That's why I got a lady. She's been wantin to spend time together anyway, so it's working out for me," I added, blowing him off.

"Oh, no worries big dawg," he rebutted. "Where you goin? I can give you a ride if you need it."

My mind started racing as I contemplated reaching for the door handle. If I refused the ride, I might look very suspicious. On the same token, if I accepted the ride, Kevin could easily drive me right into an ambush. On gut instinct, I reached for the door handle and climbed inside.

"Where you goin?" Kevin again asked as his rental car rolled forward.

I knew this neighborhood well and it had plenty of good hiding spots where I could do my business. Kevin had lived around here for several months with his ex-girlfriend before she kicked him out for sleeping with her young daughter. So, I spent a lot of time running around this neighborhood spying on him.

"Make a U-turn and at the first stop sign, make a left and then after three blocks make another left."

Kevin made a quick U-turn and accelerated down the street. On instinct, I grabbed my prepaid cellphone and turned it off. Kevin made the final left turn and I asked him to pull inside a large apartment complex. The apartment complex looked foreboding with its faded dark brown color patterns and Section 8 feel. Kevin slowed the car down and turned into the parking lot wearing a childish grin.

"Man, I use to fuck with a bitch that lived over here."

"What apartment number you at bruh?" he asked.

"Apartment 532, all the way down and to the right next to the back fence," I explained.

He pulled into a parking spot next to the fence and turned off the engine. Everything seemed to be working out for me. Bringing Kevin to this apartment complex appeared to distract him. He was familiar and comfortable here. Kevin had spent a lot of time in this very parking lot getting high and buying drugs. This was probably a better situation than I had originally planned. If there were any police around, they would stand out in this place for sure. I put on my latex gloves and grabbed the baggie of dope out of my pocket. Before I placed the baggie on Kevin's lap, I gave a quick check of our surroundings to see if anyone was lurking around. We were alone. Not even a single soul was outside with us.

"Good looking out, Kevin. This has been a fucked-up day man," I lamented while pretending to be frustrated. "This ride saved me some serious walking. Good looking out."

Ignoring me, Kevin opened the baggie and tested it with his index finger before pulling out his spoon, needles, and other equipment. The look in his eyes was frantic and rushed. It was like a switch had been flipped inside of his soul. Was he stalling or trying to send the police a signal? I had no idea what Kevin was up to, and my sense of urgency skyrocketed.

"Don't shoot this shit up while I'm in this fuckin car with you bruh," I warned. "Give me my cash so I can bounce. Then you can do all this shit."

While letting out an aggravated sigh, Kevin reached into the center console of the car and pulled out a small stack of hundred-dollar bills. He impatiently counted my money, while I discretely reached underneath my hoodie to grab the knife handle. As he looked up at me to hand over the cash, I thrust the sharp blade into his throat. Kevin's eyes held a gaze of shock and terror as he looked at me. His small fist delivered a weak defensive blow to my head. Immediately, I knocked his hand away from me while twisting and pulling the knife out of his throat. I watched as the blood poured out of the wound and soiled his expensive shirt. Kevin pissed on himself and the strong smell of his urine only added fuel to my thirst to kill him. There would be no stopping me now since I was in full control. I had played the long game with this bastard and it was finally my payday.

Kevin instinctively reached up to cover the large wound in his throat. He attempted to scream but instead began to choke on his own blood. I took the knife and plunged it into his unguarded midsection. With hateful indifference, I pulled and twisted the knife before ripping it away. Blood spatter was sent flying and red droplets covered the forward compartment of the car. I could feel the warmness of Kevin's blood through my thin latex gloves and I felt the rush of power. He would certainly not survive my attack. There would be no amount of cooning that could save him from God's justice. White daddy could offer him no protection for a life spent betraying his people. Kevin fought for his final moments on earth as I stared into his terrified eyes. I watched a river of his tears fall from his face and mix with the red blood that soiled his designer clothes. As he began to fade away, I emphatically whispered to him. "Eric Davis."

Chapter Two

Never in a million years did I ever think my life would end up this way. Never would I have ever dreamed that I would become this type of person. Not even once did I desire this sort of unworthy life for myself. As a young black girl, I had seen plenty of movies and read scores of books about women like me. Growing up, I was taught to despise and ridicule women like myself. Everything was so much easier back then and far less complicated than this haunting present I was currently living. Now as a grown woman, the card game of life had dealt me a surprising hand. My cards of life were now those of a loveless home wrecker. I had become a woman who had made an idol out of a man that didn't belong to me. Despite knowing this, I still chased after him with all my heart.

I tried my best to put my feelings away and just focus on my job, but it was a struggle to pretend that the deep feelings I harbored for him were merely a harmless physical attraction. Rationalizing away the knowing stares and telling smiles we exchanged was even a more difficult task. It was hard to ignore the burning excitement that exploded between us when we found ourselves alone together, fucking away the boredom of long night shifts through our sweat and lust. The excitement of secretly making forbidden love in spontaneous, yet hidden places became a sort of an addiction for us. We indulged in a reckless passion for each other that we both quietly understood could never be given the light of day. A passion neither the world nor our co-workers at the New Orleans Police Department would approve of.

There were so many times I wanted to just end the charade and live my truth. To finally come out and tell everyone how I felt and who I was in love with. Holding in this hidden part of myself was slowly eating away at me. At one time I once believed that I needed Daniel as much as I need life-giving oxygen. Now, I had to teach myself the painful lessons of trying to move on from a married man I coveted deep down in my soul.

These torturous lessons were hard for me to learn and indeed old habits do die a painful death. Without consideration, I grabbed my cellphone and scrolled through my list of contacts to Daniel's number. My lonely soul yearned to hear his soothing voice, even if it was just for a few seconds. I selfishly pressed the green call button before allowing myself to fully think through what I was about to do. What if he was with his wife and kids? Even scarier, what if his wife answered my phone call? If that happened, my excuse had to be ready and believable.

"I was his partner and we simply needed to discuss work-related issues," I quickly convinced myself on what to say if my thoughts happen to be the reality.

My excuse would be normal cop stuff that partners usually share, and not the intense intimacy and burning passion in which we both exchanged during our private moments together.

My call was connected, and the phone began to ring on the other end. After two rings, Daniel's groggy voice answered the call.

"Hello."

"Hey, Daniel. It's Jessica," I began. "I just need to talk to you."

"What's wrong Jessica? Is everything OK?"

Daniel was wondering what was wrong with me again. At this point, I knew that he was not alone. This time, we weren't going to be able to spend time together. The images of him sitting next to his wife blasted holes into my woeful spirit. The thought sent me vivid reminders of who I really was as a person and where I truly stood in life.

"I'm OK.... I'm OK," I stumbled.

"It's just hard dealing with work. I'm just having a hard time with all of this."

Daniel went quiet and his long guilty pause dominated my thoughts. Daniel understood what I was trying to say. I could almost feel his mind searching for the right words to break our silence. Words that we both knew would be useless given the hurtful situation we were in. This thing between us had completely gotten out of hand. We tried to stop it or at least slow down, but it wasn't happening so easily for me. Unlike me, he had a family to worry about. Daniel had been married to Judith for fifteen years and they had two children. Daniel was the man of his house. The man his family looked up too and believed in. I was just his pressure valve, his gateway into another world away from the stress of being a husband and father. I understood our relationship could rob him of all that he cared for. Yet, all of this left me feeling alone and profoundly inadequate.

"Jessica, you are one of the best damn cops I have ever known," Daniel explained with measured words.

"You just need to find some sort of release for yourself. You can't bottle all this stuff up and hope it magically goes away."

"Jessica, I have the same problems sometimes. I just…I find a way to deal with it and move on. I don't make an issue out of it. Harping on it only worsens the problem."

"Call your friends. Have a few drinks and go paint the town. Go have a good time and release all this bad energy. Just find a way to get your mind off all this stuff," he explained.

The advice sounded so easy and caring coming out of Daniel's mouth. Yet, receiving it felt impossible to me and the reality of his detached words made my soul drown in sorrow. Daniel was rejecting me while making me feel like I was crazy. I was certain I was frustrating him in some way, but I just wanted him to understand me and sympathize with me. The reality was that Daniel could never understand or sympathize with me. Understanding me was something he could not afford to do, at least while he lay next to his wife.

"It's hard Daniel."

"It so damn hard because I love you. It's hard spending every minute wanting to be with you. Thinking about you and having to hide my love for you from the world. It is so hard and I'm so tired. I love you and I'm hurting because of all of this Daniel."

"I understand, but we can't go through this crap every night," he mumbled in a frustrated tone. "I'm your partner. I will always be there for you when you need me. All of this will get better. Just trust me."

It was the kiss of death from Daniel, and I knew it. He ended the phone call, and I just stared up at my powder-white ceiling as I lay alone in my king-sized bed. Tears flowed from my eyes as the feeling of Daniel's soft rejection overwhelmed me. I didn't want to move. I could not bring myself to raise out of the bed. The pain of this love was like emotional chains holding me down in a pit of blazing sorrow.

My thoughts wandered to the childhood memories of my late mother. I desperately needed her advice at moments like this, but she was gone, and the wisdom of her life experiences would be forever denied from me. As a little child, I wondered how she managed to still love my father despite his many hateful betrayals and the nearly constant arguments they would have. There were nights I would sneak into her bedroom, only to find her face filled with tears and anguish as my father would spend yet another night away from us. I witnessed the pain my father had delivered upon my suffering mother, but as a curious child, I often wondered how my father made the other woman feel. Now as a grown adult, I found myself living out my childhood curiosities, almost as if it were my cruel fate.

A few weeks after my mother passed, my father decided to send me to live with his younger sister. The day he dropped me off at my Aunt's house, he stated clearly to me that I needed to learn how to be a woman, and that this was something he could not properly teach me as a man. The memories of my father being barely able to look into my eyes as he spoke to me or recognize my tears as they were shed still haunted me. I remember feeling alone and scared as I watched my father's car back out of my Aunt's long grey driveway to disappear from my view forever. For days, I asked my Aunt when my father would come to see me, but she would always give me a comforting smile before telling me that my father was too busy, or that he was out of town. As years passed, I finally came to realize that for him, I was both a burden and a shameful reminder of his failures.

Suddenly, my cellphone vibrated and shuttered, breaking my painful train of thought. Its vibration was a telltale sign of a new text message arriving into my phone's inbox. I bolted up from the bed to grab the cellphone from my nightstand, hoping in the back of my mind that it might be Daniel texting me to let me know he loved me. I hoped it would be his sweet words letting me know how he needed me and how much he cared about me. In my heart, I hoped that he would finally reveal his plan for us to somehow be together forever.

As I opened the text message, I quickly noticed that it was Achim Jeffers who had texted me. Immediately, I felt the sting of disappointment cascading within my already broken spirit. I tried to catch my raw emotions and stop the negative thoughts because my thought process wasn't fair to him. Achim was a great guy. He didn't deserve my negativity, but my feelings now were indeed my reality. No matter how much I tried to move away, I still wanted to be with Daniel. Achim and I had only known each other for a few weeks. I wanted to give him a fair chance at my heart, but I was finding it almost impossible given my situation with Daniel. Part of me wanted to totally ignore Achim but in a funny way, he reminded me of my father with his charming demeanor and self-confidence. He was cute for a black man and could be extremely sweet when he wanted to be. He treated me with kindness and respect, always presenting himself as the perfect gentleman.

"Hey Jessica, I'm so sorry. I may be about 20 to 30 minutes late tonight. I called and made reservations for 8 PM & they will hold our table for us," Achim's text explained.

If I needed an excuse to skip out on the date, Achim had given it to me on a silver platter. He was running late but unbeknownst to him, so was I. In fact, I hadn't even picked out any clothes to wear for the outing. My issues with Daniel sidetracked me, and now I wasn't even in a good mood to go out on a date that I had already agreed to have with Achim. After rereading his text, I took several moments to ponder my response. Would I make my excuses or pretend to be angry? Hoping that if I did either, it would ultimately lead to a disappointing cancellation of our date. Maybe I should just suck it up and go out with Achim. Maybe Daniel was right. The few hours I would spend with Achim not thinking about Daniel would probably help me deal with the pain. Maybe I just needed to trust Daniel and do what he wanted me to do.

I typed several responses to Achim and ended up erasing several of them before I could press the send button. For some reason, I wasn't quite sure what I wanted to do or how I wanted to say it. Finally, I made myself type a response and sent it to him.

"No worries. See you there!"

Upon arriving at the address Achim sent me, I cautiously squeezed my unmarked police car into a small parking lot. The restaurant sat across from an old decaying military base that was fenced in with a large DO NOT TRESPASS signs displayed at the front gate. This restaurant was off the beaten path. It was away from the bright lights and picturesque eateries in the French Quarter. The smell of fried and boiled seafood pulsed from the small restaurant that looked like it had been someone's home in earlier years. From the smell alone, I knew there was surely going to be some very good food in the place.

Walking up to the front door, I fought the instinct to ring the doorbell. Instead, I opened the door and walked to a small brown podium that blocked the entrance into the seating area. Behind the podium was an old grey-haired white lady wearing a long plastic apron. She wore a huge gold wedding ring and sported a black writing pen resting in between her ear and her gray hair.

"Thank you for visiting us, Ma'am. How many guests are with you tonight? One or two," she asked with an eager smile that exposed her pearly white dentures?

"Yes. I'm here for a reservation for two. Achim Jeffers. 8 PM." The white lady looked down at a small note pad and shook her head before grabbing two menus. "Follow me please and I'll get you seated, Ma'am."

I took my seat and ordered a glass of ice water. Achim hadn't arrived yet and was likely still on his way. Taking out my phone, I saw that I hadn't missed any calls from him. Now all I could do was wait and hope those reoccurring thoughts of Daniel didn't send me into an emotional tailspin. I tried to distract myself by watching the people around me. Rudely, I intruded upon an elderly white couple conversating at the table next to me. But then, I decided on distracting myself by sipping my ice water and playing a game of solitaire on my cellphone.

Then I saw him as he calmly walked up to the old white lady standing at the podium. That soft and silky straight brown hair with a few strings of grey was unmistakable. He looked handsome in his tight-fitting yellow polo shirt and khaki pants. His face was filled with joy that had been utterly absent from my life in recent months. I watched his blue eyes light up as Judith Fitzpatrick wrapped her arms around their two children and ushered them towards the podium. Both Judith and Daniel Fitzpatrick gave familiar hugs to the old white lady as all three exchanged in small talk. I watched in horror as the old lady leaned over and kissed both of their children on the cheek like a loving grandmother.

They were having a family outing and I would be here to watch it all. There was no place for me to run, no place I could go without them seeing me. I felt the spirit of embarrassment swarm over me as I watched Judith hang at the arm of her husband. She looked proud and secure with him as she strolled into the seating area. Her perfect brown hair seems to glow, and her petite frame drew more than a few glances from old white men eating in the restaurant. Judith was a good-looking white woman and she knew it. Part of me wanted to crawl under a rock. There was no way I could compare myself to who she was for him. There was no way I could be Daniel's Judith.

I had to prepare myself for what I knew was about to happen. When Daniel saw me, there was no way he would understand or even believe my side of the story. This was uncomfortably close. Too damn close for either of us. I had to prepare myself for the inevitable, so I pretended not to see them and again focused on my cellphone hoping our eyes would never meet.

"Oh, my goodness. It's Jessica!" a smiling Judith loudly proclaimed as she and Daniel walked closer to my table.

Daniel's gaze snapped right towards me. I could see his eyes briefly widen, then fill with fury before he forced himself to dawn a phony smile.

"Hey, partner! Great minds think alike I see," he jokingly stated with an insincere tone of surprise.

"Only if the great mind you are trying to emulate is mine," I shot back.

I rose from my seat and took a step towards Judith. Out of the corner of my eye, I could see Daniel's body tighten as Judith and I exchanged a hug and a few girlish pleasantries. Daniel's children walked up to me. "Auntie Jessica," they shouted. I briefly kneeled and hugged the children before standing back up.

"Do you eat here often, Jessica?" Judith asked curiously.

In a millisecond, I considered outright lying to Judith by telling her that I had eaten here a few times before, but I decided against it. No amount of lying was going to make any of this less uncomfortable for me.

"No. This will be my first time eating here," I began to explain.

"A friend of mine recommended this place to me. He kept going on and on about how great the seafood is here. So, at my friend's behest, I decided to finally give this place a try."

"Awesome," a smiling Judith replied as she wiped away her long brown hair.

"Since we're all here. How about having Jessica join us at our table for dinner tonight?" Judith asked while nodding her head and turning towards Daniel. The phony smile on Daniel's face was now beginning to fade into a scowl.

"No…. No," I quickly interrupted. "I'm here tonight on a date, Judith. I just…. I can't."

Judith's face lit up with a playful smirk as if I had told her I had just won the lottery. She reached out and gave me a friendly pat on my shoulder, almost like she was trying to transfer some sort of self-confidence to me. I knew Judith was trying to be supportive, but when she combined her friendliness with that belittling look in her eyes, it bothered me. I wanted to lash out at her and tell her the truth about her husband. It would have felt so good to send the white bitch in to the abyss of sorrow, but I forced myself to hold my tongue.

"Wow, I remember those good ole days," Judith explained with a smile. "A romantic dinner, a few drinks, and then a movie. Daniel and I use to be masters of the dinner date, but life happens and so do kids," she concluded.

"Well partner, enjoy your date," Daniel broke in. "We are going to get out of your hair and let you get to the rest of your evening."

I walked back to my table and sat down feeling crushed. Daniel and his family walked to a large table well behind mine and they sat there. Daniel gave me a quick glance filled with discomfort and fury. He probably assumed that I had planned to ambush him and his family tonight. I'm sure he thought I might be sending him the veiled threat of destroying him. The misunderstanding made my heart sink. That wasn't what I was trying to do. I wanted to leave the restaurant and drive myself home to hide in my bed. At that moment, all I wanted to do was cry myself to sleep and engross in my pain like I had done so many nights before.

Just as I had begun to debate my exit, Achim Jeffers walked through the front door. He wore a dark blue sports coat with a white button-up shirt and light blue jeans. His bald head appeared to shine as the light from the lamps above him reflected on the top of his head. In his hand, he held a bouquet with a small brown envelope tucked away inside of them. Achim arrived at the podium. His tall muscular frame towered over the old white lady as he stood there looking dignified and handsome. He easily looked over her head, scanning the room until his eyes found me. Our eyes met and his face seemed to explode with a smile, which dutifully employed his prominent yet adorable dimples. After a quick hand gesture towards our table, the old lady quickly stepped aside and Achim walked towards me. A feeling of immense relief overwhelmed me as he presented me with the bouquet of red roses. Achim had just saved me from this embarrassing situation. I was indeed here on a date and not some vain attempt to ruin Daniel's life.

"I feel awful for being so late, Jessica. So, I decided to stop and bring you something special. I apologize for inconveniencing you," Achim sincerely explained.

I took the flowers and thanked him. The roses were big, red, and fresh. Uniquely delicate in their beauty. Their sweet scent captured my senses as I laid them on the table in front of me for all to see. I caught several onlookers fixating on us as Achim and I exchanged in a bit of small talk. White women in the restaurant, looked at us with admiration, while annoyed white men gave us stares of jealousy and contempt. In the back of my mind, I knew Daniel and Judith were watching as well, and for different reasons, I needed both to see this moment I was having with Achim.

"Sir, would you like something to drink?" the old lady kindly asked Achim.

"I'll take a Patron Margarita, on the rocks. No salt and no sugar, Ma'am."

"Oh my! He's super polite and he bought you those really pretty flowers," the old lady gushed.

The now smiling old lady reached over towards me and gave me a playful tap on the back with her receipt pad. "He's a keeper, honey," she loudly whispered with a flirty grin.

I tried to hide my cheesy grin, but I couldn't once I looked across the table and saw Achim's coy smile. This handsome black man was smart, and he knew what he was doing. We then shared a quiet and wordless chuckle. It was a comforting and welcoming moment. It was almost like we were able to non-verbally connect despite the entire restaurant spying on us. It felt good.

"What should we order?" I asked as I reached for the menu.

"Well, I love fried redfish. I always order it with baked mac & cheese. You can't go wrong with that," Achim offered.

"I'm game," I replied tossing the menu back down. "I want to see what they are working with here, and I want to see if you really know what good seafood is."

The old lady came to our table with Achim's drink and took our orders. Achim leaned back in his chair and slowly sipped his margarita. His whole mood was one of confident relaxation. He was different from most of the other black guys I had dated in the past. He wasn't overly eager to endlessly ramble on about how great he was or talk about frivolous things. He seemed to enjoy and relish the moments of comfortable silence we shared, instead of letting the moments make him feel insecure. He wasn't here to let me entertain him, nor was he here to entertain me. This man seemed to be after something deeper, much deeper than I had anticipated. Most intriguing to me were his eyes. His attractive brown eyes seemed to calm me down and put me at ease. I had never felt that from a black man before, not even my father. The cool confidence in his stare reminded me of Daniel. Daniel was a south of I-10 white guy from a well-off family. An Army veteran that went to LSU and earned a Criminal Justice degree before joining the force. Achim was a black nomad that had moved here from Houston to work as an Uber driver. They were worlds apart, yet they both shared a knowing stillness. A stillness that comes from being in control.

"So, what was it at work that had you troubled today, Achim?"

Achim took a sip of his drink. I watched him swallow, then lean forward in his chair, purposely closing the distance between us.

"I had a long conversation with my big boss today," he started. Achim's face turned serious as did his demeanor.

"I'm told I may get a promotion here soon."

"That's great news right," I interrupted.

"No…not really," he shot back." My boss is trying to talk me into taking the gig and I'm torn about it."

"This position they are offering me is time-consuming and will demand a lot of me. Yes, it pays better, but I'm tired of working for someone else. Busting my ass to help someone else reach their dream is not what I'm built for. I have my own goals, so I want to control my own destiny."

Achim pulled out his cellphone and unlocked it before scrolling thru his screen with his finger. After a brief pause, he turned the screen towards me, showing me a picture of a long black limousine with pitch-black tinted windows and shiny chrome rims.

"I've saved up enough cash from driving for Uber to pay for this beauty," he began. "She is a little old and she needs some TLC, but I'm pretty good at turning wrenches. I can soup this baby up and make her my own."

"You want to start your own business?" I asked.

"Hell yeah."

"That's the main reason I came to New Orleans. With all the celebrities that come here, I could do well for myself."

"Paul Coffee transportation services, that's the name of my dream. I want to be the biggest name in transportation services. I envision it to be more than just cars on a phone app. More than just driving. I want to connect with people while they travel to connect with the rest of the world."

With every word Achim spoke, I could feel his inner ambition dripping out of his mouth. The cool abyss that once dominated his brown eyes had grown into a blazing inferno of desire that was consuming me. This guy was not just some Black Uber driver from Houston, not just a Black man content with the idea of rubbing two dimes together to buy a pair of Jordan's. There was something more within this man and now I could feel it.

"This has always been my dream," Achim continued. "I want to be the Lakers or the Cowboys of the transportation business."

"Not just a business owner, but to be a pioneer for Black America. To create something special for my future children and our people." Achim leaned back in his chair and took another sip of his drink before flashing a broad smile at me.

"I guess I'm a little tipsy right now."

"Oh no, Achim. You're fine. You really are," I reassured him.

"I know I'm fine Jessica, but you sister......are absolutely beautiful. But more importantly, you are a beautiful person. When I look into your beautiful brown eyes, I see greatness in you Jessica. You motivated me to reach for my dream. You make me want to do better for myself. I really enjoy spending time with you."

"Thank you, Achim. You're not bad on the eyes either and I really love that you're all about starting your own business."

"It's refreshing," I expanded. "I know you will succeed. I can sense it in you."

The old lady came to the table and served us our food. We talked about our love of the Saints and real estate while we devoured every drop of food on our plates. The food was good, but the conversation was even better. It was clear that Achim was an intelligent man and uniquely witty at just the right moments. A full hour flew by as we fully engrossed in each other. Old customers left and new customers took their warm seats and finished their meals as we both spent time with each other. Even Daniel and his family left without them making much of a fuss. All they offered me was a quick hand wave from Daniel and a wide smile followed by a girlish eyebrow raise from an admiring Judith.

"Wow," Achim stated after checking his wristwatch. "We've been here a while."

"Yeah, we have totally hogged this table for over an hour," I opined.

Deep inside, I did not want the moment or the night to come to an end. As Achim pulled out his credit card to pick up our tab, I tried to conceal my disappointment by looking at the menu.

"Hey, I know this great cigar bar in the French Quarter that makes handmade Cubans. Maybe we can go hang there for a while." Achim said.

I hated the smell of cigars, but I wasn't missing the chance to pick this man's mind further. We exited the restaurant and walked towards the parking lot. I pulled out the key to my car and clicked open the doors.

"Jessica, this may sound silly coming from an Uber driver, but I didn't drive here today, and I don't want to make you feel uncomfortable by asking you for a ride...."

"No...No problem, Achim."

"I'm not worried about you. I can handle myself. I'm a cop, remember," I declared while pointing towards a set of blue lights in the backseat.

We both hopped in my car and left the restaurant. Achim gave the directions and we found ourselves driving down North Peters Street in the heart of the French Quarter. After driving several blocks, we found public parking and began our walk to the cigar bar. It was a warm evening and the streets of the French Quarter were alive with nightlife. Live music pulsed through the air and made the historic scenery of the French Quarter come to life. We made it to Decatur Street and walked past the House of Blues towards the cigar bar. The sidewalks were crowded with partygoers, mostly young college students enjoying an evening away from their studies. Achim grabbed my hand and held me close, leading me through the sea of drunk bodies. His grip was firm, yet loving as he held me like I was his very own. Sensing that Achim wanted to lead us both, I followed him and allowed Achim to make a way through the crowd for me.

"Alright, we're here. The Cuban Stick Cigar Bar," he proclaimed with a boyish smile.

As we neared the entrance, I could hear my cellphone's blasting ring. I reached down into my purse and pulled out the ringing phone. It was Daniel calling me from his cellphone.

"Hold on. I will meet you inside, Achim. I have to take this phone call. I'll only need a few seconds," I explained. Achim nodded his head and continued inside. I walked out to the edge of the sidewalk and pressed the answer button.

"What Daniel."

"What?" he angrily declared? "What the fuck do you think!"

"You stalk me and my family tonight....and you have the nerve to get lippy with me. This is getting outta hand Jessica. Its gotta stop. We are both playing with fire right now."

"You actually think I was stalking you, Daniel? You believe I would try to hurt you like that?"

"What the hell am I supposed to believe Jessica? You call my house balling in tears. Calling me when you know its family night for me. Trying to pull all types of guilt trips on me. You know our situation and still decided to do this to me."

"This has gotten out of control. I can't deal with this anymore!"

Daniel's words were far from calculated this time. His voice was loud and demonstrative. I knew he wasn't at home and had to be away from his wife since his tone was high-pitched. There was no way he would allow himself to be this emotional around Judith.

"Where are you, Daniel?" I asked.

"I'm in my car driving to Algiers. Where you need to be going right now."

"And why do I need to stop what I'm doing and go meet you in Algiers, Daniel?" I flippantly asked.

"Because Captain Wolf called me and told me we needed to be there tonight. We both have been called in to work. Some residents over at the Oakwood Apartment Complex found a dead man's body stabbed to death inside a rental car. We've been given the case," Daniel explained.

"So, kiss your buddy Shaq good night so we can do our damn jobs, partner."

Daniel hung up the phone on me, leaving me all alone on the crowded sidewalk in the French Quarter. After shaking off Daniel's rude behavior, I turned and walked into the cigar bar. The atmosphere in the bar was relaxed and humid as loud reggaetón music blasted from a huge speaker box. Achim was standing in front of the cash register, clipping the end of a fat dark cigar. A young-looking Hispanic man pulled out a small silver torch and lit the flame. Achim leaned over towards the flame and took a big pull of his cigar before turning towards me. He playfully blew heavy smoke out of his mouth and gave me a cute smile.

"I can buy you a small cigarillo if you want to try one," he said.

"Achim. I'm so sorry," I began, before stopping myself to collect my words.

"I can't. I have to leave. I've been called in to work."

Guilt washed over me as I watched his reaction to my words. As the recognition of what I had just told him began to sink in, Achim's smile evaporated into a look of disappointment. I knew he figured that I was lying to him and was making up a convenient excuse to abandon yet another date with him. Achim must have believed this date was going well up until now, and I felt the same way too, but there was no way for me to convince him that I wasn't ditching him.

"Damn work again huh," he replied. "Don't be sorry. It's all good, Jessica. We both know all about work drama....... don't we?"

His words made me feel worse. I wasn't sure if he was pretending or he really didn't care. If I were in his situation, I would understand his sentiments. Somehow, I wanted him to know that if I didn't have to go, I would have stayed with him.

"Maybe we can pick this up next weekend?" I said.

"Yeah. Next weekend sounds fine. Just let me know," he lazily replied.

"Do you need a ride home? I can drop you off really quick if you need one."

"Nah. I'm good. I can call an Uber. There are plenty of them around here."

Achim took a big puff of his cigar and blew the smoke skyward as he silently examined me with his eyes. Without thinking, I reached out and grasped his large hand, to briefly squeeze his hand before I turned around to head for the exit. I hoped he might reciprocate my comforting squeeze, but I soon realized Achim didn't return it. His hand remained limp and his eyes were filled with frustration.

"I'll call you tomorrow", I declared while putting on my best smile.

"And I'll be waiting on that call," he responded with a stoic expression.

I made my way back to my car and turned on my police radio. As I began to weave my car through French Quarter traffic, I turned on my blue lights and blasted my siren. The congested roadway parted, and I sped my way out of the French Quarter. Algiers was on the Westbank of the Mississippi River, so I jumped on the bridge and got off on the first exit on the other side. Within ten minutes, I had made it to the Oakwood Apartment Complex. It was a dingy looking place, better known for its reputation as a haven for recently released ex-convicts and struggling drug addicts. The multitude of flashing blue lights near the back fence guided me to the crime scene.

As I pulled up and parked, I saw Daniel. He was talking to Derrick Reynolds, the lead Crime Scene Technician on duty. In the background near the fence, I saw a blue sedan. It had a Florida license plate and lightly tinted windows. I got out of my car and walked back to my trunk, opening it before reaching into my duty gear bag. I found my handgun, a pair of latex gloves, and a pair of plastic booties. I grabbed a few bobby pins and tied my hair back before dawning my plastic head wrap. Then, I heard a voice.

"Don't forget to put on your eye protection."

The slow country twang of the deep voice told me it was Derrick Reynolds, a short chubby black man who was originally from Shreveport, Louisiana. According to Derrick, he had come down to New Orleans to experience his first Mardi Gras 25 years ago. He met a pretty light-skinned woman from Slidell at a parade and just decided he didn't want to go back home. Now, he was working for NOPD and was one of the best Crime Scene Specialists we had. Derrick was focused, detailed, and patient. He would never allow anyone to rush him at a crime scene. He always took his time and collected evidence the right way. Derrick handed me a pair of goggles and I quickly put them on.

"Someone poured bleach all over the front cab of the rental car," Derrick explained as he pointed towards it. "The powerful smell is strong enough to make your eyes well up."

"What are we working with this evening?" I asked while closing my trunk.

"We have one victim. A black male, about 5-11, 170lbs with a massive puncture wound in his throat area and a knife wound in his abdomen."

"No signs of forced entry into the car. No signs of any sort of struggle, just a Ziploc baggie filled with a powdered substance on his lap, a shit load of money on the dashboard floor and a weird photo laying on the passenger seat."

"What do we know about the victim, Derrick?"

"We believe his name is…. Kevin Donaldson. Once we figured out that the victim was in a rental car, we called the rental company. The company emailed us a copy of the renter's State ID and it looks like the victim."

"From the receipts they emailed, it looks like the victim just rented the car today. He was supposed to keep the car for a week."

"Are we running his name and address for any priors?" I asked.

"Yeah, we haven't heard back from dispatch yet, which is weird," Derrick lamented. "Follow me, Jessica. I need to get you and Daniel caught up before I officially start working this scene."

I followed Derrick as we both headed towards the blue sedan. Daniel stood a few feet away from the passenger side door, peering into the car through its lightly tinted windows. Before we arrived next to Daniel, Derrick turned back to me and whispered.

"What's wrong with Daniel?" he asked with a confused facial expression? "He looks pissed off tonight."

"Derrick, you would be pissed too if you got called in to work on your off day," I immediately deflected. "NOPD really needs to start hiring again, or it will be a long summer for us."

"Yeah, we're going to be burning both ends of the candle if they don't do better," Derrick added.

We arrived and stood beside Daniel as he continued to examine the inside of the car. He turned, raised his goggles, and looked at me with a somber expression. Dealing with the sight of death was always tough, no matter how seasoned a cop believes they are. Daniel's eyes were slightly watered, and he bit down on his bottom lip. He didn't utter a word before stepping away from the window. With his hand, Daniel motioned for me to step forward and take a closer look for myself.

I stepped forward to look. Behind the wheel sat the corpse of a black man appearing to be in his late 30's. Aside from the pool of blood and his massive throat wound, the victim had the look of someone who had fallen asleep as his head leaned up against the driver's side window. The victim's mouth was wide open, and his face seemed to display an agonized expression. He wore a white Ralph Lauren T-Shirt with dark blue designer jeans. The victim's hair appeared freshly cut and the line up on his fade was nearly perfect. His eyes were wide open, emitting the ominous stare of death. In the middle of his throat, there was a wound about the width of a quarter. A pool of blood had run down his body and it was clear that he bled to death. Some of the blood dried on his neck, while a large amount of it pooled in his blood-soaked shirt and pants. His shirt also sported a long tare near his stomach area, exposing a knife wound in his gut. Blood spatter was all over the place; on the windows, on the steering wheel and the dashboard.

I scanned the entire interior of the car and couldn't find anything that looked like it could be the murder weapon. No knife. No blades. Nothing. My nose finally caught the heavy stench of bleach. I could see the spots where pure bleach had changed the cars dark upholstery into a whiteish color. Hundred-dollar bills appeared to have been tossed on the passenger side floor. Then,

I noticed the Ziploc baggie in his lap and the awkward-looking photo laying on the passenger seat. The photo appeared to be an image where everything had been blurred except for one black face. A black face that looked like the victim.

"What do you think partner?" Daniel nervously asked me.

"I think whoever did this wasn't trying to rob him. That's for sure," I replied.

"I don't see any major indications of a struggle or fight. This looks a lot like the victim was surprised. Almost like an ambush. An ambush set up by someone the victim had no reason to fear."

"An ambush?" Derrick curiously stated. "An ambush inside of your own car?"

"Jessica's right, Derrick," Daniel jumped in. "She's spot on."

"This was well thought out. This parking lot is isolated enough to get a good amount of privacy, but if you walk down this back fence, there is an exit gate at the end," Daniel explained while pointing.

"It's the perfect place to silently kill someone and walk away without attracting much attention."

"Given that there is a deadly wound to the victim's throat. I'd venture to say that it was the first wound. Once that wound was inflicted, it was over and the ripping open of the victim's guts was merely insurance."

"It was professional insurance, Daniel," I broke in, turning my gaze towards him.

"Whoever did this is a pro. There is no overkill here. It's too lethally efficient and far too logical to be some street thug or crime of emotion."

"And street thugs don't use knives," Daniel added. "Or purposely throw bleach around to contaminate the murder scene."

We were on the same page. Like always, we had that deep connection when we dug our claws into something. This was what we loved to do; solving the riddles of life. This was our calling. All the tension between us seemed to melt away as our minds raced to solve this new riddle together. Solving murders was the essence of our unique bond with each other.

"So, you think this could be some sort of hit?" Derrick asked.

"Maybe," I replied. "Either a hit or we have a very accomplished and patient serial killer on the loose. You don't kill a man by surprise like this in his own car without doing lots of groundwork prior to attempting it."

Suddenly, another car pulled up behind the blue sedan and parked. It was an unmarked police car and from its dark tinted windows, I intuitively knew who had come out to visit us.

"Alright guys," Derrick sighed as he adjusted his camera. "I better start the collection process."

"You two need anything else?"

"No, Derrick," Daniel answered. "You're good to go."

Daniel and I made our way over to the unmarked police car. The driver's side door swung open and Bill Devers rose from behind the wheel. Then the passenger door opened, and Captain Wolf emerged from the passenger's side. Both wore very casual clothing, loose-fitting pants, and comfortable but faded T-Shirts. When they saw Daniel and I, they walked right towards us.

"Hey, Daniel," Bill offered with his heavy New Jersey accent.

"Detective Baker, how's it going my friend?" Bill asked with a smirk.

"As good as it can be on my day off, Detective Devers," I replied.

"I hear that," he mumbled as his eyes widened and rolled.

I hated Bill Devers and we hardly got along. He was one of our most senior Detectives in the New Orleans Police Department. Bill was a muscle-headed Narcotics cop that loved to present himself as a "been there done that" type of guy. Aside from his ego, Bill treated female cops like shit. He was always trying to find shit wrong with everything I did. Thankfully, Daniel always had my back, keeping Bill and his hateful attitude at bay. Still, there were many times when I had to deal with Bill directly and they weren't pleasant at all. I had a morbid fear that Bill would find out about my affair with Daniel. I was certain that he at least suspected we were sleeping together. Our affair was against the rules. We would surely lose our rank as Detectives or get fired if our relationship was outed.

Captain Wolf, on the other hand, was one of my most feverish advocates on the force. She was the ideal image of a powerful and dedicated professional black woman. Along with the encouragement from my Aunt, Captain Wolf was the main reason I had become a cop. A long time native of New Orleans and a 23-year veteran on the force, Captain Wolf was one of the first black females to skyrocket up the ranks of the NOPD. There were many days she would pull me aside and provide me with extra guidance and tutelage. She understood how lonely it could get being a black woman on the force when certain men were always gunning to embarrass or shame you. Her successful presence alone motivated me. Yet, I also was in fear that she would discover what I had been doing with Daniel. She had warned me many times about the dangers of maintaining inappropriate relationships with co-workers and partners. Deep down, I knew she had given me sound advice, but hearing advice is a lot easier than living that advice when you're lonely.

"Sorry I had to call you two in on this one," Captain Wolf began. "We might have a really big problem with this case. I gotta have the best we got on this one, and you two are it."

"But before I get into any of that, Bill, please go over and have a look at the body to confirm."

Bill eased his way towards the car, pausing briefly to glance over at Derrick, who was in the middle of taking photo evidence. Derrick gave an encouraging wave of his hand, allowing Bill to walk over towards the passenger's side window. Bill peered into the car and didn't move. After about a half a minute, he dropped his head then uttered a loud curse word before backing away and walking towards us.

"It's him, Captain," Bill proclaimed.

Captain Wolf let out an audible sigh. I looked over at Daniel. Our eyes met and we exchanged concerned glances during our confusion. "Who is this guy, Captain," I asked.

"He is one of our informants," Captain Wolf admitted.

"He's one of my guys," Bill further explained. "His name is Kevin Longstreet. Kevin Donaldson is one of his aliases."

"He's been working for me for about 10 years now. I've been using this informant's information to build cases against dealers. Only a few people knew he was working for me. This is a huge problem for our department because it means there is a mole somewhere in the office. This is very concerning to us right now."

"What?" Daniel barked!

"With all due respect, Captain. The streets are smart enough to realize when somebody is a snitch. Any number of drug dealers around here could have wanted to see this guy dead and put out a hit on him. We could be looking for anybody."

"Your right, Daniel, but it's not that simple," Captain shot back. "There is a reason nobody killed Kevin before now."

"Kevin worked with our undercovers, but he also was an informant for the DEA. He was a guy who knew a lot."

"Kevin was due to testify in federal court in front of a Grand Jury next week."

"A lot of active cases, both locally and on the Federal side just went up in smoke tonight. I'm talking about big-time drug dealers, not local punks. Dead men can't testify. Now, we are going to have a lot of questions to answer when the DEA finds out about this. Bill and the DEA went out their way to keep this guy on the streets and away from trouble. Now, he is dead."

"So, you are thinking we have a mole?" I asked.

"Exactly," Captain Wolf answered.

"Either we have a mole, or the DEA has one."

"Who was he going to testify against?" Daniel curiously asked.

As Captain was attempting to elaborate, Derrick walked among us and everyone went quiet. The look on his face was one of both urgency and confusion. In his hand, he held a clear evidence bag that contained the photo from inside Kevin's car. I watched as Derrick raised the bag to eye level and turned it backward for all of us to see.

"Excuse me, Captain but I'm going to need Daniel and Jessica to look at this. I found something really weird."

I moved closer to view the bag and saw that someone had written a message on the back of the photo. It read:

"Revenge is a cold dish prepped with tenderness and lots of spice. COONS and traitors shall never be allowed to prosper. ERIC DAVIS IS INNOCENT!"

Chapter Three

Heavy raindrops poured down the windshield and blurred my vision as I struggled to get a clear view through my binoculars. Reaching for the lever behind the steering wheel, I flicked on the car's windshield wipers allowing them to run their course for several seconds before disengaging them. Now my view was clear, and I could see my targets down the road. The four FOWL members were moving with a sense of urgency. Their clothes looked heavy and wet as they scampered to load up the van. The mostly white neighborhood in Westwego, Louisiana, looked gray and somber as the dark rain clouds hovered above. All four of the bastards had decided to carry out their dirty work despite the bad weather. I pressed the binoculars to my eyes and strained for a look before mother nature once again blurred my windshield with its heavenly raindrops.

It had been two full days since I had eliminated Kevin Longstreet. I was certain that his suspicious murder would have stirred these white bastards to execute this move much sooner. For some reason, they had chosen to wait. From behind the lens of my binoculars, I could see all four of them carrying small cardboard boxes, moving them from the trunks of three parked cars and into the cargo compartment of the van. There was no talking amongst them. They were hastily loading the van with an almost military efficiency. Within minutes the whole operation was complete, and they all hustled towards the cover of shelter.

Two men jumped into the van while the two others sprinted to one of the cars. The vans headlights lit up as the engine started. The loaded van backed out of the driveway and drove towards the intersection. After making a rolling stop at a stop sign, the van turned left, increased speed and zoomed past my parked car. Close behind the van was the car with the two other men inside. I was able to catch a glimpse of who was inside the car and spied both Ryan Foster and Josh McRoberts as they rolled past me. I saw Ryan on the passenger side, coolly smoking one of his trademark hand rolled cigarettes as Josh sat behind the wheel.

Once both vehicles were well past me, I started my engine and pulled away from the curb, before making a sharp U-Turn. I pressed down on the accelerator, speeding through the quiet neighborhood until the car and van were back in my sight. As I followed, the caravan hit the freeway and drove east towards New Orleans until they made an exit near the suburb of Harvey. I knew exactly where they were going, and they weren't heading towards Andy's Tavern today. Instead, they were heading down a road leading towards their secret storage facility. Several blocks before reaching the storage facility, I pulled into a gas station parking lot. Using my cellphone to access the internet, I logged into my internet camera hidden away in the storage unit. As the camera activated, it displayed a dark screen. No one had arrived yet. It would be several more minutes before the caravan of bastards arrived at the storage unit. I sat my phone on the passenger seat and walked into the store. It was around dinner time and I was a bit hungry after a long day of spying on these Godless assholes.

After buying myself a bag of chips, a honey bun and a bottle of grape juice, I went back to my car. As I nibbled on my honey bun, I anxiously waited for my black cellphone screen to display any semblance of light. Five more minutes passed, and nothing had changed. I began to wonder if I had made a mistake or if I had missed something. Part of me wanted to leave the gas station and drive to the storage facility to see if they were indeed there. I had spent two years tracking these bastards every movement; they all had to be there, this was there routine. Why would they suddenly break from their routine? I fought the self-doubt springing up inside of me and instead opened my bag of potato chips, forcing myself into a state of patience.

Suddenly, my cellphone screen lit up with activity. I reached over and picked up the cellphone and noticed that I had received a text message; it was Jessica Baker. Before skipping out on our date, she had promised to call me the very next day. I wasn't at all surprised that she had made herself out to be a liar. Not only did she not call me, she didn't even return my phone call to her. Now she is texting me after two whole days of silence. I opened the text and immediately began to laugh to myself as I read one of her predictable excuses.

"Hey Achim. Sorry so silent. Been really busy," she texted.

I threw the phone back on the passenger side seat and refocused my attention back on my bag of chips. The text felt disingenuous and I wasn't responding to that filth. She was trying to feel me out and see if I was angry with her. In all honesty, I was indeed very angry with Jessica and I wasn't going to pretend anymore. I really cared about her, but Jessica's habit of jumping up and running from me told me a lot. Plus, if you make a promise, you keep that promise; that's how I was raised. Several minutes passed and my cellphone erupted, this time a phone call.

"Hello," I answered.

"Hey," Jessica responded with a humble tone.

"I'm sorry I didn't call you back Achim."

"I just got so busy here at work that it slipped my mind to call you back. The last two days have been hectic. I've been assigned this very demanding murder case. Everything is just so complicated right now."

"Achim you're a great guy and I really enjoyed our date the other night. I have enjoyed all the time I have spent with you."

"I just wanted you to know that I'm really…really sorry."

"Jessica, I'm not going to lie to you. This is all disappointing to me." I replied. "I really like you. I do."

"But sometimes you seem sort of…. distant."

"Every time we have a moment where I feel we are finally connecting; you pull away from me."

"At first I just chalked it up to you being a cop, but lately it's been feeling a lot like there is something more to this," I explained barely hiding my frustration. "I don't know what it is, but I'm willing to give you enough room to work it out."

"I want nothing more than for us to grow together Jessica. I think you're a special black woman. A beautiful black woman that I adore, but you're confusing the fuck out of me right now."

I felt my cellphone vibrate and I took the phone away from my ear to look at the screen. It was my internet camera. My camera was sending me a message telling me that my hidden camera was on active mode, so it was time to refocus myself. Worrying about Jessica was getting me nowhere.

"Look Jessica, I'm going to cut this short," I informed her.

"And when you get yourself ready, we can have a serious conversation. Until then, I'm giving you space."

"I've laid my concerns out to you. I'm very much interested to hear your perspective, but unfortunately I have to go right now." I hung up the phone, not even bothering to wait for

Jessica to respond to me. She would have to decide about us, and that decision needed to come from within herself without my influence.

I clicked on to my camera app and enlarged my video feed. The garage door had been lifted open and the lights inside the space were turned on. Ryan Foster and Josh McRoberts stood still as the van came into view. I watched as the van slowly backed up towards the open entrance and came to a stop. Ryan walked over and opened the back doors of the van. The entire group swiftly removed more than six boxes, a large grandfather clock, a canvas painting and several large handfuls of clothes from the van. Before the van's doors were shut, Ryan crawled into the back and pulled out a heavy looking burlap sack and threw it on the garage floor. Josh kneeled and cut open the sack with a pocketknife before removing its contents. Seconds later, I watched as kilos wrapped in plastic wrap began to litter the garage floor.

The sight surprised me. Two years of investigating these guys and never once was I able to uncover any evidence of them being involved with drugs. Had I missed something big? All the photos and video of them breaking into homes. All the cleverly planned robberies I recorded, not one hint of drugs. Then the obvious answer hit me. It dawned on me that they had been involved with drugs the whole time. These white bastards had been playing dress up and selling drugs to the black community, thereby, pulling the wool over black criminals' eyes while they robbed them blind of their possessions and drugs. These were clever drug shake downs. Criminals would never report stolen drugs or stolen merchandise to the police. It was a brilliant hustle and I could only smile.

My suspicions immediately brought me back to the erroneous Eric Davis conviction. Eric had been found guilty of the murder of two black men during a home invasion four years earlier. The star witness in the state's case against Eric Davis was none other than Kevin Longstreet. Kevin would testify under oath to seeing Eric Davis break into the home of Jeffery and Thomas Roberts and hearing gunfire afterwards. Arresting officers from the NOPD found the gun used to murder the Roberts brothers in Eric's car during a subsequent search. To the public, the guilt of Eric Davis seemed like an open and shut case. The only issue was that the accused, Eric Davis, happened to be the nephew of the very influential State Senator Rodney Davis.

State Senator Rodney Davis had been embroiled in a fierce political battle with Democratic leadership over the systemic gentrification of historically black neighborhoods in South Louisiana. Rodney Davis had been spearheading a campaign to expose the nefarious practices of powerful lobbyist that forced poor black people off the properties their families had owned since the end of slavery. In this heated battle, opponents of Rodney had leaked damaging information about Eric Davis to the press, initiating a smear campaign against him. The media eagerly reported on Eric Davis's extensive drug history, numerous run-ins with the law, and attempted to make a direct connection between Eric's criminal activities and Senator Rodney Davis. Weeks before Rodney Davis was due to present an Anti-Gentrification Bill to the state senate, Eric Davis was arrested and charged with the murder of the two Roberts brothers. The two brothers had recently inherited their grandmothers' home in the 9th Ward of New Orleans and there were rumors that their murder was simply some sort of drug turf war.

Eric's high profile arrest smothered the momentum of Rodney Davis's Anti-Gentrification campaign, as the media fixated on the arrest and ultimate conviction of his nephew. Due to the bad press, Rodney Davis's Anti-Gentrification bill quietly died in the state senate and nearly ruined Senator Davis's political career. As the years passed, the Davis family reached out to Robert Charles to help clear Eric's name. That's when I and Mr. Darryl were given the task of finding out what really happened during the murders of Jeffery and Thomas Roberts.

During my investigation, I discovered that these four white men were the murderers of the Roberts brothers, and with the help of Kevin Longstreet, they had set up Eric Davis. The gun found in Eric Davis's car was likely planted by the NOPD, and with the help of Kevin's false testimony, the NOPD was able to convict Eric. Both Mr. Darryl and I knew we could never deliver the evidence we found to the NOPD; they had no interest in righteous justice for the two murder victims. As far as they were concerned, their suspect for the double murder was already convicted and in jail. Now that I had killed Kevin, I could slowly begin the process of showing the NOPD the undeniable and painful facts surrounding Eric's conviction.

The four bastards opened a small door on the back of the grandfather clock's base and tucked away the kilos of drugs inside of it. Afterwards, all four men took several moments to tidy up the cluttered space. Ryan turned off the lights and lowered the garage door. My cell phone screen went black as the garage door closed, so I shutdown my camera and logged off. They would certainly make their way back to the highway, so I needed to get myself ready to intercept them. Looking down the road, I saw the van and the car rapidly traveling towards me. I cranked up my car and coolly pulled out in front of them, positioning my car in the far-right lane so they could pass by me. The van and the car drove by not even noticing me as they swiftly passed. Hitting the accelerator, I sped up and stayed several cars behind them. As we neared the highway on ramp, the van got into the left lane to enter the highway heading back to Westwego, while the car got into the right lane to head towards New Orleans. They were splitting, so I needed to follow Ryan because he was my target today, but I was uncertain which vehicle Ryan was in.

My gut told me to follow the car that Ryan had rode in earlier. I felt my heartbeat quicken as I glided over to the right lane and fell in behind the car. I drove close and looked through the car's back window, trying to see if Ryan was indeed inside the car. Even from one car length behind them, it was hard to see inside due to the heavy rain. All the car's windows were closed and no one inside the car was smoking. Ryan smoked a lot, especially when on the road. I decided to check out the van as best I could. When I looked over to the left, I saw the van was long gone. The van had hit the highway and long since disappeared from my sight. Now I was committed to following the car. I had to be right or my plans for tonight would be a total mess.

When the stoplight changed to green, the car turned right and sped down the service road before hitting the highway towards New Orleans. The two men drove over the bridge to the East Bank of New Orleans and took the Tchoupitoulas Street exit. They drove through the Garden District passing by its historic store fronts filled with affluent white shoppers spending their cash on a rainy day. As I inconspicuously followed them from several cars behind, they drove past all the store fronts and turned into a residential area. It was then that I knew where the two men were going. I had been down here before spying on them. After parking, Josh McRoberts exited the car and sprinted up the steps into his home, to escape the rain. On the contrast, another white man slowly got out of the passenger side and calmly walked towards the sidewalk. His clothes were soaked from the rain. The white man struggled to light a cigarette while using his hands to cover his lighter from the monsoon. I felt an instant sensation of relief once I recognized Ryan's face. Several minutes later, Josh walked back outside and handed Ryan a small stack of clothes. The two men appeared to share a few words before they both walked into the house, disappearing from my view.

This stage of my plan looked like it would be a go for tonight, but given the fact that Ryan might have company, I needed to audible. I would have to call in a favor to keep my plans rolling, so I reached over and grabbed my cellphone. My fingers instinctively swiped my screen and opened to the very phone number I knew I needed. Within seconds, Mr. Darryl's phone was ringing on the other end.

"Achim Jeffers," Mr. Darryl answered. "What do you need son?"

"I'm getting this first bastard tonight," I began. "In order for me to do it, I'm going to need assistance from other friends of Robert Charles. Two friends that are sympathetic and down for our cause," I further explained.

"You need two friends. Sympathetic and down for the cause," Mr. Darryl repeated with a heavy sigh.

My last-minute request was clearly a burden for him. I could hear the anxiety in Mr. Darryl's tone as he pounded away at me with a series of follow up questions. Mr. Darryl abhorred surprises and I worked hard to provide the answers that would sooth his tender nerves. In the world of covert operations, unplanned surprises undoubtedly lead to unpredictable mistakes and gross errors. This business was a business of calmness, coldness and precise calculation. Haste and imprudence were not the hallmarks of Robert Charles. If I needed it, Mr. Darryl would surely supply it, but not without having a robust discussion first.

"I can get you what you need Achim, but it's going to cost Robert Charles a few more stacks," Mr. Darryl conveyed.

"I'm going to have to ask Robert Charles for permission before I send any help your way. They may not want to pay any more cash or involve two other agents in your operation, so give me a few minutes. I'll get back to you and let you know what the answer is."

"Achim," Mr. Darryl stated before I could hang up. "Anything new on the black female cop? Is she with them or not?"

"No," I responded. "She's not with them. Detective Baker isn't a threat. She's just a lost black woman in the middle of all this."

"Ok," Mr. Darryl replied. "Still keep an eye on her. She could still turn out to be a load of trouble."

Satisfied with my answers, Mr. Darryl hung up the phone and I returned my attention to the task at hand. Thirty-five minutes passed, and Ryan was still inside the house. I grabbed one bag of candy and began to nibble, occupying my boredom with a sweet snack as the heavy raindrops subsided into a hazy mist.

After an hour, I saw Ryan emerge from the house alone. He walked out the front door and made his way towards the car. Ryan had changed out of his wet clothes and in his left hand he carried a small grocery bag. He opened the trunk of the Chevy Impala and placed the bag inside, then he got behind the wheel and drove down the street away from me. I cranked up my car and pursued from a safe distance as Ryan slowly made his way through the narrow back streets of New Orleans. Ryan eventually arrived at his Mid-City home and parked inside of his small driveway. I was familiar with this neighborhood as well. While staking out Ryan's home on numerous occasions, I would often see middle aged white women pushing baby strollers as they walked by me. This neighborhood was now a far cry from the days when Section 8 Housing had dominated it. Now it was a newly gentrified area, completely cleansed of its African American legacy with its elaborate hipster coffee shops and its expensive neighborhood grocery stores. I found an open parking space several houses down from Ryan's home and parked my car.

Within five minutes, Ryan came back out of his home and set his house alarm before walking down the sidewalk towards my car. He wore a powder blue flat brim hat and a short sleeve shirt with cargo shorts. His white forearms were filled with a myriad of decorative tattoos and the silver chain that hung outside of his pocket swung with his every step. I sat still as Ryan closed in on my car, hoping that he would not notice this black man weirdly sitting alone inside. As he neared, I pulled out my cellphone and pretended to be busy with it. As he passed by, I watched out of the corner of my eye. Ryan did not seem to notice me, so I continued to watch from my rear-view mirror as he walked down the sidewalk for another block and then made a left. It was then that I got out of the car and began to walk at a brisk pace to catch up with him. To my surprise, I made the left turn and didn't see him. Where had Ryan gone to?

I decided to continue down the street. He could not have just turned here and suddenly disappeared from the planet, Ryan had to be here somewhere. I walked past several houses and a small Italian Bistro before I came upon a grunge looking cocktail bar operating out of a converted duplex home. I walked up a small flight of stairs and went inside. Ryan was in the nearly empty establishment sitting alone at the bar as the bartender washed dishes. He was talking on his cellphone and looked up at me as I walked through the door. He gave me an uncurious glance before turning his head away and continuing to try and talk over the bars mildly loud background music. I sat down two chairs from him and pulled out my wallet, sitting my wallet on the bar counter for the bartender to notice it. I was a black man in a place where I wasn't truly supposed to be. It was probably best that I put the bartender at ease as to my intentions.

My eyes scanned the inside of the bar looking for any cameras. Cameras that might record my presence there for police to review and investigate later. Once I was satisfied that the bar had no recording systems, I grabbed a drink menu and pretended to review it. Seconds later, the bartender walked by with a mixed drink in his hand and spoke to me.

"I'll be with you in just a second," he proclaimed as he sat a mixed drink in front of Ryan.

The bartender was a chubby white guy, mid to late 30's I presumed. His pale white skin was littered with dark and evil looking tattoos. He was sporting a dull looking bald head with a long reddish beard. His look was a serious one that projected a no-nonsense persona usually reserved for ultra-right wingers. The bartender swiped Ryan's credit card and printed out his receipt before walking towards me and asking me what I'd like to drink.

"I'll take a Jack and Coke, double. Light on the coke please."

Without uttering a word, the bartender nodded his head and turned towards his perfectly formed drink display. He grabbed a bottle of Jack and began mixing my adult beverage. I listened as Ryan finally ended his phone call, then placed his cellphone on the counter and began to drink. His spirit and body language seemed to be one of discreet loneliness. I was sure that he must have been reflecting on the death of his black bootlicking buddy Kevin. Kevin was Ryan's access to free drugs, loose tailed black women and a bigger portion of the stolen booty inside the storage garage. Ryan couldn't just steal things out of the storage unit himself. His white buddies in FOWL wouldn't dare allow him to satisfy his dark urges at their expense. So, he cleverly employed Kevin to do his dirty deeds for him. He needed a way to insulate himself from charges of stealing. There was no better foil than a drug addicted black proxy. A black man whom Ryan knew none of his white partners in FOWL, would truly trust and would quickly blame for goods that were stolen. It was then that I figured out that Kevin and Ryan probably had plans the night I had killed him. Most likely, they were both going to travel out of town and go to the casinos in Mississippi, which was something they usually did together.

The bartender sat my drink in front of me and I forked out cash from inside my wallet. After my first sip, I felt my cellphone suddenly start vibrating in my pocket. I pulled it out and saw that Mr. Darryl had sent me a text message.

"I have Rachel and Sharon on deck for you tonight. Where do you want to meet them?" Mr. Darryl sent.

"Have them meet me at Larry's Hookah Bar on Canal Street," I typed.

"Have them there and ready to put in work," I typed a second time.

After several minutes, Mr. Darryl sent me another text. "They are on their way now. Good luck son," he sent.

Ryan and I both finished our drinks. The bartender gave me a quick refill and then walked over to Ryan. As Ryan began to order another drink, a short black dude walked through the door. He looked to be in his early 20's and wore flip flops with ratty looking basketball shorts. His powder blue Southern A&M University shirt stood out to me as it had the school's logo on it with the word 'alumni' printed below. I knew this guy. This brother had spent a great deal of time hanging out with Ryan the last few months. I would watch as this guy would come over to Ryan's house where the two men would play video games all night long.

His name was Anthony Rice, he was a recent graduate of Tulane University, who had come to America as a foreign student from the Bahamas to study engineering. Ryan had befriended Anthony after the two played basketball together at a local YMCA. Most times, Ryan would hang out with Kevin. They would both pick up women and score drugs together. With Anthony, Ryan would mostly drink alcohol and attend Saints games with him.

Anthony walked over to Ryan and sat down after they exchanged a light handshake. The two men began to talk and smile at each other and I knew it was the perfect time to inject myself upon them.

"Hey brother," I asked looking at Anthony. "You went to Southern…. What up fam?"

"I graduated from Southern too. I love the shirt family. I'm class of 07."

I rose from my seat and moved over towards Anthony and Ryan. Both men looked at me with gazes of awkward discomfort. I reached out and offered my hand to Anthony. After he gave me a weak handshake, I motioned for the bartender to come over.

"Hey, drinks for these two fellows. On me," I requested. The bartender looked at both men and they eagerly ordered drinks. I could sense their uneasiness disappear as I smiled and paid the bartender.

"What year did you graduate?" I asked Anthony.

"I graduated in 2016," Anthony responded with a slight Caribbean accent and half smile.

"My name is Slim by the way," I introduced.

"What are you doing now?" I asked as he took a sip of his cranberry vodka.

"My name is Anthony Rice. I'm working for Entergy, I'm a computer programmer."

"Okay" I responded.

I knew he was lying to me. Anthony wasn't a computer programmer. That's probably the lie he told his immigrant parents to make them feel better. Anthony worked at a local electronic store, selling TV's and computers. Ryan and Anthony had a little hustle where they would sell partially damaged or used electronics from the store. Selling them on the street at discounted prices and splitting the cash.

"I notice your accent brother. Where are you from?" I asked.

"I'm from Freeport in the Bahamas."

"Yeah! The Bahamas," I excitingly responded.

"I've been to the Bahamas several times."

"My favorite place was the Bimini Islands with all that beautiful light blue ass water."

"I really loved the conch salad….and that… Kalat beer?"

"No. No. No," Anthony corrected me with laughter. "Kalik Beer," Anthony clarified with a broad smile.

"Yeah," I excitingly proclaimed while giving Anthony some dap.

I turned to Ryan and extended my hand to him. His eyes were a little hazy and the drink in his hand was now nearly empty.

"Hey I'm Slim," I offered.

"Ryan," he replied shaking my hand with a firm grip.

"You from around here Ryan?"

"Yeah, I'm from Laplace born and raised. I live in the city now."

"You from Laplace huh. You got to be a Saints fan then," I jokingly inquired.

"Hell, yeah dude. I got season tickets."

"Me too," I interrupted. "I have a box suite pass because I work for Mercedes Benz."

I saw both of their eyes light up. Their whole expression and body language changed in that instant. I don't know if it was Mercedes or box suite that got their attention, but I could tell I was no longer the annoying drunk guy at the bar. I was now an opportunity.

All three of us sat and began to chat about everything from football, rap music to beautiful women for just over an hour. Both men were tipsy as hell as they chased one drink after another. Ryan reached into his pocket and pulled out his tobacco. After ordering another drink, he rolled a handmade cigarette.

"Excuse me fellows, I need to go have a smoke," he declared.

"I'll join you man," I seconded. "Anthony, can you watch our drinks for us?"

Ryan and I walked outside, positioning ourselves away from the bars entrance. I pulled a Black & Mild cigar out of my pocket and asked him for his lighter.

"You don't look like the Black & Mild type of dude," he stated with a wide smile.

"What does a Black & Mild type of dude look like to you?" I asked curiously.

"Not you Slim," Ryan said with a laugh. "You look like the church going, family man type."

"Your right Ryan. I am a man of God," I replied.

"I'm not into Black & Mild's, but tonight I will be. This isn't what I really want anyway, but it will have to do for now," I added as I lit my cigar. "I got big plans for tonight."

"What are you doing tonight?" Ryan asked while blowing smoke out of his lungs.

"There is a hookah bar over on Canal Street. They sell the harder stuff I am getting into tonight. I'm celebrating my divorce from my wife. We were married for seven years."

"She gets the kids and the cars. I get the pussy and the drugs."

"Sounds like a fair deal," Ryan said barely holding in his laughter.

"It was the only deal she was getting. If you know what I mean," I further explained.

"I'm about to head out in a few. You wanna roll?"

"Shit yeah. I'll smoke some hookah with you Slim. You can't celebrate being a newly single man by yourself. That's not in the bro code."

"How about your boy Anthony? Is he willing to roll out with us?"

"Yeah, Anthony will come," Ryan said with excitement in his voice. "We planned to go to Bourbon and hang out, but we can hang with you for a while before we go."

We went back into the bar, paid our tabs and tipped the bartender before leaving. I led the way as we walked several blocks towards Canal Street while chatting about smoking weed and buying cocaine. Once we made it to Canal Street, we walked one block and arrived at Larry's Hookah Bar. The place was packed with people, mostly young college age women sitting at their tables smoking hookah and typing away on their laptops.

"Wow, I've never been to this place before," Anthony commented. "A lot of chicks in here. It looks poppin."

"Yeah, I've heard of this place before but have never been here," Ryan explained as he stumbled towards the door. "Apparently this is a good place to find easy prey."

"You like black women, don't you?" I asked with a smile.

"Buddy Yeah! There isn't nothing better than a fine ass black woman with a big juicy ass." Ryan began. "My nigga, I don't even fuck with white girls no more. I got to have me some black pussy, I'm addicted to that shit."

I forced a smile to my face as I saw Ryan examining me for my response to his intentional words. I glanced at Anthony and noticed the wide grin on his face as he shook his head in approval, barely noticing Ryan's racist comment. That is why Ryan liked Anthony. Anthony was a weak Negro. He was all too eager to accept white abuse in return for white acceptance.

We walked into the Hookah bar and were greeted by a beautiful Egyptian looking hostess. The hostess sat us at a large booth and presented us with menus. I ordered the table a round of Tequila shots with a grape mint hookah served in a large hollowed out pineapple. As we smoked and laid back, I could see that Ryan was getting comfortable and trying to feel out my barriers.

"Man, this fuckin grape mint is chill as fuck," he lamented to me. "I love this shit."

"All I need now is a big black titty in my mouth and I'm in heaven!"

"How about you Anthony? I interjected.

"Do you like black women or do you only mess with white chicks?"

"Hell, yeah dude," Ryan broke in. "Anthony likes boney ass white women. He isn't black. He's a white boy ass nigga."

I listened as both went back and forth over who was "blacker." The discussion pissed me off, but I forced myself to remain calm and in character. Wearing a phony smile and laughing loudly at their silly jokes that denigrated black culture, was making me boil inside. I was forced to listen to Ryan try and explain to me how Eminem was the greatest rapper ever. I hid my sheer contempt behind playful laugher as Ryan described how rappers like Nas, Jay-Z, LL, Rakim, Biggie and Tupac were all garbage. He foolishly detailed how he could get any party jumping with his lengthy Eminem playlist. This guy was a disrespectful idiot. I would be able to get God's retribution soon enough, but first I had to find my back up. I looked around the bar as both men distracted one another. No one in the bar jumped out to me as being Rachel or Sharon. I needed to get away from these idiots and make a phone call to Mr. Darryl. If I left, there was a possibility that these two idiots would bounce on me, so I reached in my pocket and pulled out a small baggie, tossing it on the table for both men to see.

Looking at the baggie, they stopped joking and a silent pause came over the booth. Ryan reached down and picked it up, examining it closely before wrapping his fist around the baggie to conceal it from public view.

"Dude, you just gonna use this shit right here in the booth?"

"Hell yeah," I responded. "I told you this is my celebration night."

"I know the owner of this place. We good. Nobody fucking with us in here as long as we are buying drinks and not causing problems."

"I'll be right back. I got to go take a piss. Ya'll get that shit ready," I said with a smile.

I knew right then that they were not going anywhere. They would be hanging with me for the duration of the night, or at least Ryan would. I walked towards the restroom and pulled out my cellphone. I called Mr. Darryl and got no answer. As I put my phone away, I felt a tap on my shoulder, and I turned around to see Rachel. It had been six years since I had last seen her. She looked like she hadn't aged a day since then. She wore tight blue jeans that revealed every curve of her attractive figure. Her shirt was cropped and gave a noticeable hint of her cleavage. Her long flowing black hair highlighted her beautiful brown skin. Rachel's earrings were just right, not too flashy and not big. The smile on her face made her pretty brown eyes stand out. She was a bomb shell of a woman.

Next to Rachel stood a cute light skinned woman that I had never met before. She wore tight fitting shorts and a thin crimson shirt that gave a hint of a bra that was holding back very large breasts. The lotion she wore on her light skin made it look alluring. Her hair was cut short but was very feminine and cute. She was short but her thick thighs were evidence of a gym habit. Her eyes seemed to change color as I investigated them. Switching from brown, to blue, then to green. These were two beautiful black women. They were most certainly the right tools for my mission.

"Hey Sweetie," Rachel said as she leaned towards me to give me a hug.

"It's been a while since we last saw each other."

"Yeah, like six years since that thing up in Atlanta," I expanded.

"How are you doing girl?"

"I'm good sweetie. It's good to see you again. You look fine as hell mister."

"No, you're the one who looks fantastic Rachel," I shot back. I watched as Rachel blushed. She leaned over and gave me a kiss on the cheek, leaving the scent and feel of her lipstick on my face.

"Oh, thank you sweetie. You are such a gentlemen Achim."

"Achim, this is Sharon," Rachael said as she motioned towards the light skinned woman standing next to her. "Sharon is from

Seattle. She's down here doing a little freelance work with me and I'm showing her the ropes."

"How are you Sharon?" I said while shaking her hand. "You couldn't learn this business from anybody better then Rachel."

"Hi. Nice to meet you Achim," she replied with a distinct valley girl accent.

"Well…. are you two ready to go to work? I got a tough one for you two tonight," I explained.

Rachel and Sharon looked at each other and shared a giggle. "Tough! You call those two losers you're with tough?" Rachel mockingly asked. "Sweetie, we can make quick work of those two…. but before we do anything…. we need to make sure the money's right first.'

"Money's, right?" I asked.

This was some bullshit. My back automatically stiffened at the suggestion of having to negotiate while in the heat of battle. There was an uncomfortable moment of silence between all three of us. The background noise of the hookah bar accentuated the deceptive seriousness in both ladies' smiles, as they both gazed at me. It was then I realized that they were not joking. They were dead serious.

"You're not really going to do this to me right now are you? I'm right in the middle of this shit Rachel," I exploded.

"Yes, we are Sweetie. Mr. Darryl only paid us half. Normally, I would have told his old ass to fuck off, but when I heard it was you, I decided to make a deal with him."

"Mr. Darryl said you would pay the other half."

"Other half of what?" I barked back.

"Other half of twenty," Rachel clarified.

"Twenty," I sheepishly sighed.

Either these ladies were gaming me, or Mr. Darryl had not taken care of business. It was too late in the fourth quarter for all this bullshit and these ladies knew I was in a bind. They had me by my nuts and there was nothing I could do about it. I had no choice but to grant their demand. I had stashed away some cash and jewelry that was supposed to be donated to Eric Davis upon his release. Given the circumstances, I decided that the Davis Family wouldn't mind if I used it to cover some of their own expenses.

"Look, I will get you both your other ten once this thing is done."

"I'll even add some stolen jewelry into the mix. Your just going to have to make sure that you pawn the damn jewelry out of state, but first, you got to help me do this. You got to follow my rules to a tee and deliver me what I need before you get any damn thing."

"That means, I need access to the white boy's house. That means, you get him in his house without him setting his alarm. That means once this is done, you two leave New Orleans, immediately. Not when you're rested. Not after a few days, but immediately. No hanging around to party and spend money. You do this job, and then you travel as far away from New Orleans as you can. It will be too dangerous for you both to hang around here once this is done."

"Do we have a deal ladies?"

The ladies looked at each other and nodded their heads. Rachel broke out a pretty smile and leaned up to kiss my lips. When she kissed me, I could feel her soft wet tongue against mine. In an instant, she pulled away and began to laugh at me with a flirting smile. From my time working with her in Atlanta, I knew Rachel had mastered the powers of seduction. A man could never tell whether this woman wanted to sleep with you, or she was just manipulating the hell out of you.

"Deal Achim! Sealed with a kiss between us and the world," she said as her eyes lit up like a lottery machine.

"We'll get you inside that house. Hell, we may get him to leave the damn front door wide open for you."

"Tonight, my name is Slim. The marks name is Ryan. Which one of you are going to go after him?" I asked.

"We are going to let him choose," Rachel explained with a dismissive grin. "His eyes Achim. His eyes will tell us what moves we need to make. Don't you worry yourself about that? That's why you're paying us."

I walked back to the booth and the ladies followed me. As we got close to the booth, I saw that Ryan and Anthony had open my bag of dope, just as I had asked them to do. They were both high now and my plan was working itself out magnificently.

"Hey guys. Look who I found after taking a piss," I proclaimed as I ushered Rachel and Sharon into our booth. "Two pretty ass friends of mine just ambushed me outside the men's room."

Rachel and Sharon glided over and immediately turned on the sexy. The looks on the two men's face were telling. Ryan could hardly contain the cheese smile hiding under his oversized baseball cap. As Ryan's blue eyes reviewed the women, he scooted over to the edge of his sofa in order to make room for the ladies to sit next to him. Anthony's face wore the nervous look of a brother that hadn't had a piece of ass for months; they had both swallowed the bait.

"Hi," Sharon said to Ryan with a cute little voice. Rachel moved towards Anthony and sat next to him, offering him a light handshake and an adorable smile.

The ladies introduced themselves to the men and we all engaged in small talk. The ladies told the men that they had once been Saints cheerleaders and that they met me while shooting a commercial for Mercedes Benz over in Mandeville. Sharon noticed the open baggie of dope on the table and began to glare at it. Her gaze caught Ryan's eyes and he immediately stuck his finger into the bag, pulling out a large pinch of powder on the tip of his finger.

"You want to try some don't you girl?" He said to Sharon holding it near her face. "Come on, get you some of this shit. It's good."

Sharon giggled nervously and shook her head 'no', in a halfhearted yet playful rebuke. "You try and then I'll try," Rachel chimed in encouraging Sharon. "Come on girl" Ryan continued with a mockingly sarcastic smile. "My nigga Anthony over there just tried for the first-time and look at him. He's doing really good over there right now."

Both women laughed uncontrollably at hearing Ryan call Anthony a nigga. I once again felt the prying white eyes of Ryan examining me, so I gave a dutiful wide smile and joined in on teasing the hapless Anthony.

"I must say this shit has me feeling nice right now," Anthony opined with a coonish smile.

"Ok…Ok…" Sharon began with an innocent yet flirty laugh. "But not too much though. Just a little."

"A little is all you need sexy. Relax, we havin some fun tonight," Ryan added with a grin.

Sharon leaned towards Ryan's finger and took a small sniff. Ryan then put his finger up to his own nose and sniffed up all the rest of the dope left on his finger. After dipping his finger back into the baggie, Ryan had Rachel lean over and take a sniff. Anthony dipped his own nubby finger into the baggie afterwards. His face displaying a glossy smile after taking a rather large sniff, in an obvious attempt to show off in front of the ladies. Everyone was getting high except me and no one seemed to notice. They were completely out of the moment with their minds channeled somewhere else. They were all engrossed in the cat and mouse game of flirting, teasing and elevating sexual tension.

Several rounds of warm tequila were consumed, spiced in with a few more snort sessions. The conversation among us grew raunchy as the girls continuously got more and more touchy with both guys. Anthony had his arms wrapped around Rachel and began to whisper into her ear, causing her to giggle loudly and caress his arms. After a large snort of the dope, Sharon crossed her sexy legs and leaned her head on Ryan's chest. I could see the excitement in his eyes as he looked at her alluring thick thighs. He moved his right hand and placed it over her crossed legs. Sharon responded by moving her left hand, laying it on his thigh, near his crotch. A suppressed smile burst onto Ryan's face as he glanced over at me, sharing a bit of unspoken locker room bravado. I winked while giving him a non-verbal salute for a job well done.

My cellphone rang interrupting our conversation inside the booth. I looked at my phone and saw that Jessica had just text me.

"I want to talk to you," she wrote. "I need to talk to you."

The thought of Jessica temporarily took me out of the game and caused my own frustrations to boil inside of me. This was not the right time to talk to Jessica, she would have to wait. I was in no condition to talk to her, but I decided to use her untimely intrusion to my tactical benefit. I reread her message, pretending

"Will do sweetie. So....are you buying me more drin
handsome.... or are you going to make a sister beg for
texted with a heart and eggplant emoji.

"Girl, I got something for you that's better than
eggplant. I got the bag sister," I texted back.

"You nasty boy. You know how to really turn me on d
Achim. See you in Slidell," she texted.

About thirty minutes passed and Rachel's SUV finall
rolling up the dark street. The SUV came to a sudden and cr
stop in the middle of the road in front of Ryan Foster's l
Both passenger side doors swung open, and Ryan and Sl
spilled out of the SUV drinking tall hand grenades. I could
their loud drunken laughter and it seemed to echo through
the empty and dark street. A clearly drunk Ryan was also carry
two large plastic bags sporting the label French Quarter Exoti
a popular novelty store near Frenchmen Street. I knew Rach
had purposely taken him there and her forethought regardin
this mission truly impressed me. This woman was worth ever
dime, she had pulled a genius move. Sharon shut the passenger
side door behind her and gave a quick wave goodbye to Rachel.
Rachel giggled at Sharon and straightened her wheels before
pulling away from the couple. Her SUV came towards me and
I watched as she gazed down at me from above, in her perch
behind the steering wheel. As she slowly passed, she gave me a
naughty smile and blew me a kiss before speeding off into the
darkness of the night.

I watched as Ryan and Sharon made their way up the porch to his front door. He struggled to handle his house keys with full hands, forcing him to place the two bags on the porch. Finally, he opened the front door and disengaged his security alarm. This was show time for the newbie, Sharon. I began to worry that she might not be able to distract Ryan long enough for him to forget about the alarm system. It would be a disaster if she failed in getting that done. I knew Rachel could charm any man into doing what she needed them to do. I had seen her in action and experienced it for myself. Sharon on the other hand was an unknown quantity, still learning the ropes of this business. She walked through the open door and Ryan reached down to grab the bags off the porch. With full hands, he walked in the house and the front door quickly shut behind him. I watched my cellphone as the time slowly passed by, hoping that Rachel & Sharon's creative novelty store ploy had prevented Ryan from setting his alarm. Sharon would have ten minutes before I would come in after them. Ten minutes to have Ryan engrossed fully in her, so I could strike.

Ten minutes passed, and it was do or die time. I got out of the car and gave a quick check of my surroundings. The streets were clear, not even a stray dog or cat in sight. The Mid-City neighborhood was quiet as hell. I walked towards Ryan's front door and paused before going up the steps, hoping that I might hear something inside. Not even a peep could be heard from

within the house. Now was the moment of truth. Had Sharon done her job?

I walked up the steps and twisted the knob before slowly pushing the door forward. As I added force the door began to move, and it didn't stop, it was opening. As the door swung half open, I heard the first faint sounds of music. Ryan had Post Malone playing in the background and the sound of that music sickened me to my core. I walked inside the house and slowly closed the door, locking it behind me. Following the music, I made my way through the passageway towards the living room. Slowly I moved forward, not making a sound while walking up against the wall. Eventually, I made it to the wide living room entrance and peered inside from behind the wall.

I noticed Sharon's shorts and shirt laying on Ryan's plush dark brown carpet. A few feet away laid her white bra and laced panties. Ryan's clothes were in a neat pile near the long brown leather couch. Towering above the couch were a pair of wall mounted home studio speakers. The speakers rattled as the annoying music poured out of them. At the end of the couch, were the two Exotica bags, a large black strap on dildo, lubricants and several other sex toys all hastily dumped on the floor. Sharon was laid back on the couch completely nude. Her light skin tone looked beautiful and soft. I noticed her long erect brown nipples and perfect pedicured toes, sporting shiny pink nail polish. Her legs were spread wide open and Ryan's face was buried in her crotch as he kneeled on the soft carpet indulging himself in her.

He was totally nude as well, aside from wearing a pair of dirty white socks. His hairy back shined with sweat, as one of his hands reached up to fondle Sharon's exposed breasts while he tasted her. With his other hand, he masturbated, pleasuring himself while fueling Sharon's excitement.

Sharon's eyes darted towards me as I eased myself from behind the wall. Our eyes locked and she flashed an ecstasy filled smile at me. Showing off, she placed her hands behind Ryan's head and pushed his face into her before letting out a slight moan of joy. I watched as he squeezed her breast harder, while feverishly moving his face into her and stroking himself wildly. I grabbed my sharp knife and the small towel from my pocket. Sharon kept her eyes locked on me. She moaned louder as I looked into her eyes and slowly walked toward them. She was enjoying this shit and I could tell she was about to orgasm. As she came, she again pressed Ryan's face into her, while letting out a loud cry as her muscles began to spasm. Seconds later, Ryan let out his own loud moan, then continued to devour her as he ejaculated on the edge of his brown couch.

I rushed over and shoved his face deeper into Sharon. Then I took my blade and in one decisive move, I slit his throat. Blood shot out all over the couch and onto Sharon's crotch. We released his head and a bloody Sharon nervously jumped up from the couch. I threw him down on his back before handing Sharon the towel.

"Clean yourself up sister," I calmly instructed.

Ryan was on the floor, bleeding profusely as his body wrenched in pain. Finally, he looked up at me and saw my face. We exchanged a cold stare of instant recognition and I could see the telling surprise in his eyes as the blood poured out of his slashed neck.

"Fucked up ain't it? You'll never say the word nigga again, now won't you," I declared. Bending down to one knee, I took the sharp blade and shoved it into his guts and ripped it out after a few painful twists.

"Have you touched the dildo?" I asked Sharon.

"No…. No…He opened it," a very shaken Sharon replied.

After reaching over to grab the large black dildo, I took it and shoved it into Ryan's bloody mouth as his body involuntarily fought for air.

"Eminem sucks cock, just like you", I playfully informed Ryan.

"Do you remember everything you touched in this house?" I asked a now rattled Sharon.

"Yes……I do."

I walked into Ryan's laundry room to grab two towels and a half-filled jug of bleach. When I came back to the living room, a clothed Sharon was now sitting on the arm rest of the couch in tears.

"Sharon, I need you to pull it together right now," I explained.

"Right now, you are falling apart on me. You have done a fabulous job so far."

"But right now, you ain't helping us Sharon," I insisted.

"You're actually leaving more evidence that I will have to clean up after. Do you understand sister?" I said as I pointed to her teardrops falling on the carpet.

"When we get to my car, you can cry your eyes out. Hell, I'll even console you, but right now I need you to get your shit together. We got a damn job to do."

Pulling a pair of latex gloves out of my pocket, I handed them to her. Then, I took one of the towels and lightly moistened it with bleach.

"Put on the gloves and take this towel."

"Everything you touched in this house get it cleaned up with that fuckin towel. Understand?"

"Yeah, I got it," Sharon softly mumbled as she wiped away her tears with the back of her hand.

"And please turn that stupid ass music off," I added.

Now it was time to set my stage. I walked to Ryan's bedroom and opened his closet. After moving around a few items, I found what I was looking for. I took it and brought it to the living room, neatly laying it out next to his now lifeless head. Then, I took the photo out of my pocket and placed it on his forehead.

"Sharon, go in the kitchen. In the second drawer to the left, there are two large Ziploc bags. Please bring them to me."

"How do you know all this about this guy's house?" Sharon softly asked.

"Do you really want to know, how I know?" I angrily shot back. "Just go get the damn bags. Time is running short."

She came back with the bags and I wrote a message on them with my black sharpie. Once the ink dried, I took the bags and placed Ryan's dead hands in each one. I watched as Sharon began scrubbing everything from the door frame, the couch and the kitchen counters.

"Did you pay for any of these sex toys?" I asked.

"No," she whispered. "His sick ass paid for them."

"Make sure you collect all your stuff, including that drink you brought in here."

"Leave nothing behind. Double check everything."

It was getting close to move out minute. Glancing down at my watch I noticed we were a little behind schedule. It was critical that I got both of us out of Ryan's house at exactly the right moment or his neighbors may witness us both leaving. I took one of the Exotica bags and emptied it. After placing the bloody towel inside of it, I handed the bag to Sharon.

"Take this with you and put it in my car. Do you know which car I'm in?" Sharon shook her head 'no' and I pointed in the general direction.

"I'm in the brown sedan parked a block away towards Canal Street. Walk directly to it and open the door like nothing unusual is going on. Get inside and wait for me out there. If something screwy happens while I'm in here, get behind the wheel and drive to Slidell," I instructed while handing her the keys.

Sharon took the car keys and walked to the front door. Once she opened it, she gave a quick glance outside to see if there were any spectators. When she was satisfied that she was alone, she removed her latex gloves and gently closed the door. I heard her light footsteps as she walked down the porch and calmly hit the sidewalk. It was then that I knew she was a keeper. She was what a true strong black woman is made of, not this wholly destructive caricature that white society likes to promote. Sharon was a rider. Robert Charles should surely be proud to have such a committed black woman like her on our team.

Chapter Four

The loud humming sound of the hotel's broken air conditioning unit interrupted my sleep. My eyes abruptly opened, and I felt the sticky humidity choking me in this dark smothering room. In frustration, I tossed back my thin bed sheets in a vain attempt to dry and cool my sweaty skin. The more I tried to make myself comfortable, the more nothing seemed to work. The room was so stuffy, and I was feeling this heat that felt like I was slowly roasting from my insides. What I needed was some cool fresh air, a totally new environment that would allow me to breathe instead of having to struggle for each precious ounce of oxygen. I decided it was time to get out of the bedroom and get some fresh air.

I looked over at Daniel as he laid quietly asleep in the bed next to me, seemingly without a worry in the world. He was completely naked aside from wearing his silver wedding band. The look on his face was one of peace and tranquility, and I wondered how he got so much sleep in such conditions. It had been weeks since we were last together in this manner. Just the two of us together, without having to pretend or hide our feelings, making love and exchanging our passion without fear or inhibitions. Daniel told me he missed me. He told me, the sight of me laughing and smiling with that other guy had driven him to mad jealousy. I didn't mean for us to take it this far. It wasn't my plan for us to have make up sex. I was just supposed to listen to him explain how he was feeling, but it took another twist. When he told me, he wanted me to be his without anyone else being involved, somewhere in between all that talk, I somehow lost my way. This was not what I wanted. Yet, here I was, once again in a hotel bedroom with that other woman's husband. Despite all the lies I tried to tell myself, the mixed truth was evident every time I looked into Daniel's eyes. My heart was trapped, and I could tell it was at war.

I rose out of the bed to put on my shirt and panties before quietly creeping out of the bedroom unnoticed. Closing the bedroom door behind me, I walked over to the small sofa in the living room and sat in front of the wooden coffee table. Since I couldn't sleep, I might as well work on the Kevin Longstreet case. Daniel and I were now past those critical first 48 hours of the case. We had zero leads and no clear motive to hang our hat on. Moreover, this whole investigation was going nowhere fast. Both the DEA and the NOPD brass were clamoring for answers as to how their number one informant and star witness had suddenly been murdered. The possibility of us having a mole inside of our police station was not something Daniel and I wanted to entertain. All the evidence we could collect from the crime scene was badly contaminated with bleach or completely unreliable. Kevin's cellphone was missing and all his phone records from his service provider were a dead end. The only clue we had was a blurred and cryptic photo with a message written on the back proclaiming the innocence of Eric Davis, a man convicted of double murder years ago.

Kevin's NOPD contact, Bill Devers, had given us all his records on Kevin Longstreet. The records confirmed that the NOPD had been using Kevin as a protected informant for years. Bill had used Kevin to set up several major drug stings, resulting in the arrest of scores of drug dealers in the 9th Ward and in the Bywater Area. Yet, something in Bill's records did not seem right to me. The records indicated that Kevin had been arrested for other serious crimes and Bill had somehow kept him from being charged. Because of Bill's influence, Kevin had skipped out on serving time for sexual assault, rape, child abuse and several other minor felonies. It was clear that Kevin's informant status had been the reason this hardened criminal was allowed on the streets to cause havoc. Due to this, many people in the community could have a host of reasons to want to see Kevin dead. Both Daniel and I wanted to ask Bill about this, but we knew better. Bill would take it as a personal attack if we questioned his judgment or seem to assign blame to him in any way. Bill Devers was a guy that was best left alone when his pride was up, so we focused on the Eric Davis angle instead.

Daniel and I had argued over whether we should drive north to the David Wade Correctional Facility and interview Eric Davis. I wasn't in favor of doing it, but Daniel was adamant about interviewing him. I knew Eric's lawyers would righteously object if we seemed to attempt to implicate him in another murder. A murder that he obviously could not have committed while sitting in a prison cell. Additionally, Eric's influential uncle, Rodney Davis, would frame our questioning of him as a further attempt to formulate another massive police cover-up. The bottom line for me was that we didn't have anything on Eric for us to even consider interviewing him. Until we had something solid, Eric had to be off limits. As far as I was concerned, going to interview Eric was a waste of time.

"Where did you go partner?"

Hearing Daniel's voice startled me. I sat Kevin Longstreet's case file down on the coffee table and turned around towards Daniel's voice. His pale white face wore red pillow scars and his hair was in shambles. Daniel's bare chest looked enticing as my reddish bite marks from last night were on full display. The only piece of clothing he had on were his navy-blue boxers.

Behind them, I could see his erection as he stood at the bedroom doorway, flashing an immature yet devilish smile at me.

"Daniel, we really need to get to work baby."

"We don't have any leads on this case. Captain Wolf is counting on us and I don't want to let her down."

"Oh, all right Jessica" Daniel lamented with a touch of sarcasm. "It's good to know at least one of us is trying to be somewhat of a responsible officer of the law. Captain Wolf would be proud of you right now if she could see you."

Daniel walked over to the small kitchen and began to brew a pot of coffee. I used my hand to fix my hair and grabbed my cellphone off the table. Looking at my screen, I saw that there were no missed calls and I was surprised. Achim hadn't even bothered to return my call or text me back. Was he mad at me? I wanted to talk to Achim. I wanted to let him know that I did need him. I needed him to somehow help me out of this prison that I had built for myself. For Achim to truly help me, I knew I had to be honest and lay it all out on the line. He deserved my honesty and I in turn, needed to be honest. So far, I hadn't been honest with him and he was starting to see through my lies. He was a black man I couldn't fool. Now Achim was frustrated with me, and I was frustrated with myself.

"Here's your coffee partner," Daniel offered as he sat a cup down on the table in front of me. "Black coffee just the way you like it. No sugar, no cream."

"Where are we at on this shit today Jessica?" He asked me while staring at the case file.

"We are absolutely no fuckin where," I began while scanning over my notes.

"None of the residents we interviewed at the apartment complex noticed anything noteworthy. Kevin's closest next of kin is his mother. She lives at an old folks' home over in Baton Rouge....so we can count her out. The only option we have left is to focus on the drugs we found."

"Maybe if we found out who Kevin's drug providers are, that could potentially lead us someplace? Other than that, we are looking at another cold case here."

"Good luck finding every drug dealer in New Orleans and asking them to help you out," Daniel jokingly remarked before taking a small sip out of his coffee cup.

"You know this case is a self-licking ice cream cone, don't you?"

"The more you attempt to dive into it, the more it just gets all over you."

"What are you trying to say Daniel? That we should just fall back on this case and give up?" I inquired.

"I'm saying sometimes there are no good answers in life partner."

"The more you try to find a good answer, the more problems you end up creating for yourself. Sometimes the best answer is to just walk away," Daniel explained.

"If it was your son or brother, you couldn't just fuckin walk away Daniel!"

"Then what do you expect us to do here Damnit!" Daniel replied.

"Are we to start wasting our time questioning every low life thug in New Orleans? Is that what we gonna start doing for some snitch ass drug addict?"

"Life is about decisions Jessica," Daniel barked before grabbing the case file and angrily raising it above his head.

"Kevin Longstreet made a bunch of bad decisions. Decisions that hurt a lot of people who trusted him. Nothing we find out about this case is going to justify his life or erase the fact that life sometimes administers its own form of justice. It's called karma Jessica."

Daniel slammed the case file back down on the table, then walked back in the kitchen. He was frustrated and I understood Daniel's point. We both were being asked to investigate the circumstances of karma upon a man that led a harmful life. Yet, Daniel's sudden anger at finding the truth made me feel a certain way, and I had to let it out.

"Yes Daniel, we have no choice but to judge Kevin now that he is gone. Judge him for all his bad actions because this damn world won't be turning a cold shoulder to his sins."

"But what about us Daniel? How much better are we than Kevin Longstreet, the drug addict and snitch?"

"What about the truth about us? You the narcissistic adulterer and me your lying home wrecking mistress?"

"How does either of us have the audacity to not only judge Kevin Longstreet, but also condemn him for his misdeeds when we deserve the exact same karma that he received?"

Daniel picked up the coffee pot and threw it up against the wall. The sound of breaking glass echoed throughout the hotel room. He was angry as hell and his eyes looked at me with a level of fury that I had never seen from him before. Without thinking, I rose up from the sofa signaling my intention to not retreat. Warm tears rolled down my face as I felt myself shaking uncontrollably.

"So, tearing shit up is going to make you feel better Daniel? Is breaking a coffee pot going to make our ugly truth go away?"

Before I knew it, Daniel was towering over me, staring down into my eyes with an expression of pure contempt and anger. My body felt a powerful jolt from the force of his hands, and I suddenly realized that I was falling to the ground. After landing on my back, I could feel the coolness of the hotel's hard floor. Then I realized what had happened, and how I found myself to be on the ground. Daniel had struck me, and now I was at his mercy as I stared up at him with my eyes focused on his tightly balled fists.

"Don't you ever straighten your back at me again! Do you understand?" Daniel ordered.

He stormed back into the bedroom, slamming the door behind him. As he disappeared, I stood back up and went over to the couch, where I cried and sobbed into the palms of my hands. Part of me regretted what I had said to him. He would never forgive me for exposing the lie we were both living in. The other part of me, knew it had to end like this. I needed to take my first critical steps into this pain that would surely set me free and bring a halt to my inner war.

After several minutes, a fully clothed Daniel came bursting out of the bedroom with his night bag in his hand. As he walked past the couch, he didn't even look at me. He went straight to the front door and walked out without saying a word, leaving me alone in the hotel room. I got myself up from the couch and walked to the window that oversaw the parking lot. Pulling back the curtain, I looked down at him and watched as he drove away in his car. It was over; this was truly over. The feeling was half pain and half relief.

I wiped the tears off my face and grabbed my cellphone. After a few sips of my coffee, I unlocked my phone and sent Achim a text message. He had always been so good at listening to me, yet because of my poor decisions he would not listen to me now. Then the realization that he may never come around to listening to me again struck me. As my tears began to flow, I typed out a text to Achim. I could not control what he felt or what I had done in the past. All I had left to control was my present and future decisions. I began to let my honest feelings out in typed words. Rereading them to ensure I got it right. Then, I pressed down on the send button and hoped for the best.

After sending Achim the text, I sat on the couch for several minutes, hoping that he would respond; hoping that my phone would ring, and I could confide with him, allowing him to save me from my own despair. Finally, the unnerving silence of my loneliness crushed me. Looking at the broken coffee pot glass scattered about the floor, I decided to use a few small towels to clean up the mess. Afterwards, I forced myself to go into the bathroom. I needed to take a hot shower to calm my nerves. As the hot water ran down my naked body, my thoughts were consumed with my many mistakes. My ignorant obsession with Daniel; a married white man who used me for cheap sex. My neglect of Achim, a black man that adored and valued me when I hardly valued myself. For a long time in my life, I believed that I had been making all the right decisions. I had a successful career. My lifestyle allowed me to see the world and experience things I had only dreamed of as a child. I was the black woman every little black girl looked at with awe.

Yet, I was still empty and unfulfilled. Something was missing and until now, I hadn't been able to figure out what it was. I simply filled this empty hole with things that were hurting me. Looking to people like Daniel and Achim for some form of selfish satisfaction. As I rinsed the soap from my brown wet skin, I knew I had to change my approach to life. The problem wasn't Daniel or Achim, it was me.

I dried myself off and put on a new set of clothes. It was time to pack up and mentally prepare myself for work. Daniel would be there, and I had to be emotionally ready to confront him. The days of pretending and hiding myself away were over for me.

From now on, Daniel was my work partner and that would be it. There would be a new reality between us and this time, I would set the boundaries of that relationship. As I was about to walk out of the room, my cellphone rang.

"Hello," I answered.

"Good morning Jessica, this is Captain Wolf," she said in a dull voice.

"I need you and Daniel to head over to Mid-City. There has been another murder."

"It looks like this may be the same guy that killed Kevin Longstreet. It's the same MO, using a knife, bleach and leaving photos. It looks almost exactly like Kevin's murder."

"The only two differences are that this victim is a white male," Captain Wolf further explained. "And he wasn't killed in a car."

"Yes Captain. I'll call in to dispatch when I get to my car and head that way," I replied. "Is CSI on scene already?"

"Yeah, I believe CSI is there already. If Derrick isn't already there, he and the rest of CSI should be their shortly," she elaborated.

"Is Detective Fitzpatrick with you Jessica? If he is, just inform Daniel for me as well. That will save me the trouble of calling around for him."

"No, Daniel isn't with me this morning Captain."

"I'll have dispatch reach out to Daniel and inform him."

"Okay…" Captain Wolf said with surprise in her voice.

"Are you two alright girl?"

"Yeah. We're good Captain," I conveyed before ushering myself off the phone.

After leaving the hotel, I got inside my car and contacted dispatch. They gave me the Mid-City address and I put it into my GPS before asking the dispatcher to contact Daniel. As I met New Orleans morning traffic, I turned on my police lights and sped through the congested highway. Exiting the highway, I pulled up to the victim's home and parked across the street from the house. A white four door Chevy Impala was parked in a small driveway in front of the residence. Derrick and another member of CSI were dusting the outside of the car and collecting prints. Yellow police tape barricaded the homes front entrance. Behind the flimsy yellow tape, stood the homes bright white front door. I was amazed when I saw that someone had drawn a huge black swastika on the victim's front door.

Out of the corner of my eye, I noticed Daniel parking down the street from me. Before getting out of my car, I grabbed my gloves, note pad and other gear.

"Hey Derrick," I blurted out as I crossed the street. Derrick looked up and noticed me. He walked towards me and began to shake his head in frustration.

"Hey Jessica, it looks like your boy is at it again. This time it's even worse," he said.

"The victim's name is Ryan Foster. A 28-year-old white male and an aspiring jazz musician from Junction City, Arkansas."

"Good morning Daniel," Derrick said as Daniel approached me from behind.

Daniel nodded his head at Derrick barely acknowledging either of us. He reached into his sports jacket and pulled out his small notepad and pen. He began to flip feverishly through the pad until he eventually found a blank page to write on. All was done in silence with a stern expression that betrayed his hidden frustration.

"You OK detective?" Derrick asked. "These cases seem to be touching a nerve with you lately."

"Let's just cut the shit Derrick and get through this, alright," Daniel shot back.

A shocked Derrick looked over at me and our eyes briefly met. I turned my eyes away from Derrick and ignored addressing the obvious. Derrick looked back up at Daniel and pointed towards a slightly overweight white man with thinning brown hair, wearing a pair of large silver glasses.

"That gentlemen over there is the victims neighbor," Derrick explained with a pissed off demeanor. "You two may want to start there before you start trampling through my crime scene."

"Why the hell are you dusting this car for fingerprints Derrick?"

"Who the fuck gave you that order? Was its Jessica?" Daniel demanded.

"I'm dusting the car because it isn't registered to the victim, and the neighbor told me he saw the victim driving it yesterday."

"And if you haven't noticed, it's fuckin about to rain Daniel!"

"Would you rather me wait on your ass and let the damn rain wash away potential evidence? Or will you let me be proactive and collect evidence before it disappears?"

"I'd rather you show some damn respect and call me to get permission before you jump the gun and start making decisions Derrick," Daniel barked back with a laser glare. "I'm responsible for this case, not you. Remember that."

"Well, excuse me boss," Derrick sarcastically yelled back.

Daniel turned away and walked towards the victim's neighbor. I looked at Derrick and his bottom lip quivered as he balled his fist in anger. "Be cool," I whispered to him.

I followed Daniel over towards the man and pulled out my badge. "Morning sir. I'm Detective Jessica Baker from NOPD and this is my partner Detective Daniel Fitzpatrick," I began as I flashed my badge.

"If you have a moment, we would like to ask you a few questions if you wouldn't mind."

"No problem officers," he eagerly responded. "I'll do all I can to help you out."

"May I ask your name?"

"My name is Cliff. Cliff Roberson, Ma'am."

"Cliff, I understand you discovered your neighbor deceased this morning?"

"Yeah, I noticed that Ryan's music was way too loud. It woke me and my dog up from our sleep at about 3AM."

"I was about to call in a noise complaint to you guys, but I figured I'd go walk my dog and maybe I'd knock on Ryan's door while I was out here or see if I could get him to turn the music down. I didn't want to call the cops on the guy. We are neighbors and we got to live with each other."

"What happened when you walked by Ryan's door?" Daniel asked.

"Well, I noticed the swastika drawn on the door. That got my full attention."

"It concerned me enough that I put my dog's bathroom break on hold and walked up to the door to see if Ryan was alright."

"I rang the doorbell twice and no one answered. The music just kept playing, so I started knocking pretty hard to get his attention."

"When I started pounding on the door, I noticed that the door wasn't completely shut. It started sliding open. So, I put my dog in my arms and opened the door all the way."

"That's when I walked in and saw Ryan laying there in a pool of blood. I ran out of the house and called you guys."

"The sight of Ryan just layin there like that, and the look on his face is just freak in me out guys…. I'm a veteran of the first Gulf War. Twenty-five years in the Marine Corp and I've never seen anything like this. He was butchered."

"You said that his music woke you up out of your sleep. Did you notice or observe anything unusual at the victim's residence before going to sleep last night?" I asked.

"No. Not really."

"Our houses are really close to each other, so I can definitely hear each time Ryan comes and goes. I'm a disabled vet, so I don't work, and I spend a lot of time in my living room watching TV. Aside from my bathroom breaks and my late evening meal, I pretty much sit in my living room all day."

"Yesterday afternoon, he left the house carrying two small boxes."

"Someone driving that white Impala came and picked him up yesterday," Cliff explained. "A few hours later, he drove up in that car by himself and parked it."

"It caught my attention because Ryan hasn't had a car in the six years, we've have been neighbors. He is always walking, catching a ride with someone or using someone else's bicycle to get around. I've been telling him for years that he needed to bite the bullet and go buy a cheap used car."

"What did you notice after Ryan drove back with the car?" I pressed.

"Well, he went in the house and then not too long after that, he came back out and left again."

"Did he drive away?" Daniel asked.

"No, he didn't drive. He just walked out of the house and kept walking. I didn't think much of it. Ryan is always walking around places. That's why he liked living here in Mid-City. Everything is close enough to walk to. Easy living is what Ryan used to call it."

"Did you notice Ryan when he returned home and if so what time?" I followed up.

"I would guess sometime before midnight for sure because I hadn't eaten my evening meal yet.... so maybe 9PM or 10PM. I was sort of surprised to see him home that early on a Saturday night. Ryan moonlights as a DJ you know. He usually is gone all night long on Saturday's."

"So, it was sort of early for me to see him. That got my full attention. I saw him get out of a dark colored SUV. It looked like a Cadillac or maybe a Tahoe but definitely American built."

"Ryan had a young black girl with him. She was a light skinned black girl, about 5-8 or 5-9, short black hair, wearing shorts and a very skimpy red shirt."

"They both got out of the SUV carrying drinks and stumbling around with several bags. Ryan was drunk. He walked up to his porch and I watched as he fumbled with his keys trying to open the door. The black girl came up from behind and wrapped her arms around him, then started tongue kissing his ear. After that they both disappeared into the house."

"That was the last time I saw Ryan alive," Cliff lamented.

"Did you get a good look at who was driving the SUV or its plates?" Daniel interjected.

"No. From my window view, I couldn't see who was driving. I just saw the SUV pull up and stop in the middle of the street before pulling off."

"I didn't think to look at the plates. The damn SUV was gone before my brain could figure out what was going on. Plus, I was getting myself and my dog ready for our evening meal."

"Is it normal for Ryan to bring guests back to his place?" I asked?

Cliff looked over at Daniel and then darted his eyes back at me. I could sense him gauging me out. Trying to get a sense of me and where I was coming from. I had interviewed enough people to know when brutal honesty was about to pour out of someone. His next statements would not be rehearsed or calculated. Cliff was about to let it all hang out.

"No disrespect officer, but Ryan always has black street ladies running in and out of his house. Aside from him being home early, seeing that last night ain't unusual. If it isn't the black working ladies running around his place, it's the young black hoodlums he keeps around here."

"I've talked to him about the company he kept around here," a now sweating Cliff expanded while looking at Daniel.

"It's alright to party with them and DJ for them, but he needed to keep them away from here."

"Ryan called me a paranoid old bastard and labeled me as old school. I told him man! I told him. I've lived in New Orleans for twelve years, I told him. He just wouldn't listen!"

"Alright…Alright," Daniel interrupted, stopping Cliff's train of thought.

"What happened after they went into the house? Did you see or hear anyone leave the house?"

"About an hour after they arrived, the black girl left and walked off. She came out of the house with her drink, a plastic bag and what looked like a used condom. I watched as she shut the front door and slowly walked down the sidewalk towards Canal Street."

"You didn't see this black woman take a marker and draw anything on the front door?" I asked.

"Well…. No," Cliff admitted. "She just put the used condom in her bag and casually walked off like it was another day at the office for her."

"What about after she left. Did you notice anything else?" Daniel broke in.

"No. About five minutes after she left, I went to bed like normal."

I had heard enough and was done with Cliff. Daniel wrapped up the interview with him and recorded his contact info, while I walked back over to Derrick. He was almost done with pulling prints off the driver's side of the Chevy Impala, so I stood by in silence while he and his partner bagged the evidence.

"How many were you able to pull, Derrick?" I asked in a soft voice. His demeanor was still combative and now was not the time to ruffle his feathers.

"I got one, maybe two," he answered. "Both on the driver's side. Both not really of the best quality."

"Thank you Derrick," I chimed in. "It was really a good idea. I liked it and appreciate you for trying."

Derrick looked up at me and gave a slight grin before shaking his head at me. I could sense the frustration pulsing from his spirit. He was a good Crime Scene Expert. One of the best and most hardworking guys we had. He didn't deserve the way Daniel had treated him.

"How about you and I take a cruise around the house?" I asked him.

"Whenever you're ready Madam Detective," Derrick replied with a bit of sting.

We put on our protective gear and I followed Derrick up the porch towards the front door. As we got close to the front door, my nose caught the strong scent of bleach. Derrick pushed the door open and we both ducked under the yellow police tape, entering the house. Looking down the passageway into the living room, I could see feet laying on the carpet. The feet were wearing dirty white socks with small reddish marks of blood on them. Near the feet was a plastic bag with the words French Quarter Exotica written on it.

"Derrick make sure you get a good photo of that bag and dust that bag for prints. I believe that store has secret surveillance cameras inside of it."

"Jessica, I don't want to know how you might know about cameras being in that place," Derrick jokingly lamented.

We walked down the passageway and into the living room. Ryan was laying on his back, in a carpet filled with blood. His throat was slashed almost to his spinal cord and his abdomen cut wide open exposing his internal organs. His eyes were open, displaying a stale look. A large black prosthetic penis had been shoved into his mouth. Then it hit me all at once. The overwhelming smell of the bleach pulsing from Ryan's corpse was

Chapter Five

Two days had passed; a busy two days that put everyone at the police station on edge. The worried faces of my co-workers was telling. There was something rotten going on inside of the NOPD and everyone at my district office was looking for cover. At the time, the media was not asking too many questions about the two murder cases I was investigating. No one outside of the NOPD had correlated the brutal stabbing of a black drug addict with the grizzly execution of a white musician. The historic racial divide in New Orleans was doing us a favor. It kept people from immediately seeing both murders in the same vein.

Although both men were brutally killed by the knife, the media and the citizens of New Orleans viewed both cases as worlds apart. To the citizens, Ryan Foster was a white man and his murder was likely a story of some sort of robbery gone wrong. Just as expected, Kevin's murder was simply labeled as street business: Black trash taking out black trash. That's how this world worked. This was what we all knew to be true in our society. Yet, inside the police station, we knew the uncompromising truth. The more we dug into the cases, the less we were able to separate them from each other because they were linked. For some reason, the murderer had made sure to make that obvious to us.

Suddenly out of nowhere, I was distracted by a familiar voice coming from the TV. I looked up from my desk filled with case files to catch a glimpse of the mounted flat screen on the police station wall. The channel was on a local news station and the news anchor was interviewing an older-looking black man wearing large glasses and a phony cheese smile that showed his perfect white dentures. The news anchor asked the man a question about Kevin Longstreet's murder and the on-screen image changed to old footage that showed Kevin testifying on the witness stand at the Eric Davis trial. As the screen shifted back to the older black man, I once again heard his booming voice and knew who he was.

"The death of Mr. Longstreet is certainly a heart-breaking tragedy," State Senator Rodney Davis slowly began. "In fact, his entire life is a sad reminder of how vulnerable Black Americans are today. The false testimony Mr. Longstreet gave at the trial of my nephew Eric Davis, was an abomination that negatively affected my family and the entire black community of New Orleans."

"Although I am disappointed that Mr. Longstreet intentionally lied in the court of law, murder is not something any reasonable human being would wish on anybody," he continued.

"I and the entire Davis family have nothing but the most heartfelt condolences for the loss of Mr. Longstreet and want to let his surviving family know that we are praying for them in their deep moment of grief."

The painful memories of my Aunt losing a hard-fought state senate election to this man flooded my mind as I watched Rodney Davis smile wide for the camera. The mental images of my Aunt and her devoted campaign staff weeping tears of sorrow, while being forced to watch Rodney Davis give his pious victory speech, always stuck with me. Now Rodney Davis had his eyes on bigger prizes and more influential offices. He smoothly plugged his upcoming campaign for a vacant U.S. Congressional seat before pivoting to a clearly rehearsed talking point about race and inequality. Rodney Davis's words sounded magnificent, but the purpose of his statement was just more of the same.

Rodney Davis's insincere words ended the interview segment and the local station went to a commercial. I turned my attention back to my desk, flipping through the two case files, trying to find some hidden link between the murders of Kevin and Ryan that might reveal who murdered them. Every time I searched and compared the two cases, I continued to come back to the same unsavory result; the double homicide conviction of Eric Davis. Kevin was the state's star witness in the prosecution of Eric Davis. It was his sworn testimony that helped a jury convict Eric Davis of the murders of Jeffery and Thomas Roberts. We ran Ryan's fingerprints and to my utmost surprise, Ryan's prints matched unattributed fingerprints collected at the Jeffery and Thomas Roberts's crime scene.

I had a DVD with several videos of Kevin and Ryan together frequenting a bar named Andy's Tavern and several strip clubs. I also had videos of the two men bringing women to Ryan's home. There were also images of the two men doing drugs and sharing needles. If that wasn't bad enough, the DVD contained a video of Ryan dressed in a NOPD uniform and driving a police model vehicle with police issue lights and mirrors. The DVD also contained videos of Ryan Foster and an unknown white male handcuffing black men, laying them face down on the street, and robbing them of their jewelry and cash. It was horrifying for me to watch. As I reviewed the videos of these guys pretending to be police officers, I knew that there was no way they did this without some support from within the NOPD itself. These videos alone could be enough for Eric Davis to win an appeal of his conviction since the DVD was reasonable doubt in spades.

The door of the police station opened, and I watched as Captain Wolf walked inside, followed by her life partner, Debbie Wolf. At the time, it was noon, and Debbie was carrying a half-filled plastic bag from a popular restaurant in the French Quarter.

Captain Wolf was silent as she walked past the reception desk, barely acknowledging the uniformed officers that enthusiastically greeted her as she entered.

She walked through our bullpen of open cubicles and unlocked her office door. Before she slipped inside her office, she took the bag of food from Debbie and gave her a passionless kiss on her cheek. Debbie smiled and whispered a few soft words before turning around and walking away towards the exit. It wasn't unusual for Captain Wolf and Debbie to go out on lunch dates, but Captain Wolf's despondent attitude was something totally new. As Debbie walked by my cubicle, she gave me a quick hand wave followed by a hearty smile. I had never spoken to Debbie, but she was always kind and seemed to make it a point to wave when she saw me. She was a middle-aged white woman that had come from a wealthy family, as her late father and mother were owners of a natural gas company that operated in the Gulf of Mexico. Captain Wolf would playfully tease that Debbie was always trying to get her to retire from the force, so the two of them could sail their superyacht around the world fulltime.

Captain Wolf popped back out of her office and our eyes met. She waved calmly at me before she turned around and slipped back through her doorway. Sensing her urgency, I dropped everything I was doing and walked to her door. I walked into her large office and she asked me to have a seat. Captain Wolf closed the door behind me and slowly walked to her desk. It was clear that this was going to be a private conversation. I felt like I was a twelve-year-old again and had been summoned to the principal's office to account for some unknown misdeed. My heart rate started to rise, and my nerves began to bother me. Had she finally found out about me and Daniel?

"Jessica, we need to have a moment alone. I have a few things I need to share with you and just you alone," Captain Wolf started.

"But first, what are your thoughts on these two Bleach murder cases?"

"Well Captain, the more I dig into these two cases, the more they start to correlate with each other. I mean...its beyond just the knife and the bleach and the photos. This looks like someone trying to send us a message."

"I know", Captain Wolf interrupted. "They are trying to send messages that aren't going to be pleasant to hear."

Captain Wolf moved from behind her desk and walked over to a promotion plaque adorning her wall. Next to the plaque was a photo of her in her younger days wearing a police uniform, holding flowers, and hugging her deceased husband. Back then, she was beautiful. Now, her long curly black hair showed more than a trace of gray and her frame was a bit more robust. Her skin was now considerably more wrinkled when compared to its state in her younger years. She stared at the photo with wide eyes. I watched as her bottom eyelid began to quiver. I could see the tears forming as she attempted to blink them away as she began to speak.

"Two years before the Jeffery and Thomas Roberts double murder, the NOPD began soliciting from within our ranks to form an Anti-Drug Task Force. Members of the Task Force were to be voted in by our peers. No brown nosing to bosses. No pulling seniority or rank, just pure street cred and respect to get in."

"As a seasoned Lieutenant, I put my name in the hat for selection into this Task Force. At the time, I thought that I'd be a shoe in for selection. I worked harder than the next guy. I was smarter than the next guy and everyone in that office knew it. This Task Force was going to be my validation. Not only was I one of the best, I was part of something special. Something I belonged in."

"Then the day of voting came around. Everyone in the office smiled in my face. It made me feel like I had already been selected. I was super confident."

"When the votes were counted, I hadn't received one vote," the Captain said with wet eyes. "Not even one damn vote!"

Captain Wolf wiped a tear from her eye and sniffled her nose. It was the first time I had ever seen her emotional. For me, she had always been sort of a professional robot, impervious to the emotional torture chamber that is police work. All through the years I had known her, she seemed incapable of displaying human emotion. Now, I finally realized that Captain Wolf was indeed a real person. A human being with real feelings and real-life disappointments.

"I was devastated," she continued. "Not just because I didn't make it into the Task Force, but mostly because after not getting selected, I came to realize something painful about my life."

"I was nothing more than a black woman pretending in a white man's world. Everyone appeared supportive of me before the voting. They smiled in my face and patted me on the head."

"In truth, they were all liars and phonies, and so was I."

"It was the first time I ever felt that in my career. The first time I felt like an outsider in a place I had dedicated my life to. After that vote, I knew for certain that I was not part of their team."

"That very thought still hurts me to this day."

"I had worked so hard to get their respect. I ruined my marriage, passed up on having children…all for the team…. or what I thought was my team."

"When it was time to cash in my respect, respect I thought I had earned, I got nothing in return."

Captain Wolf paused and walked back towards her desk. Reaching down into a pile of paperwork, she pulled out a photo and slammed it down on the desk in front of me.

"I went back and looked at the Eric Davis's investigation and what I found scared the hell out of me."

"Eric was arrested by that same Anti-Drug Task Force I put in for. The Task Force included cops from narcotics, homicide, robbery, every division we had here at the time."

"I found out that this Task Force had been following and tracking Eric for months prior to his arrest. They monitored and even sold drugs to him."

"All this surveillance took place during the time Eric's uncle, State Senator Rodney Davis, was putting all kinds of political pressure on the city government here in New Orleans. Senator Davis was ruffling feathers in the city by attempting to outlaw the gentrification of historically black neighborhoods."

"Do you see where I'm going with this Jessica?" Captain Wolf asked.

Immediately, I knew where Captain Wolf was going with this. She did not have to take it there with me because I had already arrived. As black people, we all knew about the invisible hand of white influence and power. She didn't have to waste any more of her words to explain the situation to me. Someone with power was using the NOPD to influence politics. It was a dirty white trick as old as time.

"Captain," I whispered. "Now we aren't just talking about one corrupt police officer. This wouldn't just be one bad apple."

"Jessica, look at the damn photo," the Captain ordered as she pointed towards the picture, she had placed in front of me. My eyes instinctively followed her hand and I saw an image of the familiar white flag with the large black X. It was the same flag I had seen in the Ryan Foster photos.

"Now tell me what you see there in that photo?" Captain Wolf asked.

"I see a flag. An ugly weird looking flag."

"Yeah. At first, I thought the same thing too, but there was something about that damn photo of Ryan wrapped in this flag that bothered me. So, I reached out to a good buddy of mine in the FBI."

Captain Wolf lifted her laptop screen and hit a few buttons before turning the screen around so I could see it. "Here is an FBI field report that was sent out several years ago," she explained. "My FBI buddy sent it to me this morning."

"Come closer, Jessica and take a look at it."

I leaned forward to get closer and read the report. On her screen was an image of the exact flag with its powder white background and large black X. Under the image were the capitalized letters F. O. W. L. As I read further, I was shocked to discover that FOWL was short for the name Freedom of White Life. FOWL was an underground Neo-Confederate White Supremacist organization that advocated for what they termed as the peaceful genocide of the Black race. FOWL trafficked drugs, ran guns, and performed other illegal activities to fund their terrorist organization. The FBI reported that FOWL had successfully infiltrated the ranks of Law Enforcement and were now transitioning to sending its members into the Armed Services.

I sat back in my seat as my thoughts began to race. Why would a White Supremacist hang out with black people? Why would a racist who believes in the genocide of the black race be seen openly bringing black women into his home? None of this made sense to me.

"This is what's bothering me, Jessica," Captain Wolf began using a hushed tone. "We have photos of this man boldly wrapping himself in a White Supremacist flag. In this same man's house, we found an NOPD uniform with video of him detaining and handcuffing black men."

"Not to mention the video of the man partying and doing drugs with a murdered NOPD informant."

"This is going to look like a shit show, Jessica. The press is going to eat us alive when they find out about all this."

"So, what are you trying to say. Captain?" I asked. "That we hide all this to spare ourselves the public embarrassment?"

"No, Jessica. That's not what I'm saying…"

"Then what are you saying, Captain?" I interrupted. "That our pride is worth more than the truth?"

"All I'm saying is that we need to have some semblance of order in this city", she sternly barked back at me.

"Without order, we will have chaos. With chaos, everything you and I have committed our lives to goes away."

"What did we commit our lives to, Captain?" I asked. "Because right now, I'm not sure what it is that we are supposed to be protecting. It seems like we are more committed to protecting ourselves than producing justice. I didn't become a police officer to hide from justice. I became one to deliver it."

A hush fell over the office as Captain Wolf stared at me with eyes filled with disappointment. We were talking to each other without really getting to the fundamental issue that hung over us like the undeniable blue sky. We were discussing racism and black fidelity without using those forbidden words. Questions about black fidelity aren't supposed to be asked between polite black company.

Captain Wolf sat down in her chair and pulled open a cabinet. She retrieved a large folder and sat it on her desk in front of her. "You and I have to protect each other, Jessica," a stoic looking Captain Wolf began.

"Girl, I have been protecting you for a while now."

"Protecting you from the likes of Bill Devers and every other white man around here who dislikes you."

"Bill Devers knows all about you and Daniel, Jessica. He knows about your affair and so do I."

"Bill noticed you two kept popping up at a hotel he was staking out. At first, Bill suspected that you and Daniel were involved in some sort of illegal trafficking. I didn't buy his theory, so we agreed to have you two followed for six months."

My heart sunk. The words that came out of her mouth shot chills down my spine. I fought to hold on to my outer dignity, but deep inside, I felt ashamed and exposed. Raw emotions ran through me as Captain Wolf and I exchanged poker stares. I knew what she had in her folder. She had been spying on us and she had the goods on me. Captain Wolf had the power to end my career and destroy my life, but I had given her the power to do so. My bad decisions were ultimately my decisions. Now it was only a matter of time for her to decide when she would finally destroy me professionally.

"I think we both know what I have in this file, Jessica," she explained with a combative tone as she slammed her index finger down on the folder. "Photos of you and Daniel at hotel rooms.... On duty at your apartment....in the back seats of police vehicles.... Even in Daniel's own home."

"Do I have to continue, Detective Baker?"

"No Captain," I sighed.

"I don't make the laws Jessica. My job is to enforce...or decide not to enforce them," she declared.

"Whether you believe it or not Jessica, we are both in this together. I need you here. The NOPD needs you here and the black community needs you here too."

"We are a part of this family, even if the family members don't want us here. No matter how they feel about us, we are still a part of this family. That's the message we need to send back to whoever is doing these murders."

"Whenever family problems happen. We can solve them with our family, behind closed doors. Not in the media. Not out in public. Not someone else demanding for it. This is because once we allow that to happen, the order will be disrupted. The family will be thrown into chaos and chaos can lead to bad things for us."

As I listened to the Captain's words, I became angry. I wanted no part of this insane family, especially if the family was going to hide the truth. My father had done enough hiding. My mother had done enough hiding. Now I had done enough hiding and it was time that I put all the hiding to an end.

I was in love with a married man and Captain Wolf was in love with white acceptance. Those were the truths we both had purposely hidden from ourselves as black police officers. I knew that if I continued arguing with Captain Wolf it would be of no use to either of us. We both knew where her loyalties lied, and she would extinguish me if I even hinted at not toeing the family line. There would be a time to give voice to my truth, but it wasn't this time. I needed to play along until I had the advantage over her.

"I'm a family member, Captain," I started while letting the tears flow. "But it's just so hard sometimes. It's hard to see what's going on and not speak out."

"That's when you have to remember what's important," Captain Wolf stated as she shot up from her chair and walked over towards me.

"We can't forget about the goal of our people. We can't forget why Martin Luther King and Rosa Parks fought so hard for us to be here today. That's why I stood up to Bill Devers and defended you from him. We have to make sure we both survive this craziness."

"The truth is that there will always be some form of oppression in this country, Jessica. The quicker you accept that fact, the easier life in this country will become for you."

"Our forefathers loved this country enough to fight to better it, not to destroy it. Our ancestors built this nation. It is ours. We have a right to it," she continued while kneeling to wipe away my tears with her rough hand.

Suddenly, I felt her lips up against mine and the sensation of her tongue touching mine followed. Her hand flowed down to my breasts and I felt her gently squeeze them. Disgusted, I pulled myself away as the tears again showered down my face upon realizing what was occurring.

"Captain, what are you doing?", I asked in terror.

"I've been looking at those sexy photos of you and Daniel fucking for a while now."

"I always wondered how it felt to be Daniel," she said with a strange smile before walking away.

"We are having a meeting about this Ryan Foster murder in the conference room in about thirty minutes."

"Just remember that we are all family, Jessica."

I exited her office almost in a state of panic. When I sat at my desk, I couldn't help but re-live repeatedly in my mind what had just occurred. I took a napkin and dried my face, attempting to hide my tears and sense of betrayal. Co-workers passed by my desk without the slightest clue about the rage and terror that was burning inside of me. It seemed to me that the world had stopped at this painful moment while everyone else's life moved on in normalcy. I was vulnerable. Captain Wolf had violated me and there was nothing I could do about it. She has details of my affair with Daniel ready to be used against me at a moment's notice. Who would believe me anyway? Captain Wolf was an officer with an impeccable service record, while I could easily be portrayed as just a thirsty hoe with a badge.

"Jessica. You know we have a meeting in about ten minutes, don't you?" Daniel proclaimed.

The sound of Daniel's voice broke my silent stream of consciousness. I looked up at Daniel without saying a word. My face contorted as he looked into my eyes. Daniel knew something was wrong. I was tired of hiding it all. My soul couldn't take it anymore. I was tired of projecting what I thought the world wanted me to be. This was my day of defeat, a defeat that had laid me bare. Daniel lowered himself onto my desk and put his hand on my shoulder.

"Hey partner, what's wrong?" he asked.

"You don't want to know, Daniel. Don't even ask OK."

"I do want to know, Jessica. That's why I freakin asked you"

"Please, Daniel. Just stop with the fake sincerity."

"Let's just get this damn meeting over so we can move on."

Daniel rose from the desk. He knew I was done confiding in him. He was the last person I wanted to lean on anyway. There was nothing his empty promises and sexual comfort could offer me now. I had come to realize that leaning on Daniel for strength only served to weaken me as a black woman. This was my struggle to overcome. It was my opportunity to start relying on who I was as a person. To believe in myself and to trust myself before trusting someone else who would clearly, hurt me when the rubber met the road.

Daniel pulled his cellphone from his pocket. After unlocking it, he placed his phone on my desk and clicked on a video. "Well, before we go into this meeting partner, we need to get on the same page."

"I went to that French Quarter Exotica store this morning. You know, the place where the victim bought all those sex toys before he was killed."

"Well, it turns out that the joint has recorded closed-circuit cameras in it," Daniel relayed with a smile.

"Go ahead Jessica, press the play button."

I wiped away my tears and pressed the button. The screen on Daniel's phone came to life as an image of the inside of the French Quarter Exotica burst into view. The store looked bright and sterile. A white male cashier stood alone behind the register that sat on top of a long glass counter. There were no customers inside the store, just the white cashier looking bored while harmlessly typing away on his cell phone.

Then the store's front entrance swung open. A white male wearing a powder blue hat and short sleeve shirt came into view. Behind him was a light-skinned black female wearing a pair of skimpy blue jean shorts and a crimson-colored top. As they both walked into the store, I noticed the cashier fumbled with his cell phone before hastily hiding it. The couple began to browse and playfully giggle as they examined items in the store. It looked as if they were both a bit tipsy as they laughed uncontrollably and shared over the top displays of affection. After the white man grabbed several sex toys, he coolly walked to the glass counter while the young lady amused herself with a pair of edible panties. The cashier began to ring up the man's merchandise and the store's camera was finally able to capture the man's face. I saw his face as clear as day. It was Ryan Foster. I looked at the time stamp on the video and it read 9:15 PM.

"So now we know for sure that Ryan was alive at 9:15 that night," I mumbled to myself.

"Yeah", Daniel lamented. "That would probably put the time of death sometime after 10 PM."

I continued to watch the rest of the video. Ryan paid for his merchandise then walked away from the counter and back towards the young lady that came into the store with him. Straining to look, I couldn't see her face clearly or make out any of her features. She seemed to almost be aware of the camera, always positioning her face away from it. It was frustrating.

"Yeah, I noticed that too," Daniel chimed in instinctively, confirming that he understood what I was attempting to ascertain.

"She definitely knew that there was a camera in that store. Look at how she positions her face away from the camera."

"What do you think she's up too?" he asked.

"I would say robbery," I began. "But Ryan isn't rich, and he has nothing that is worth stealing. Ryan is essentially a poor ass white boy."

"Plus, nothing that we know of was stolen from him or taken from his home."

"That leaves us with some sort of planned ambush or revenge, which fits in with all the Eric Davis clues and links to the murder of Kevin Longstreet we keep finding."

"So, you think this is Senator Davis trying to clear his nephew's name by framing Ryan?" Daniel followed up.

"That's a big stretch, Daniel. We have zero evidence to support that."

"And if we go sniffing around and asking the wrong people any questions, we will certainly start a media shit storm. I don't think Captain Wolf wants that either."

"There are a lot of people invested in the idea of keeping Eric Davis in prison, all while there is somebody out there who is willing to kill to get Eric out."

"I guess we are in the middle," Daniel said with a sigh.

"So, what does that mean, Daniel? Are we on the same team on all of this?" I asked.

Daniel leaned his head back to collect his words. I could see the somber look flashing on his face. His blue eyes began to moisten as they filled with tears. Then he leaned down towards me, placing both of his hands on my desk and looking into my eyes as he came closer to me.

"I am on your team, Jessica, and I always will be."

"That's what I love about you, Jessica."

"You are driven to do what's right," he whispered. "This whole thing has been painful for me because I know that I haven't done right by you."

"I was supposed to be your partner, not your source of pain and agony."

"You deserve better than all of this."

"I want you to know that I'm so…so sorry for all of this. I didn't mean for all of this to happen to us."

"You are a brilliant woman and I just got selfish."

"I was wrong, and I hope that you can forgive me."

A tear rolled down Daniel's face and he quickly cleaned it up with his sleeve. I could feel his remorse and it was genuine. I leaned towards him and wrapped my arms around his neck. The familiar smell of his aftershave was comforting. We exchanged a soft all telling kiss before we both broke away to collect ourselves.

Chapter Six

The smell of the fresh coffee was strong. Its scent was dominated by a unique boldness, which hid a hint of Caribbean spice. A piercing noise from the bean processor sent shock waves ricocheting throughout the entire building and briefly startled me. The interior of the coffee shop was painted with an extravagant, yet comforting revision of yellow. Patient customers eagerly stood in line, each awaiting their opportunity to pay for their favorite brand of liquid comfort. All of them trapping themselves in their own private little world as they stood alone, waiting for their fix. As one customer finished their business, others slowly moved a few steps closer to the front of the line. When a new customer approached the register, the black owner of the coffee shop entered each customer's lonely world with a seasoned smile and an accommodating tone. I could hear the cash register pop open with each purchase. The black owner's smile and sense of urgency increased with each order. Business was good and the owner's thoughts were surely thoughts of victory. For the owner, it must have been the successful realization of God's blessings and achieving a hard-earned dream. A dream of running his own business and owning his destiny.

I looked at my cell phone to check the time and I noticed that Anthony Rice was once again running late. Anthony always made it a habit of making me wait for him, and I abhorred having to wait on anyone, especially my subordinates. Abandoning my meeting with him was not an option. Just like Rachel and Sharon, I needed to make sure that Anthony disappeared and got the hell out of New Orleans. After today, Anthony would become a full-fledge member of Robert Charles's family. All his training wheels would be taken off and Anthony could expect to perform real duty out in the field by himself. For Anthony, it would be an exciting beginning to a new life as a counter-racist hitman.

The thoughts brought me back to my own rebirth back in the day, and the struggles of having to somehow learn to put away the horrifying memories of my murdered family. Trying to silence the inner sounds of sudden gunfire that echoed within my dreams was painful. Erasing the ghostly look of fear that the white gunmen wore as he walked into my church and began to slaughter us was nearly impossible. Unlike Anthony, those bitter events were my induction into the life of counter-racism.

As it once was for me, it was now time for Anthony to realize the newfound purpose in his life. He had done a great job befriending Ryan Foster, stealing his house keys, and giving me access to the bastard's storage space. Anthony had been my key into the circle of bastards and my gateway to all their secrets. He had been the trusted and happy foreign negro who always smiled at the White Supremacists. They never feared him, and I used that to my advantage.

As I munched on my Apple Danish, I finally saw Anthony walk through the door. On instinct, I rechecked my surroundings, placing my hands in my pocket for easy access to my concealed pistol. I wanted to make certain that Anthony hadn't brought any unwanted followers. Any of those bastards could have been tailing him so I wanted to make sure he was alone. Anthony walked to a table and sat down by himself. After five minutes of observation, I was satisfied that he was indeed by himself. I waved for Anthony to come to my table and he nervously made his way to grab a seat next to me.

"I did good…didn't I?" he confidently asked.

"Yeah Anthony. You did very well."

"Robert Charles is proud of you."

A smile splashed across Anthony's face, followed by an audible sigh of relief. I sat one of my Danishes in front of Anthony, before handing him a small cup of black coffee. Underneath the table sat a small paper bag, I took the paper bag and slid it over towards him.

"That coffee is really good. It's black and strong."

"Make sure you don't waste a drop."

Anthony took a small sip of the coffee before he broke the Danish into several pieces, devouring it all within seconds. He was clearly hungry, and I liked that. Robert Charles needed hungry young brothers like him.

"Is it all here?" Anthony asked as he reached down to look inside the bag.

"Anthony!" I cautioned him.

"Robert Charles doesn't lie about business, my man."

"And neither do I."

"If I tell you it's all there. Well…. It's all there, brother. Trust us."

A now embarrassed Anthony closed the paper bag and took another sip from his coffee cup. After a few seconds, he reached into his pants and pulled out several sets of keys, tossing them on the table in front of me.

"Here they are sir. I'm a man of my word too. That's the key to the cop's house and the extra keys are to the storage unit," Anthony relayed in his Bahamian voice.

"There is no honor amongst these thieving bastards, Anthony", I began. "That's why we eliminate them without prejudice. You saw how they set up Eric Davis and ruined his life."

"In your paper bag, you will also find instructions. Once I leave this table, you are to read them and follow them to the letter."

"Do you understand, Anthony?"

"Yes sir," he replied curiously. "So, I'm leaving New Orleans sir?"

"Yes," I confirmed.

"Just like we discussed, Anthony. Once you finished your objective, you are to leave New Orleans. Don't count on coming back unless Robert Charles needs you here."

"Right now, the city is too hot for you to stick around. The cops will eventually get around to you and we don't need them questioning you about Ryan Foster's murder."

"Robert Charles needs you to disappear and lay low for a while. We are paying you handsomely to do so."

"Don't try to go back home to the Bahamas either, and don't stick around here. Don't even stay in the state of Louisiana. Pack your bags. Get in your car and get the fuck outta here," I explained as I rose from my seat.

"Oh, by the way."

"Congrats on your promotion," I said offering him a handshake.

"Thank you, sir," Anthony replied.

"When will I get a chance to work with Rachel again? She's really good," he added with a naïve smile.

"If you are lucky your new job will keep you far away from her", I jokingly shot back. "Our friend Rachel is a handful."

"What can I expect from this new job?" Anthony asked.

He stared at me with his eyes wide open while sporting a shaded grin. Having been in his situation once myself, I could imagine the twisted cocktail of excitement, fear, and wonderment that was brewing inside of him. He was still a very young man, still fresh to the challenges of manhood and adult life. The question Anthony had asked of me required an answer that mere words could not properly convey. There was not enough time in the world to explain the many mistakes I had made in this life. Yet, he had asked, and it was my duty as a black man to offer him the best I could deliver.

"Expect loneliness. Your journey will be one of solitude," I began.

"No one will know you when you enter. No one will remember you when you leave. You will love your people but none of them will love you. No one will appreciate you or what you sacrifice for them. There are no heroes in this business Anthony, only winners and losers."

"Your love for your people is all you're going to have. That's what's going to wake you up when you're tired, and that's going to keep you alive when you want to die."

"Hold on to that love, Anthony. Never let anyone compromise your love or we as a people will all die if you do."

Anthony looked away from me and glanced down at the table. His grin disappeared and was replaced with a more solemn and worried expression. From his obvious disappointment, I knew my words weren't what he expected to hear. This life was no CIA novel. It was hard being a warrior for black people in this world. He would have to find his own way of making sense of it all. This life was one of never-ending struggle, filled with competing ideals of morality. Anthony would have to make his own tortured decisions as to what he believed was morally right and unacceptably wrong. Then, he would have the duty of living with the outcome of those decisions. This was the life Robert Charles asked us to commit to, a life of becoming the tortured hands of black justice.

"Thank you, sir," he gently whispered as I walked away from the coffee table.

I walked to my car and drove myself home. These few days had been exhausting form me and I hadn't slept in my bed since Ryan Foster's murder. Rachel and Sharon had convinced me to go to Gulfport, Mississippi, with them to gamble at the beachfront casinos. We partied every night, drowning ourselves in liquor and losing more than a few dollars at the blackjack tables. The ladies had worn me out. They were simply too much for me, especially Rachel.

After showering and cleaning myself up for bed, my cellphone rang. I looked at the screen and saw it was Jessica Baker. There was no way I could avoid her call this time. I had purposely let

Jessica chill out for a while and if it went any further, she would most certainly resent me for it. So, I took a deep breath and mentally prepared for her bullshit before I made myself answer the phone.

"Hello," I answered.

"Hey," Jessica said in a low tone. "Are you busy?"

"No. I'm just getting out of the shower."

"How are you, Jessica?"

"I'm OK, I guess," she sheepishly responded. "We need to talk. I mean I need to talk to you, Achim."

"I've been thinking a lot about what you told me the other day and I'm ready to discuss it with you. Are you free tonight?"

I didn't know what to make of Jessica calling me. What was she truly up to? Could she and the rest of the NOPD have found out about me? Was she trying to lure me into some sort of trap so I could be arrested? After all, this woman works for the NOPD. I had followed her enough to be able to conclude that she was not only a dedicated police officer but that she slept with the enemy. I had watched all the late-night excursions with her white partner, fucking this white boy's brains out while they both earned a paycheck. The thoughts of them together angered me and the sight of Jessica allowing herself to be used as some white asshole's private concubine broke my heart. Every time I saw them together sneaking around, I wanted to run up and snatch her out of his white hands. She was better than that and she deserved more then what he was giving her.

Yet, the look on Jessica's face as she looked at that white man drove me crazy. From my painful concealment, I could see her blazing desire for that man in her eyes. Jessica had placed her hopes and dreams into this man. A white man that didn't value her the same way I did. She had never looked at me with that same sense of dedication, not even once. It was almost like I somehow killed that loving spirit within her. Almost like I drowned her hopes and dreams. I wasn't the slick-looking white boy. Instead, I was the Uber driving broke ass nigga. In a white man's world, I wasn't good enough for Jessica. As a black man, I was somehow beneath him, no matter who I was.

Part of me wanted to blow Jessica off. Doing so would make both practical and professional sense. Spying on Jessica was no longer needed or even a viable source of information for Robert Charles. There were only three bastards left, and if I continued to mess around with Jessica, it would be a waste of my time. Yet, deep down in my bones, I did truly want to go see her. To hear her voice and look into her eyes again, hoping to God that she would finally open her soul and feel me. From the first day I saw her, I knew that there was something special about this woman. Something in her that I selfishly wanted all for myself.

"I'm free tonight," I finally uttered after a long pause.

"Do you mind seeing me tonight, Achim?" Jessica humbly asked.

"Yeah, we can meet up tonight. How about you meet me at my favorite hangout spot."

"Meet me at Little Dizzy's Café, over in Treme", I said. "I'll be there in two hours."

"OK," Jessica agreed.

I got myself ready and fought my way through New Orleans rush hour traffic as I headed to Little Dizzy's. My thoughts again began to wonder if this was indeed a wise decision. Was this date a necessary risk? There was nothing Robert Charles stood to gain from involving ourselves any further with Jessica Baker. Only chaos and danger could result from this endeavor of my own heart's making. However, I convinced myself that this was my own decision and I alone would take responsibility for its outcome. Reaching into the hidden compartment of my car, I pulled out my handgun and laid it down on my lap. If she was setting me up, I wouldn't be captured alive. In my mind, this would be the end of the road for us.

I found an open parking spot several blocks away from Little Dizzy's Café and parked my car. Before leaving the car to walk to the Café, I looked around, searching for anything that didn't look normal. Nothing jumped out at me. No unmarked cars. No suspicious people standing idle on the sidewalk. No white people walking dogs or pushing baby strollers. It was just another evening in New Orleans. After more self-deliberation, I decided to put my gun back into its hidden spot. This was a gamble I had to take, and if Jessica betrayed me, then so be it.

I exited the car and walked to Little Dizzy's. The Café was half full and I was quickly ushered to an empty table. A black

Radio DJ sat behind a long table in a corner. He was wearing large earphones and giving out traffic updates into his long silver microphone. The Café was quiet as couples sat at their tables engaging in conversation. Sitting at my table, I watched the time slowly tick by. I felt my nerves bubble, as reminders of my sudden vulnerability flooded my senses. The sound of customers leaving and coming through the entrance almost spurred me to panic. It would be easy work for a SWAT team to come rushing in and subdue me. I was in a building that I had failed to case out hours beforehand as I typically would. Now, I felt cornered and trapped in a small restaurant with only one exit.

The waitress came to my table and asked me if I wanted to order any food. She was a nice-looking older light-skinned black lady. An obvious Creole woman with an attractive and seductive accent. Her warm smile and jovial spirit comforted me as she went out of her way to make me feel at home. We both made small talk while I scanned the menu and asked for her expert advice about the various entrée's they served. After much discussion, I decided that a large bowl of gumbo would be my poison for the night.

As the waitress departed my table, I heard the front door open. My eyes locked onto Jessica as she walked through the doorway. My heart began to race as I witnessed her unique beauty add life into the room. Pushing my selfish thought away, I refocused myself to the task at hand. No matter how beautiful this woman was, she was still a cop. I examined Jessica, looking for any signs of an impending sting operation that might arise. She wore plain clothes that fit her perfectly. Her pants weren't baggy, and her shirt wasn't concealing any wires. There were no handcuffs, no radio, and no gun. It was just her.

Jessica's eyes looked tired and weary. Her hair wasn't in its usual neat and pretty state. She almost looked like she had just woken up from some horror-filled nightmare. The door closed behind her and she approached me. As she neared the table, I stood up out of respect to greet her. Without notice or even a hello, Jessica walked up to me and gave me a tight hug. She wrapped her arms around me and tenderly buried her head into my chest. Her hug momentarily unnerved me. I looked around to recheck my surroundings for any suspicious moves. Had I missed something? I returned her embrace while searching for the inevitable SWAT team members to come rushing through the door. Was this all a clever setup? As I held her close, my mind raced but my heart raced faster.

After a long second, Jessica released me from her arms and took her seat across from me. I handed her a menu and she politely pushed it to the edge of the table while looking directly into my eyes. Her demeanor was different, and her eyes were serious. I had never experienced her like this before. She looked determined. I could almost feel her mettle as I stared at her from across the table. Her defiant, yet vulnerable body language boldly told me everything I needed to know about her intentions for the evening. There would be no surprise invasion by SWAT teams or police units. Tonight, would be all about me and her.

"Thank you for seeing me today," Jessica stated while forcing a smile to appear on her shaken face.

"No problem, Jessica," I replied. "Do you want to order any food?"

"Before I order anything, I have to talk to you, Achim."

"I've lied to you about a lot of things and I've also lied to myself. I want to be honest with you right now."

"I'm giving you an opportunity to decide whether you still want to have dinner with me or not. After I tell you the truth about me, if you want me to leave, then I will go."

"I need to tell you that I've been living a double life, Achim. I'm not the person you think I am."

"Right now, I'm at the point where I'm at rock bottom," Jessica declared while quickly wiping away a tear from her eye.

"I'm about to lose my job. A job I worked my ass off to get."

"Everything that I worked hard for in my life is about to go up in smoke. I've made a lot of bad decisions recently. I trusted people that hate me and pushed away people that cared for me."

"I pushed away people like you, Achim and I want to say I'm sorry."

"I feel like I'm so lost. Lost and using a map that has been misleading me into a trap. I don't know where to go anymore and I'm ready to admit that."

At this point, she was crying heavily. Her shaking hand could not keep up with the task of hiding the river of tears that flowed down her face. I calmly grabbed a few napkins and handed them to her. The other couples in the restaurant had noticed this beautiful black woman crying in front of me at my table. Many of them gave us polite, yet nosy stares as they quietly ate their meals. Out of the corner of my eyes, I could see our curious waitress stop herself as she headed towards our table. The waitress and I made eye contact. Without uttering a word, I gently waved the waitress away with my hand. The waitress accommodated me by nodding her head and walking away from us without a protest.

"I don't want to lose you, Achim," Jessica passionately continued. "I didn't realize it until recently, but you have been a blessing to me."

"Why did it take so long for you to see me, Jessica?" I asked curiously.

"Because I have been sleeping with a married man," she explained as she looked directly into my eyes. "I have been secretly sleeping with my partner at work for a few years now."

"The affair has gotten so bad that our boss and our co-workers know."

"At first, it was all just physical attraction combined with my loneliness and his curiosity. But as we continued to see each other, the affair became more intimate. I fell in love with him and thought he had fallen in love with me."

"I realize now that he didn't love me. He never loved me. He was just using me. For him, I was exotic and prohibited sex. A dangerous little bit of dirty fun while on the job. For me, he represented the world; a world I so desperately wanted to be a part of."

"I wanted to so badly believe that he loved me, and I made myself believe it. I forced myself to believe that lie," Jessica humbly described.

"Deep in my soul, I knew better. My mother and my Aunt taught me better. I should have learned from the mistakes of my father, but instead, I internalized them. My pride and self-confidence wouldn't allow me to be honest. The allure of it all was too much for me, I guess."

"I desired something that I would never have. Something that realistically, wasn't mine to ever truly own. I ignored my better judgement because I bought into my selfish fantasy. I readily accepted the world's version of what I should be by deceiving myself, while feeding into my own vanity and insecurities.

"Instead of fulfillment, I experienced emptiness and want. Instead of love and appreciation, I struggle with permanent discontent and shame."

"What was it that you desired Jessica?" I curiously interrupted. "What caused you to stray so far away from who you are?"

Jessica reached for another napkin and cleaned her face of the tear trails that had come streaming down. As she considered my question, I watched her shake her head in frustration. The answer to my question was obviously embarrassing to her, so I gave her a moment of silence to formulate her answer.

"I wanted to be accepted.... I guess," Jessica finally shot back in a low voice.

"Accepted by whom?" I immediately asked.

"I don't know," Jessica replied with urgency in her voice. "It's so hard being a successful black woman nowadays. I oftentimes look around and find myself all alone."

"I'm black and I'm a woman, Achim. Nobody can relate to the stuff I deal with every day. Nobody is here to encourage me when I'm feeling down. No one is able to understand the pressures I feel every day as a black woman."

"So, because you experience the pressures of life, so that's an excuse for sleeping with a married man?" I asked boldly.

"No. It's no excuse," Jessica replied. "I'm just describing how I felt at the time. Not trying to make excuses."

"Jessica," I began as I leaned in close to her. "This man you're fooling around with...is he a white man?"

I watched as Jessica's eyes began to water and filled with embarrassment. Suddenly her eyes darted away from me. It was Jessica's last attempt to shield her shame from the world. What Jessica didn't know is that I already knew about the affair. I had known even before I had first met her. I saw how she looked at that white bastard. The look in her eyes was one of reverence. Now, this white man had filled Jessica's eyes with tears of pain and confusion.

"He's white, isn't he?" I asked again.

"What does it matter, Achim?" Jessica barked back. "Love is blind. I didn't fall in love with him simply because he's a white man. Truth be told, he was the first white guy I was ever with."

"Are you trying to say I somehow betrayed our race because I was with a white guy, Achim? It's not fair for you to question my loyalty because I fell in love with a white man."

"I didn't say that Jessica," I interrupted. "You're the one who brought up loyalty sister, not me."

"Then why did you ask if he was white? Why make an issue of his race? Would it have been better if I slept with a married black man, Achim?"

"I asked because I'm trying to understand what happened here. I can't lie or pretend away my own feelings about that, anymore then you can."

"Well, how do you feel, Achim? Please tell me," Jessica interrupted.

"I think you know how I feel Jessica. I wouldn't be here if I didn't have any feelings for you."

"I care about you. You are so special to me. You are a woman that I adore. You are the woman that is on my mind when I wake up. A black woman I daydream about before I go to sleep at night. I catch myself wondering about you all the time, hoping to hear your sweet comforting voice and anxious to look into your beautiful brown eyes. I lust to feel your perfect brown skin."

"It hurts me to know that I can never be like that white guy. I'm just a man that loves you. You're not just exotic to me. You're my perfection. My motivation."

"To you, I'm just a broke Uber driver. A negro who isn't walking around waving a degree or bragging about my fancy job. I'm a black man that wants to build something special for the both of us. I want to give the best of me to you. It hurts to realize that my best may not be good enough for you in this crazy selfish world."

"You motivate me to push myself. I want to build with you. I want to build something special with you. Without you Jessica, there is no reason for me, as a black man, to build anything in the first place."

Jessica's tears were flowing even more now. Yet, these tears were of a different type. A slight smile flashed across her face as she looked into my eyes. For the first time, I noticed that Jessica looked at me differently. In her beautiful brown eyes, I saw both of our futures and I was humbled by the magnificence of it all. As she gazed at me with something more than merely human recognition, I reached across the table and grabbed her menu. I placed it in front of her before motioning for Jessica to look.

"You're hungry, so you better order your dinner, my love."

We ate dinner and decided to leave Little Dizzy's for the French Quarter where we walked and talked along the Riverwalk. We enjoyed the romance of each other's company as the swirling brown water of the Mississippi River jetted southward. I could feel Jessica's comfort and ease around me increase as the minutes passed by. Jessica described how she felt alienated at work. She explained how the two murder cases she was investigating were connected, but how some of her co-workers wanted to cover up any connections to the conviction of Eric Davis. I quietly listened with a concerned ear as she described how several of her co-workers, including Bill Devers, wanted to discard any notions of potential police misconduct. I made a mental note of everything she told me about the NOPD. It was clear that Jessica hadn't been involved in the framing of Eric Davis. In fact, Bill Devers was deeply involved in the framing of Eric Davis. I had known this from the onset of my investigation. Jessica's words only proved to me that he was still up to his old tricks. Bill Devers would have to be dealt with. This bastard's time had come.

"Jessica, how do you continue to work as a cop if you know that justice wasn't the main priority?" I asked. She looked up at me and a long pause ensued as she fished for the right answer.

"I guess I always believed that I could change the system from within instead of from the outside," she replied.

"Well, how do you feel about that theory now?" I shot back.

"No comment," Jessica said with a chuckle.

We walked towards my car and prepared to end our evening. I reached for Jessica's hand and she readily gave it to me. It just felt like there was something different going on between us tonight. When I looked into her eyes there was no more guessing. I could see that she was feeling something for me. We made it to my car, and I drove Jessica back to Little Dizzy's.

"Thank you for such a great evening. I really needed this, Achim," Jessica lamented.

"No problem", I eagerly responded. "I enjoy spending my time with you, Jessica."

I reached over and held her hand and Jessica began to caress my fingers as we both sat still in knowing silence.

"I want to let you know that you are special, Achim. You are such a great guy."

"I'm so thankful that you are in my life. You gave me so much strength today."

"Things have been so hard for me lately, but I'm so appreciative that you're here with me."

"That's what I'm here for, Jessica. I'm here for you," I eagerly responded.

Jessica leaned over towards me and kissed my cheek. As she pulled back, I turned, and our lips met ever so gently. We began to kiss. With each soft kiss, I could feel the passion build between us. I reached down and began to gently massage her thigh. She reciprocated and began to caress my shoulder. Her skin was soft and perfect. I could feel my excitement bulging and I could sense her passion increasing. At this point, I was getting myself lost in Jessica. My inner gentleman made me pull back, as I didn't want to obligate her.

"I want to be respectful, Jessica," I blurted out. "But if we keep going like this, I'm going to need you."

"Well, let me stop teasing you and take you home with me," she said.

The kissing session began again and this time it was even more intense and passionate. My hands made their way up her chest, as I began to feel her breasts. The feeling of Jessica's warm tongue only served to pour more fuel into my already burning excitement. The curious thoughts of experiencing her soft touch and warm feel flooded my desires. The mental images of making love to Jessica crushed my senses and dominated me. There is nothing as intoxicating as the touch and feel of a black woman, especially this special one. I found myself lost in that time old fleshly instinct as I gazed into her deep brown eyes. This was meant to be for the both of us. It all felt like destiny as our souls interlocked with each overwhelming kiss and each burning touch. As my curious fingers reached down to feel her, I could feel the explosion of manly motivations erupting within me. The earthly desires to taste her and indulge myself in this uniquely beautiful black woman were taking control.

"We have to stop now,", Jessica whispered. "We need some privacy. Not here."

"I'll ride with you," I whispered obediently.

We hopped in her car and she drove us to her place, which wasn't very far from Little Dizzy's. Jessica lived in a long duplex that had been converted into a single-family home. It was a typical

New Orleans style house with colorful window shutters and a tall vaulted ceiling. We walked into her house and she ushered me into her living room. I coolly sat down on her cream-colored couch, and she handed me the TV remote before heading to the kitchen to open a bottle of wine.

"I hope you like red wine," Jessica said while waving two empty wine glasses.

She opened the bottle and poured out our wine. We sat in each other's arms, flipping through the channels and sipping out of our glasses. We shared silly stories about our past love lives. We playfully relived the accounts of both conquests and failures of our yesteryears as the nearly silent TV seemed to watch itself. As our wine glasses emptied, our eyes began to meet. We both knew what was coming. I wanted to take my time and savor this moment with her. Jessica was happy and comfortable as we cuddled on the couch. I had never seen her smile so wide and her eyes so intoxicating. We enjoyed being close to each other as I gently caressed her soft arm. No words needed, just the knowing touch of love. The joyful anticipation of intimacy finally overwhelmed me. I leaned down and kissed her lips. She slowly reached her hand up towards me and began massaging the back of my head. One of my hands made its way underneath her shirt, while the other hand began to rub her back. In an instant, Jessica reached back and unsnapped her bra, giving me access. My hand moved up past her stomach to her soft breasts. Her nipples were erect, and I was eager to taste them. I began to massage her as we exchanged ever-increasing passion in each kiss.

I worked my tongue down to one of her long brown nipples. I sucked and licked them very slowly as Jessica's hands rubbed my back. On the instinct of passion, my fingers unbuttoned her pants. I slid my hand underneath her silky blue panties. As my fingers reached their destination, I could feel Jessica widen her legs to receive me as my curious fingers entered her wetness.

"You're a naughty little gentleman," she murmured with a half-smile.

I sucked her nipple faster as my fingers experienced her ever-increasing wetness. Jessica's warm softness had me ready to bust her wide open. I felt her fingers clumsily undo my belt and pants. Her small soft hand grasped my hardness in a tight grip as I continued to play in her.

"I want you," she whispered into my ear with a fog of hot breath.

It wasn't long before we were both naked. Relieving ourselves of our bothersome clothing, I enjoyed touching her soft brown skin. My natural urges were beyond control as her mouth explored my body and I explored hers. Tasting Jessica was amazing. Hearing her softly moan as her body tensed up around my neck motivated me to continue pleasing her. While I indulged in Jessica's satisfaction, I massaged her breasts. Tasting how bad Jessica wanted me inside of her, I knew it was time. She was exactly right. I entered her and immediately felt her sharp fingernails plunge into my lower back. After filling her out, in a burst of passion, I grabbed Jessica's legs and pushed her knees towards her head. Pounding away at her, I stared deep into her eyes as she let out the four-letter words of pleasure. Her pupils were wide and telling as I stared into them as she began to climax. She was so beautiful and sexy. It all felt so good. It all felt so right as I tried to fight off my own end. Fuck it. It was at that moment, that I decided I wanted some more of this. For us, this would only be our warmup for the rest of the night. The ball game was just getting started for the both of us. Our second round would be the tip off.

Chapter Seven

Bill Devers was going to die today. It was time for this damn Race Soldier who pretended to be an honest police officer, to be taken out. It's been two weeks since I murdered Ryan Foster and Kevin Longstreet. Both killings quietly fell out of the local news cycle as the NOPD had starved the media of necessary information about the cases. For most citizens of New Orleans, both murders were simply chalked up to the typical random acts of violence the city had become accustomed to. Neither of the murders were thought to be a symptom of the wrongful conviction of Eric Davis. Jessica Baker told me all about the steps Bill Devers and her black boss Captain Wolf took to restrict the spread of any evidence that would cast doubt on

Eric Davis's conviction. They instead peddled the idea that there might have been a mole within the NOPD. The NOPD wanted these murder cases to disappear, hoping whoever had committed them would ultimately catch the hint that there would be no justice rendered for Eric Davis. The NOPD and the city of New Orleans had no intentions of freeing Eric. They were intent on using their enormous power to keep Eric Davis imprisoned for murders he did not commit.

Unfortunately for the cops, I had planned for their stubborn injustice. The police are the Enforcement Arm of White Supremacy. They would have to be made to bend towards the will of justice. Every instance of abuse towards a black person was somehow justified in this system of white power. The time had come to air out the NOPD's dirty laundry. Air their dirt out in such a way that they would have no choice but to confront the undeniable truth. This was the time for Robert Charles to shine. We would strike a major blow against our opponent and they would have no clue who had struck them.

I found myself about a few miles north of Grand Isle, Louisiana, pretending to be fishing inside a small motorboat in the shallow waters of Caminada Bay. Boater traffic was heavy on the water this weekend. I noticed that I was the only black boater, as every white boater that passed by kept staring at me. This was a good thing. I wanted to be seen. I wanted every racist inbred fucker to see this black man and wonder within themselves, 'how did this nigger get a boat?' I needed them to wonder and wanted them to get curious.

As I anchored my boat, I finally saw Bill Devers and his fellow bastard, Josh McRoberts. They were in a long flat boat speeding towards one of their favorite fishing holes that hid among the grassy bayous. The day I murdered Kevin Foster was the last time I saw Josh outside of his house in the Garden District. Kevin borrowed his car that evening and ever since Kevin's murder, Josh had purposely kept a low profile. He was able to keep himself out of the limelight. He was a spoiled white bastard who had been born into wealth and had failed up his whole life. After dropping out of Tulane University, he inherited his parent's luxurious home in the Garden District where he lived off his trust fund. He spent most of his time online trolling liberals or hanging out with his racist mentor, Bill Devers. Bill had tried to get Josh into the police academy, but due to Josh's weight problem, he couldn't pass the physical exam. Weeks after Ryan's death, the two bastards were together once again, re-invigorating their weekly fishing trips. They neared my anchored boat and I saw Bill Devers pull back the throttle and slow himself down. Their boat slowly motored passed me while they both emptied their gaze at me, giving me curious looks. I waved my hand to greet them and they both returned a half-hearted and annoyed head nod. After passing me, they stopped their boat in the water and dropped anchor.

I sent my fishing line into the water and watched as Bill and Josh began to fish. Luck was miles away from me, as I could see them pulling redfish out of the water within thirty minutes of casting their fishing line. An hour passed with no luck shining on my path. I could see both looking at me with concealed grins as they laughed hysterically amongst themselves. They were surely observing my inability to catch even one fish in such a target rich environment. Little did these bastards know that I had my eye on a much bigger catch. The moment I got their attention, I set out to put my plan into action. While both men wrestled to reel in a big fish, I walked over to my outboard engine and ripped out my boat plug. Slowly, the water of Caminada Bay began to seep into my boat.

As the water began to rise, my boat began to slip under the waterline. I was clearly sinking. With a great sense of urgency, I began to shout and wave my arms in distress.

"Hey!" I shouted. "Help me!"

I pulled the starter on my engine, attempting to crank it up and nothing happened. My engine made a strange sound as it seemed not to turn over. I again turned towards the men and screamed for help. When Bill and Josh both realized what was going on, they quickly pulled up their anchor and motored towards me. Bill pulled up alongside my boat and Josh threw over a tag line to me.

"You're taking on water, bud," Bill shouted over to me as he surveyed the brown water filling up my boat.

"Pull up your anchor man! We can tow you to shore," Josh ordered.

"Okay," I responded in my best panicked voice.

I yanked up fifty feet of anchor line and threw my anchor on deck. Josh sent over a towline and I quickly attached it to a bit on the bow of my boat. Bill engaged his throttles and pulled me over towards a marshy shoreline, not far from our fishing spot. My boat came up on plane and I used a small bucket to bail the raising water out of it. The marshy beach in front of us would be my salvation, otherwise, I would have to swim for my life in the Bay's nasty brown water. Bill gunned his throttle as we got close to the marshy beach. I could feel both of our boats bouncing off the bottom of the bay as we powered towards safety. In an instant, I felt my boat suddenly come to a jerking stop, which threw me off balance. It was clear that my boat had run aground. Bill still had his throttles engaged to full power and his engines were roaring, churning out a cloud of thick white exhaust into the air. Within a few seconds, I watched as the towline on my bow tightened under the heavy strain, storing hundreds of pounds of energy. It was only a matter of seconds before the line would part and break in half. I dove to the deck and curled into a ball, seconds later I heard the line snap into two. The dangerous recoil of the line that was shot back missed me by inches and burst a wide hole in my center console. I luckily escaped death.

"Are you alright bud?" Bill asked as he struggled to pull his boat alongside mine.

"Yeah." I cautiously replied. "That line almost took my damn head off."

"Well, you're alive." Bill half-jokingly replied. "It's better than swimming out in the bay."

"We got to get you to shore." Josh declared. "Tie a line to your boat and come over here with us."

The beach was less than forty yards away, so I grabbed a long line and tied one end on a bit. I stepped over to their boat and Bill slowly nosed his flatboat onto the marshy beach. Once on the beach, I began pulling my boat ashore and Josh joined in to help me. He was a balding and heavy-set white man, short with stubby arms and small hands. I could feel his strength diminish with each pull. Exhausting ourselves, we both pulled my boat through the sticky mud and onto the marshy beach. Bill set an anchor for his flat boat and joined us ashore.

"What the hell happened out their bud?" Bill asked with a heavy New Jersey accent.

"I was fishing. Everything was all good, but then I saw water coming into my boat. When I started looking around to stop it, the water kept rising and I panicked."

"Thank you for saving me," I added. "I probably would have been in a world of hurt if you weren't out here with me."

"You damn right man." Josh sternly interrupted. "Look at your boat dude! You don't have a radio. No life jackets. No safety equipment at all. You could have been killed!"

"What the hell were you thinking bud?" Bill shouted at me with an intense stare. "Are you trying to kill yourself out here?"

"No…I just came out here to do some fishing and relax." I stuttered.

Both men began to inspect my boat. Again, noting that I had no life jackets or any type of safety equipment, Bill then questioned why I was using the wrong type of fishing rods for the area. Josh found my cellphone on the deck of the boat, totally submerged under water. Then Bill showed me the removed boat plug.

"Bud, this is why your boat is taking on water," Bill explained with cockiness! "Your fuckin boat plug is not installed."

"What!" I shot back faming ignorance.

"Dude, if you don't have your boat plug installed, your boat is going to take on water," Josh began. "Before you put any boat in the water you have to make sure the boat plug is inserted…. Where are you from dude?"

"My name is Damon. I'm originally from St. Louis, Missouri." I began. "I moved down to New Orleans eight months ago."

"Well Damon, I'm Bill and this is my friend Josh," Bill explained. "You owe us both for saving your black ass."

"It's nice to meet ya'll. Might be dead if I didn't." I said with a phony smile.

"You sure would bud. This isn't the place to fuck around in, if you aren't familiar with the landscape homie." Bill sarcastically began.

"I'm from New Jersey, born and raised there before moving down here 25 years ago. Hell, I still don't know my way around all these bayous. Everything changes around here. As the Gulf of Mexico swallows up these inland marshes, navigational landmarks disappear. The damn coastline of the entire state is mostly underwater. Boating down here is nothing to play around with."

"You better know what you're doing before you decide to just start fishing around these parts bud. This isn't St. Louis."

"I know now," I replied. "I'm so thankful you guys were out here. I might have died, and no one would have known."

"How do I get back to Grand Isle now? My engine is flooded, and it won't start."

Josh walked over towards my outboard engine and pulled the cranking lever. The engine sputtered and failed to turnover. After pulling the lever for several minutes, an exhausted Josh finally gave up.

"This thing is flooded with water. It's not going to start until it is rinsed out and dried." Josh explained.

Bill threw his arms up in the air in frustration and Josh's flabby face wore a look of concealed disgust. Both men refused to even look at me as the realization of what they had gotten themselves into dawned upon them. They had acted as helpful mariners, and good Samaritans looking out for the well-being of a fellow boater. Now, their reward was to have to babysit me, instead of enjoying a fun filled afternoon of pulling delicious redfish out of the bay.

"I'm so sorry guys." I pleaded. "I didn't mean for you both to have to worry yourselves."

"We can't just let you sit out here, all alone on this marsh bud. Your cellphone is wasted. You have no clue about a damn thing out here. You're screwed and I'm screwed too! I'm a cop and if you come up missing, I will get blamed for leaving your ass out here."

"You have two choices Damon," Bill angrily continued. "Either we leave this boat here and you come back to Grand Isle with us, or we call a commercial salvage company to come take your boat back to Grand Isle."

"I can't leave this boat guys," I injected. "It's not even my boat. I don't own it. My friend does."

"So that means we can call commercial salvage to come tow you then?" Bill asked with frustration.

"No. Not exactly," I replied. "Maybe I can call my friend and tell him what happened. Maybe he can decide what he wants to do with his boat."

"Well, where is your friend at?" Josh asked.

"He lives in Biloxi, Mississippi."

"Biloxi!" Bill shouted in anger. "It will take him hours to get out here!"

"How about I call him and see if he can arrange for a salvager to come out here to help me?" I inquired. "Who knows, he may already have insurance on this boat."

After releasing a sigh of frustration, Bill reached into his pants pocket and pulled out his cellphone. He turned it on and unlocked it before handing it to me. Bill's phone took several long minutes to locate a tower signal. When his phone notified that it had acquired a strong enough signal, I hit the green button to begin a call. As I began punching in a phone number, I paused.

"I'm not sure I can remember my friend's number," I cautiously admitted.

"What!" Josh vented.

"Damn man, I'm sorry Josh. I'm all fucked up out here."

"Let me call my office and see if someone at work can give me his number."

Josh and Bill both walked away from me in frustration as I began calling several numbers. If they could have punched me in the face, I knew they would have, and I knew they wanted to. My plan was working out and I was right on schedule. I pretended to dial one last phone number and began to speak into the phone.

"Hey Phillip," I stated loudly so both Bill and Josh could hear me.

Both men looked away from me as I engaged in a fake conversation with no one. They were both falling for my deception. Out of frustration with me, they both had lowered their guard. They surely assumed that I was just another dumb nigger and not any sort of threat to them. How could I be a threat? I couldn't even operate my own boat or catch one fish. To them, I was just another black man that was totally out of his element in their world. After several minutes, I ended my fake dialogue and returned the cell phone to Bill.

"Thanks sir," I began. "My friend Phillip wants to arrange for a commercial salvager to come down here and pick up his boat. Phillip is calling them, and the commercial salvager will call us back to get our location once the business end is handled."

Bill shook his head in approval and Josh's face cracked a wide smile. Both men appeared satisfied with the good news.

"Alright bud," Bill began. "Here's what's going to happen. We can give you a ride back to Grand Isle or you can sit your ass out here on this marsh and watch us fish. Either way, Josh and I are going back out to our spot to fish."

"Yeah Damon," Josh added with a gleeful smile. "If you want to go back to Grand Isle, now is the time. Bill and I can keep an eye on your friends' boat for you. We'll be here when the commercial salvager arrives."

"You might not want to stay out here on this marsh bud," Bill chimed in. "It's filled with all kinds of snakes and shit."

This was a con game. Bill and Josh were trying to pull a fast one on me. If they took me back to Grand Isle, I knew they would come back out here and steal my boat. They could claim salvage rights and there would be nothing I could legally do to regain possession of it. I would never see them or the boat again.

I walked over to my boat and climbed in. Reaching down, I grabbed my five-gallon bucket and threw it on the marshy beach.

Then I found my long black pelican case and carried it back to the shore.

"I'll stay guys," I declared. "I want to thank you guys for helping me. Please let me know when the salvager is on his way out."

I flipped my bucket upside down and sat on it because I was determined to wait the men out and destroy their scheme. Bill and Josh both smiled and shook their heads in frustration as they silently watched me open my pelican case.

"What the fuck are you going to do out here for hours while this salvager makes his way out here?" Bill barked. "What if he gets lost or can't find you? This isn't the damn hood homie."

"We can't stay out here with you forever Damon," Josh seconded. "You have no clue what kind of danger you're in out here man. People die out here. The weather comes rolling in and people go missing. Hell, the Coast Guard can't even find their bodies half the time. It's better for you to go back to Grand Isle. Maybe we can have the salvager meet you on the island when he calls us back. We are just trying to look out for you man."

"I'll stay," I boldly proclaimed. "I'm right where I want to be anyway. There isn't nothing in Grand Isle I want to see right now. What I want is out here with me."

I smiled at both men as I flipped open the lid of my pelican case. My silver handgun shined as the bright sunlight hit it from above. My long sharp blade also smiled back at me as it shined under the sun. I was ready for action and I could feel a burst of anger coursing through my veins. Now, it was only a matter of time before I would strike my first blow. There was no turning back. It's either they both die, or they end up killing me out on this mosquito infested hell hole.

"Your gun and machete aren't going to do a damn thing for you, if you can't call nobody," Bill uttered in laughter. "I told you. You don't need to be out here boy!"

Bill walked over to where I was seated and gazed into my open pelican case. His eyes reviewed my weapons and the other items inside. I saw a look of recognition splash across his face as he looked down at one item. Then he looked into my eyes with a familiar stare.

"So, this is why you're out here huh," he lamented with a grin. "I knew you guys would eventually come after us, you black bastard. I already told your boss what you needed to do. If you can't do it, there is no deal boy. Go tell your boss I said that. Robert Charles can go to hell."

"I'm not here to make any sort of deal with your white ass, Bill Devers. I'm here to kill you."

"So, now that I'm here to execute you.... What are you going to do about me Mister Police Officer?" I laughingly responded.

Bill's hand reached towards his waist. In one quick motion, I launched up from the bucket and kicked Bill in his chest before he could aim his gun. My kick sent Bill stumbling backwards towards the shoreline, until he tripped and fell on the marshy beach. His service weapon went flying into the brown water, causing a loud splash as it disappeared underneath the waterline.

"You fucking nigger!" Bill yelled. "You're a dead man."

In an instant, I drove my black fist through Bill's face as he lay helpless in the mud. His nose exploded with blood, as it shot out of his hairy nostrils. I cocked back my left arm to deliver another punch to his face, when I felt Josh's body knock me down into the muddy ground. Josh landed on top of me and drove his flabby forearm into my neck. I tasted my own blood in my mouth as the sting of Josh's blow settled in. Using all my strength, I pushed Josh's face upwards with the palm of my hand until his body was driven off mine.

"Get your fat ass off me bitch," I mumbled.

With my right hand, I reached into my pocket and found my switch blade. Josh's huge belly was exposed. I plunged my switch blade into his stomach several times, as my hand felt his warm blood pour out of the wounds. Josh let out a loud cry before he punched and kicked me away, fighting for his pathetic life. I rose to my feet and towered over Josh as he lay in the mud, holding his hands to his stomach. He began to cry like a little baby, and I enjoyed seeing his tears of weakness. As I started to kick him in the face, I saw a bright glint out of the corner of my eye. Turning my head towards the sudden shining light, I saw that it was Bill Devers. In his hands he held my silver handgun and he had leveled it at me. I found myself looking down the barrel of my own weapon. Bill's face was filled with part panic and another part hatred as he bore down on me, giving me all kinds of commands. These were the familiar ingredients of White on Black violence and murder.

I heard a loud click as Bill pulled the trigger. Bill recognized that my gun failed to fire. He quickly pulled back the slide and chambered another bullet, clearing a perceived misfire. As he aimed once more, a panicked silence ruled the moment between the both of us. With so much fear eating him up, Bill again pulled the trigger. A bright flash and loud gunshot rang out as I ducked towards the ground for cover. When I stood back up, I heard Bill screaming in pain as he slowly fell to the ground. I walked over towards him and saw a large piece of the guns slide lodged in his right eye. His right hand was completely mangled and bloody. Several fingers on his hand had been blown off and there was a large bloody hole in the middle of his palm. My gun had exploded in his hand, just as I planned.

"You're a cop Bill. Aren't you trained to check a firearm before you handle it?" I mockingly asked.

"Fuck you," he screamed back in a distressed tone.

"No Bill…. Fuck you. You're fucked bud."

Kneeling in the mud, I took my switch blade and violently plunged it into Bill's stomach several times. His pathetic cry for help and mercy only fueled my blood thirst. His whimpering caused me to drive my knife into the bottom of his lower jaw.

"Shut the hell up!" I whispered to him as I drove the tip of my blade into the top of his mouth.

Blood shot out of his mouth and a river of tears rolled down his pale white face. He was silent now and his left eyelid was closed. It shook as he forced it shut. Bill knew his fate was sealed. I owned his life, there would be no mercy, only justice and recompense. I heard Josh moaning and trying to raise himself off the ground behind me. Standing up, I walked back to my pelican case to grab the only weapon I truly wanted to use. The weapon Bill should have taken instead of the gun; my long knife. The old-fashioned machete was sharp and deadly as hell. Just like the ones my ancestors were forced to use to chop sugarcane while being worked to death in the concentration camps and killing fields of south Louisiana.

"You know Bill," I began as I grabbed the machete. "God gave you a choice. You could have easily killed me today."

"But you made a bad decision. A decision that I am sure you are now regretting. A decision I knew you would make."

"Instead of choosing this beautifully sharpened machete…. You chose the ease and detachment of a gun."

"I knew your white ass would choose the gun because you White Supremacists are nothing more than lazy cowards. You depend on guns to do your dirty work for you and keep you alive."

"That's why you white folks love your second amendment rights."

"Well today that all blew up in your damn face, now didn't it."

I sprinted over towards Josh as he attempted to raise himself up to his knees and struck him in his head with the machete. His head split open like a juicy watermelon, which brought a smile to my face. His body fell limp into the mud and blood poured out of the back of his head. Josh was now lifeless as he laid there. I didn't give a damn about that. There would be no mercy, even for this racist bastard's defenseless corpse. I hit his torso hard with my blade until I had exposed his smelly insides to the insects. The muddy ground around him was now layered with dark red blood. The sight of it all was magnificent and my spirit was moved. The Lord had seen fit for me to conquer, and by faith, he had allowed me to do so. I stopped for a moment to take it all in and enjoy my victory, as the flies began to swarm in on his lifeless corpse.

"Praise God." I whispered to myself. "Justice is truly yours Lord."

Behind me, I heard Bill coughing up blood as he tried to lift himself off the ground. I walked over to him and kicked him back down into the mud. He opened his mouth as he fell and moved his lips in a vain attempt to plead for mercy. Red blood instead shot out and I could hear him choking as he looked up at me with his one good eye. Now, I would have his undivided attention.

"It's racists like you that I hate the most," I began. "You pretend to be an honest police officer, but, you're just a White Supremacist carrying a badge. That's all you are."

"You used your badge to terrorize my community. Sell drugs in my community. Steal from my community. Then you kill my people or set them up, like you bastards did to Eric Davis."

"Well, today is judgment day for you bud."

"Robert Charles finds you guilty of being an Anti-Black racist," stating my verdict in a formal voice. "Your punishment is death. May you burn in hell."

With one powerful blow from my machete, Bill's head was severed from his body ending his life instantly. I picked up his head and placed it on top of his chest. The fun part of my mission had been completed. Now, it was time to take care of the business portion of my responsibilities.

Inside my pelican case, was a mountain of damning evidence against these bastards. Time was of the essence and I had to arrange the murder scene perfectly in order to convey just the right message. This time I would not be talking to the NOPD. Since this crime scene was in Caminada Bay, outside of New Orleans, it would be the Jefferson Parish Sheriff's Department that would respond. NOPD's soiled laundry would be aired out for the world to witness. It would be the perfect narrative. A dirty cop is viciously murdered alongside a White Supremacist terrorist on an isolated marshy island with tons of incriminating evidence surrounding them. The entire circumstance would sound all too nefarious and would be irresistible to the press.

I took a police uniform from my pelican case and hung it up from a branch on a small tree. The uniform swung slightly as it seemed to float in the light breeze. The name tag on the uniform read J. McRoberts. Just like Ryan Foster, Josh McRoberts had been impersonating a police officer while robbing black people. Josh and Ryan would pull over unwitting black citizens in their cleverly arranged replica of an unmarked police car. They would hand cuff black men, women and children, while both Ryan and Josh rummaged through their belongings. They would steal anything of value or plant drugs on innocent black people in order to extort them.

Next to Josh's body, I laid out his White Supremacist flag with its powder white background and large black X. The white flag quickly soaked up the bloody mud as it lay on the ground, making the flag appear as though it were reddish brown in color. I took a handful of photos and tossed them on top of the wet flag. They were incriminating photos of Josh McRoberts and Ryan Foster dressed in police uniforms and handcuffing black men. Photos of both men proudly holding up this White Supremacist flag, while wearing NOPD badges and giving Nazi salutes. More photos of both men guzzling tall glasses of beer while NOPD detectives Bill Devers and Daniel Fitzpatrick, stood by watching with wide adoring smiles. The conclusion one could draw from the photos was undeniable. There was something rotten within the New Orleans Police Department, something that had harmed a lot of innocent black people.

Taking both of Josh's hands, I placed them inside of Ziploc bags before writing a message on them, "My hands are the hands that killed Jeffery and Thomas Roberts. Fingerprint me. Eric Davis is an innocent man."

Now it was time to arrange Bill's message. I walked over to Bill Devers corpse and laid several bags of dope on his body, next to his severed head. On top of the dope, I arranged more photos of Daniel and Bill, waving the White Supremacist flags while wearing KKK outfits. Then there was one final photo, which was a photo of Bill Devers sitting inside a car with Kevin Longstreet. I took my marker and wrote a message on the back of that photo, before placing the photo in Bill's pocket.

"This was your star witness in the Eric Davis case. Kevin Longstreet along with his racist white daddy, Detective Bill Devers. Kevin was a drug addict and police informant who lied on Eric Davis to keep himself out of jail and cover up Bill Devers misdeeds. Free Eric Davis NOW or suffer more consequences. Signed Justice."

I climbed into Bill's boat and grabbed a sack filled with flares and a long wooden paddle oar. Once I got out, I pushed the flat boat off the beach and sent it floating into the bay. Then I walked over to my boat and popped the cover off the top of my engine. After reconnecting a fuel line, I used the hand pump to recirculate fuel into the engine. I pulled the starter ignition and the outboard engine turned over immediately, blowing out a small puff of gray smoke upon starting.

After loading up my pelican case, bucket and other tools, it was time to leave this masterpiece of God's punishment in my rearview mirror. Wanting to ensure that no evidence of my presence could be found, I grabbed a hidden bottle of bleach and poured it over the dead bodies.

Using the long paddle, I pushed my boat off the marshy beach into deeper waters. When my paddle could no longer touch the bottom, that was my cue to lower the outboard engine and motor towards Bill's flat boat. Once alongside the flat boat, I tied my boat off to it and climbed over, as it was time to make a radio call. I turned on Bill's radio and watched as the lights on his expensive communications panel lit up. After changing the radio to channel 16, I grabbed the microphone and pressed down on the key to begin talking.

"Coast Guard! May day…. May day…. help. I'm in Caminada Bay," I shouted.

Within seconds the panicked voice of a female U.S. Coast Guard officer replied to me. She rattled off a series of questions, asking my location and for a description of my vessel. Once again, I keyed the microphone but instead of talking, I rubbed the microphone up against my shirt without uttering a response. Seconds later she called me back, confused as to my transmission.

"Vessel in distress this is the U.S. Coast Guard. Please give us your location, description of your vessel, number of people onboard and nature of distress. Over."

I turned the radio off and climbed back over to my boat. It was time to shoot off a signal flare. Reaching inside Bill's flare bag, I found an orange and red parachute flare. With a pull of the trigger I shot the flare skyward and watched as it deployed its small parachute. It slowly fell to the earth, while displaying its trademark orange and red sparks against the clear blue sky. Now it was time to shake this spot for good. The Calvary would most certainly be on its way to execute a hasty rescue. Instead, they would only find the sad and grizzly remains of two justly rewarded FOWL racist rotting under the hot Louisiana sun.

Chapter Eight

I t was a beautiful Saturday afternoon. The sun poured through the windshield as Achim drove us down the empty highway. Traffic had been light and non-existent at certain points in the city. On such a beautiful picturesque day, the sight of an empty highway was completely out of the ordinary for a vibrant city like New Orleans. Everyone in the city had decided it was better to stay at home, as opposed to venturing out in public. I could hardly blame them. After a weeklong series of protests and violent riots that followed the news surrounding Bill Devers gruesome murder, there was hardly anybody in New Orleans who could summon the energy or the courage to risk leaving the safety of their homes.

The once jovial city was now paralyzed with anger and mistrust. Rumors of White Supremacist terrorists working hand in hand with city police officers, sent shockwaves throughout every community. Most of the rumors were fanned by Eric Davis's uncle, State Senator Rodney Davis, and his large band of supporters. After receiving news of Bill Devers misdeeds, Senator Davis's anger over the wrongful and political conviction of his nephew Eric was now being openly expressed. Details of Bill Devers having orchestrated an NOPD plan that was set up to pin the murders of Jeffery and Thomas Roberts on Eric Davis, had been leaked to the national media. Shocking details of a government sponsored set up of Eric now dominated the news cycle. This was now the narrative that was being pushed by a newly emboldened black community. Conspiracy theories ran wild, as more and more of the black citizens' questions went unanswered by city leadership. How many black people had this White Supremacist terrorist ring effected? How many more other false arrests or potential setups had they executed? How many black people were robbed by this band of thieves? How many other innocent black people could this band of white thugs have killed?

No one at NOPD had real answers to any of those questions. Publicly, we all were blindsided by the evidence that two of our own had used their badges to promote White Supremacy. Privately, I was not shocked nor surprised. Ever since my dispute with Captain Wolf, I knew that there was much more going on in my office then I could ever have wrapped my head around. Now, what had happened in the darkness could no longer be hidden away from righteous eyes. Monstrous misdeeds had slipped into the light, and everyone in the NOPD was covering their back sides.

I felt Achim reach over and hold my hand. He began to softly caress my fingers, conveying his concern for me. Achim's tender and comforting touch was followed by a loving smile that highlighted his deep brown eyes. This black man loved me, and I knew I loved him too. I wiped a tear from my eye and tried to compose myself. Thankful to the man above for what he had given me. Appreciative of what I had been blessed with. Real love from someone who was so sweet and caring.

"Have you heard from your old partner Jessica?" Achim asked as he drifted over into the far-right lane. "Has Daniel tried to reach out to you?"

"No. I haven't heard from him at all," I answered.

"It's been two weeks since Daniel disappeared and if he hasn't reached out to me already that means he no longer trusts me."

"It already feels like an eternity. So much has changed since I last saw Daniel," I added.

"What about his wife and kids?" Achim inquired. "How are they taking all of this?"

"I visited Daniel's wife last week before we searched his home for evidence," I began. "She is a total mess, you know. She's heartbroken. It has to be tough to find out your husband is living a double life."

"His kids are understandably sad. They aren't quite sure what's happening regarding their father, but they can sense that it isn't good. It's a terrible situation for the whole family. Their world has been literally flipped upside down."

"You guys have any ideas on where Daniel might be hiding?" Achim followed up.

"I don't have a clue where Daniel is hiding and I can't speak for anybody else in the office, but I'm sure someone knows."

"I do know that I'm really, really scared right now."

"Daniel has a lot of friends on the force. He could be hiding anywhere. I do know that somebody tipped him off about what was found at the murder scene down in Grand Isle. Now, Internal Affairs and the State Police are crawling all over the NOPD. Everybody in the department is a suspect. We've all been questioned."

"Because I was Daniel's partner and lover, they are all over me. I got questioned for several hours without the representation of my union attorney the other day. Somehow, they thought I might be involved in all of this mess."

"What kind of questions were they asking you Jessica? I mean…just because you are Daniels lover doesn't mean you support White Supremacy," Achim said with a bit of frustration.

"You believe that Achim, but they don't. Captain Wolf has sent these damn investigators after me."

"They want to know why Daniel and I were sleeping with each other and how it was that I never suspected him or Bill Devers of misconduct. Mostly they asked if Daniel had ever confided in me, regarding the Eric Davis case."

"They had lots of questions about the Eric Davis case."

"Did Daniel ever confide with you about the case?" Achim curiously asked.

"No. He never said anything about it. I knew that Daniel and Bill were close, but I never thought either of them were doing anything illegal. I guess I was being naïve."

"When we began looking into the Kevin Longstreet and Ryan Foster murders, we started finding clues that something had gone terribly wrong with the Eric Davis investigation."

"That's when I found out that Daniel had been the officer that arrested Eric Davis. Both Bill and Daniel had testified for the prosecution in Eric Davis's trial. I had never known that until all of these murders happened."

"Captain Wolf knew I was suspicious, and she threatened to expose my relationship with Daniel if I pursued it further. I didn't know who put Captain Wolf up to threaten me, but they must have been very powerful. Whoever it was, they are willing to go to any lengths to hide the truth."

"Everyone in the department believes that I know more than I actually do. Captain Wolf and these investigators will never believe me when I tell them I don't. They think I have something to hide."

"As a matter of fact, I'm certain Captain Wolf is having me followed right now."

Achim peered back using the rearview mirror, while studying two cars that lagged us. Achim pressed down on the accelerator, increasing our pace and sending our car flying down the highway. The sudden acceleration pushed me back into my seat. Achim was focused, as both of his hands tightly gripped the steering wheel. His eyes were shut between the road ahead and the two cars fading away in the rearview mirror. I placed my hand on Achim's thigh and began to stroke him.

"No worries baby," I said calming him down. "I have nothing to hide. Let them do their jobs."

Achim stared at me with an obvious look of concern. I knew he meant well and only wanted to protect me. He was doing his best to keep me away from danger, yet he listened to me and relented to my request. Achim took his foot off the accelerator and allowed the car to coast until we were back under the speed limit.

"Where do we exit?" Achim asked attempting to change the subject.

"Two more exits down. We'll take the exit right before the airport," I instructed.

We pulled into the parking lot of the funeral home and easily found an open space. The few cars that were in the parking lot looked familiar to me as we drove past them. From the emptiness of the lot, not many people had come out to celebrate Bill Devers life. In death, he had managed to find a way to be as unpopular with his co-workers as he had been in life. This entire situation just seemed so poetic.

Achim put the car into park and killed the ignition. I put my hand back on his thigh and squeezed him before he could open his door. "I don't know what's about to go down in there," I explained. "But my main goal is to pay my respects to a co-worker. I don't want to get involved in all the damn drama."

Achim looked at me and shook his head in confirmation. "I'm here to support you," he answered back in his reassuring deep voice. Achim reached in the back seat and grabbed his Bible before opening the door and exiting his car. I followed him out of the car, and we made our way into the funeral home. As the front entrance door closed behind us, the funeral home suddenly felt dim and cold. We walked towards the seating area and more than half of the seats in the funeral home were empty. Bill's shiny light brown casket sat in front of scores of empty chairs. Around his lonely casket were a beautiful arrangement of bright flowers along with a large photo of a young-looking Bill Devers. An elderly white man somberly greeted us and ushered us to our seats several rows behind Bill's family. Achim and I both sat down and silently waited for the wake services to commence.

Out of the side of my eye, I noticed Captain Wolf turn around in her seat, two rows in front of us. Her eyes were filled with tears as Debbie rubbed her back to comfort her. Our eyes met and we exchanged a knowing head nod before she turned back around in her seat. Debbie gave Captain Wolf a kiss as they held hands and shared a few comforting words. The sight of Captain Wolf shedding tears surprised me. I never would have imagined that Captain Wolf and Bill Devers were that close. I could never envision Bill Devers shedding any tears at Captain Wolf's funeral, much less anyone that wasn't a white male.

Captain Wolf and Debbie rose from their seats. They both walked towards where Achim and I were seated, so I stood up to formally greet them. With tears in her eyes, I watched as Captain Wolf offered me a hug. Deep inside, I didn't want to touch this evil bitch who had sexually violated me in the worst possible way. Yet reluctantly, I accepted her hug to avoid causing a scene at such a solemn event.

"Hey Jessica," Captain Wolf began with the tears flowing. "Thank you for coming. I know you didn't have to, but I'm certain Bill's family will appreciate your presence here today."

"You comin here is a testament about who you are as a person. I'm proud of you Jessica."

"Thank you," I softly whispered.

Captain Wolf turned towards Debbie and introduced her to me. "This is the love of my life Debbie Wolf," Captain Wolf explained. "Debbie. Please meet one of my best Detectives, Jessica Baker."

Debbie's blue eyes, well-manicured teeth and gracefully graying hair gave her the look of money. We shook hands and exchanged polite pleasantries. I turned and introduced both women to Achim.

"Captain this is my boyfriend Achim Jeffers," I relayed. A handsome smile exploded across Achim's face as the surprising title I had bestowed upon him sunk in. "Nice to meet you ladies," Achim remarked as he shook their hands.

"So, your last name is Baker, right Jessica?" Debbie asked out of the blue.

Her question confused me, as did her disingenuous smile that she openly displayed as she waited on my answer. "Yes, it is," I admitted.

"And is your mother's name Alice?" Debbie followed up.

"Well yes. My mother's name is Alice Baker," I confirmed. "She passed away years ago."

"Oh my," Debbie said laughingly. "Because I'm certain I know your father. As a matter of fact, I can see his resemblance in your face," Debbie continued. "I know the man well. Be sure to tell your father that Debbie sends her best and give him my sincerest apologies regarding your mother."

The moment was awkward and confusing. A look of sheer embarrassment filled the face of Captain Wolf. Achim quietly wore a smile while his curious eyes probed both Debbie and I, while attempting to figure out what was occurring between us. I too was confused. How could this rich white lady possibly know my father? I asked myself.

The wake service began and several of Bill's family members stood up to speak in his behalf. None of them mentioned anything about his police service. They all told touching stories of Bill. Once the family was done, a priest rose and spoke a few comforting words before we all stood and joined him in prayer. Then it was time for the viewing. The funeral home attendants opened Bill's casket and the ushers filed us down the center aisle. When it was our turn, Achim and I walked up to the casket and peered inside. His face looked plastic and waxy in appearance. He was dressed in a huge turtleneck that bulged out from underneath his suit jacket, and his jaw and right eye were clearly deformed. It had been a painful and brutal death for Bill. The grizzly sight of Bill's body moved me emotionally, mainly because I wasn't prepared to see such devastation wrecked upon someone I had personally known. Achim leaned in over me and peered down. He wore an expressionless look, almost as if he had detached himself from the reality of what he was viewing.

I quickly turned away from the casket and walked towards Bill's family. It was then that the reality of his death totally sunk in. He may have been an asshole, but his family would have to survive without him after his death. My heart went out to them. I wiped away tears that flowed down my face. Achim wrapped his arms around me and held me tight. I relented to his comforting touch and put my head into his hard chest. After composing myself, I leaned over to Bill's wife and we exchanged sincere hugs.

She was a plump white woman with brown hair and a large frame. In her eyes were the clear signs of emotional exhaustion. Without words, I sympathized with this white woman and she understood my sympathy. Her nightmare was truly just beginning. For her, it would be a new life defending a late husband who had done many terrible things.

Achim and I gave our condolences to the grieving family and we walked out of the funeral home. It was too exhausting for me to stick around. As we opened the entrance door the bright sunlight from outside poured in and partially blinded my unprotected eyes. Suddenly, I heard voices erupting and cameras snapping. Achim grabbed my hand and pulled me through a large crowd of reporters gathered at the front door. They were shouting all sorts of questions and pushing microphones in our faces.

"Are you NOPD ma'am?"

"Did you know about Detective Devers White Supremacist ties?"

"Did the NOPD set up Eric Davis?"

"Does the NOPD support White Supremacy?"

Achim used one arm to push his way through the crazed crowd of reporters, while dragging me along for the ride. We made it to our car and Achim opened my door, allowing me to slide inside.

"Get the hell back," Achim screamed as the media scrum tried reaching their microphones inside his car!

Achim got in the car and blasted his horn several times before starting the ignition. Catching the hint, the media scrum relented, allowing Achim to back up the car. Achim threw the car into reverse and he eased out of the parking space. The media scrum once again turned their attention to the front entrance as Captain Wolf and Debbie stepped into the sunlight. Like a swarm of ants, the media gathered around Captain Wolf and began bombarding her with questions. The look on her face was one of dismay and frustration. Captain Wolf was left to answer the hard questions this whole mess had created. This was all her responsibility and I didn't give a damn about her. The hidden truth had been exposed, and Captain Wolf would finally have to account for it.

"I feel like a stiff drink baby," I whispered to Achim.

"Good because I know just the right spot for us." Achim replied as he pulled out of the parking lot.

Achim hit the highway and started driving us through the deserted streets of New Orleans. We arrived at a black owned bar and grill in the Seventh Ward named, Half Shell on the Bayou, near Esplanade Avenue. While the streets of New Orleans were empty and completely devoid of traffic, the restaurant was packed with black people everywhere. It was the first time I had been to this place and the joyful spirit inside the restaurant instantly made me feel better. I grabbed Achim's hand and began to rub him, I was glad he had brought me here. It felt good to be around our people again. In a world that was ruthlessly cruel to us as blacks, this was our own little piece of heaven. All the tables were occupied with customers, so instead of waiting for an open table, Achim and I found two open spots at the bar and seated ourselves. A cute dark-skinned brother with long dreadlocks, and light brown eyes was tending the bar. He quickly placed two white napkins in front of us and flashed a hospitable smile.

"What can I get for the both of you?" He asked.

"Jack and Coke my man," Achim instructed. "Please make it a double."

"I'll take a margarita," I added.

The bartender nodded his head and walked away to get our orders. I handed Achim a food menu and we both quietly browsed through the choices. As I looked through the menu, I debated between ordering the enticing Chargrilled Oysters or the delicious looking Seafood Gumbo.

"What are you ordering?" Achim asked.

"I don't know yet," I shot back indecisively.

"Well, I'm getting me some Shrimp Creole," he added with a smile.

"Good," I said flirtingly while placing my hand on his knee. "I will just eat off of your plate then."

"The hell you will girl," Achim blasted back playfully. "We'll be fighting up in here."

The bartender came back with our drinks and then took our food orders. Achim handed the bartender a credit card and instructed him to keep our tab open. Suddenly, the bar erupted in cheers as the basketball game shown on the television screen went into overtime. Many enthusiastic fans traded high fives, while several disappointed watchers shook their heads in frustration. Taking it all in, I took a big sip of my drink and looked at Achim.

"I just love the vibe here. How did you find this place?" I asked.

Achim raised his eyebrows at me before taking a large gulp of his Jack and Coke. "Girl, I'm always looking for black owned businesses to patronize. Usually, I find them on the internet, but I found this one purely by accident."

"An old boss took me here to eat dinner one day and I've been hooked ever since," Achim explained.

Achim and I traded basketball stories as we drank and watched the game go into double overtime before it finally ended. Our dinner arrived and we both lightly chatted as we enjoyed our meals. The bartender refilled our drink glasses several times, as we engrossed in each other's company. I was a bit tipsy and it felt good to release some of my pent-up stress. I hadn't been able to relax this much in weeks, given all the drama surrounding the Bill Devers saga. Most of all, I enjoyed being with Achim. He was so handsome and charming that he took my mind off all the nonsense happening around me. This black man went out of his way to make me feel comfortable, and special. Just the way he looked at me, made me thirst for him even more.

"Jessica, I have something I need to tell you," Achim stated out of nowhere. His demeanor changed as he looked deep into my eyes with an unflinching gaze. My heart paused at his abrupt seriousness.

"I promised myself that I'd be honest with you. So, I'm going to be exactly that."

"When I first met you, I never imagined that you would give a guy like me a chance to get with you. I have always thought you were beautiful. Yet, I have also come to find out that you are a very loving person. You gave me a chance and believed in me."

"I'm so appreciative that you are in my life. You make me better. You motivate me."

Achim leaned in close, wrapping his arm around my waist and gripping me with his huge hand. "I've fallen in love with you Jessica," he coolly whispered. "I just wanted to tell you that."

"I love you and I want us to be forever. You are the one for me. You are too special for me to live life without you."

"I hope that doesn't scare you away."

Achim leaned away and nervously took another large gulp of his drink. Tears began to well up in my eyes upon hearing his words. Something inside of me just knew that he wasn't lying to me. There was more than mere physical attraction between us. This wasn't just dating; this was something special. Something that I thought I'd never achieve.

Without thinking, I lean towards him and grabbed his chin, pulling him towards my lips. We exchanged a passionate kiss.

A long kiss, undeterred by the thought of nosy or offended onlookers. It all felt so seductive and intoxicating. As our lips broke apart, I could see the look of excitement in his glossy eyes. He wore a look of sincere longing mixed with naughty thoughts of lust. I could feel his heavy hand caress my thigh, engulfing my leg with his probing fingers. He wanted me and in turn, I wanted him.

"I guess you love me to," Achim murmured in a halfhearted attempt to ask the question.

"Yeah. I do Achim. I do."

"Are you ready to leave?" Achim knowingly asked.

"Take me anywhere. I'll go anywhere with you. I'm yours," I whispered to him.

Achim began flagging down the bartender, it was time to close out our bar tab. As the bartender approached us, I felt my phone vibrating inside my purse. Reaching to grab it, I saw that it was an incoming call from Captain Wolf's personal number. I leaned over to Achim and told him that I'd meet him outside, before giving him a kiss on the cheek.

I felt it was weird to get a call from Captain Wolf's personal number. She rarely ever called any of us from it, so this was out of the ordinary. I walked outside the bar and answered her call once on the sidewalk.

"Hello."

"Detective Baker! Where are you right now?" Captain Wolf asked with urgency in her voice.

"I'm out having dinner," I responded. "What's going on Captain? Is there some emergency?"

"Yes, there is Jessica. You're in danger."

"Several patrol units were sent to your house to respond to a report of a break-in."

"Our patrol units got to your house and found it ransacked."

"What!" In that instant I felt a cold shiver crawl up my spine. My first instinct told me this was all Daniel's doing. He was coming after me for some unknown reason.

"Yes," Captain Wolf continued. "I was scared to death because I thought something had happened to you. I just saw you at Bill's wake earlier today. Things are getting way too crazy."

"Where are you Jessica," Captain demanded.

"I'm in the Seventh Ward."

"Well, I need you to come to the station pronto. Internal Affairs is crawling all over my ass right now."

"They think you are the key to all this mess. You and your lover Detective Fitzpatrick."

"Why the hell would they think that?" I shot back. "I don't have a clue about what's going on here. I have no idea where Daniel is hiding."

"You're going to have to tell them that story Jessica. They have a reason to believe Daniel has been at your house with you. They are suspicious as hell right now."

"Internal Affairs searched Bill's office and found his personal notes linking you to Eric Davis fingerprint evidence stolen from the NOPD evidence warehouse," Captain Wolf explained. "Internal Affairs also believes that you are connected to a black militant named Percy Darryl."

"Logs are showing that you accessed fingerprint evidence from the Eric Davis case, last year. Now Internal Affairs is suspicious that you are a mole within NOPD."

"They believe that you have been giving undisclosed information to a secret black militant organization named Robert Charles, and that you are working for Percy Darryl to pressure the NOPD to overturn the conviction of Eric Davis."

"They are going to try and pin all these murders on you," Captain Wolf stated with concern in her voice. "You need to come in right now. I need you to come clean, Jessica."

"Bullshit!" I shouted. "I have no idea what you or Internal Affairs are talking about right now. I don't know anything about Robert Charles. Bill's racist ass is full of shit. Hell, I hadn't even seen any of the Eric Davis evidence until after Kevin Longstreet was murdered. You can check the logs and see that I viewed the evidence weeks ago.... not last year. You guys can put all your faith in Bill Devers crazy notes if you want to, but I'd put my integrity up against his and yours any day. He had everything to hide and I don't."

"I'm going to go see about my damn apartment," I continued.

"Someone just broke into my place. They may have been trying to kill me and you guys are more concerned about Black

Then I saw the glint of a blade come upwards and into my view. I screamed, as Daniel thrusted his knife into Achim. Achim tried to move and dodge the knife but it was too late. Daniel stabbed him in his chest before pulling the knife out. Achim crumbled down to the ground, grabbing his chest wound. In a reenergized fashion, Daniel crawled from under Achim and got to his feet. His face was bloody and sported heavy bruises. He cocked back his arm preparing to deliver another blow with his knife.

"Let's go! Now!" Captain Wolf screamed as she used her body to pin me down.

Captain Wolf's words startled Daniel, pulling his attention away from a now vulnerable Achim. Instead of continuing to stab Achim, Daniel spit a mouth full of blood on Achim's face and yelled several curse words before leaving him to bleed alone on the sidewalk. Daniel ran over to the driver's side of the car and got inside. I screamed out loudly for Achim as I made one last frantic effort to free myself. Daniel cranked up the car and I felt Captain Wolf power her weight into me. I couldn't move and I felt helpless as she had me pinned down. Now, I was kidnapped and at the mercy of two people who had every reason to want me dead.

Chapter Nine

I could feel the heat pulsing from the light bulb in the lamp next to my bed. Its bright white light wasn't pleasing to my sensitive eyes, causing my brain to scream for shade. A pretty light skinned black lady wearing scrubs and latex gloves, walked up to my bedside. She wrapped the blood pressure gauge around my arm before pumping air into it, tightening the gauge until my fingers began tingling. Satisfied with her readings, she deflated the gauge and moved towards the IV drip hanging over my bed. After checking my IV, she adjusted the dressing on my wounds, then patted me on my shoulder.

"I see you finally woke up," she said with a slow country drawl? "How are you feeling Achim?"

The lady looked at me with the concerned smile of a loving parent. Just her smile alone made me feel like I was in good hands. Hands that cared and gave a damn about me. Her tenderness prompted me to ask the only question that mattered to me at that moment.

"Where is Jessica?" I mumbled fearing the answer I might receive.

"We don't know," she softly responded. "But I'm sure you guys will find her. The NOPD is searching all over the city for her."

"Don't worry yourself about all that yet. How are you feeling Achim?"

"I'm a bit thirsty," I feebly responded. "Can I have something to drink?'

"Yes, you may, dear sir," the lady happily responded.

"Hi. My name is Rita," she explained while fluffing my pillow. "If you start feeling worse. Just holler at me. I'll be right outside the door there."

I looked around the room and noticed I wasn't in a hospital. My bed was small, and the mattress was stiff like a board. An abundance of comic book posters hung from the walls. An assortment of stuffed animals sat on an oversized rocking chair, next to a baby's crib. It was obvious that I was in someone's bedroom, most likely a young child's room.

"Where am I?" I asked.

"It doesn't matter," she coyly replied. "You're safe. That's all that matters right now."

"Just know that you're in the hands of a friend of Robert Charles, agent Achim Jeffers."

She flashed her right hand in my direction, showing me her gold ring with a deep green colored emerald bulging from the center. It was the secret symbol of a deeply covert friend of Robert Charles. She was a non-paid sleeper cell. A Robert Charles cell that was only called upon in the direst of circumstances. I was certain that her real name wasn't really Rita. It was probably just her call sign. There was only one person who was able to call up sleeper agents of Robert Charles like these.

"Where is Mr. Darryl?" I asked.

"He should be here soon," Rita replied.

"Mr. Darryl wants to talk to you, and now that you're awake, I'll call him for you."

"How long was I out?" I broke in interrupting her.

"Just a few hours Achim. I gave you a sedative to put you out. You lost a lot of blood brother. That gunshot wound was superficial, but the knife wound could have killed you."

"Your partner Anthony is here. He's outside right now. I'll have him bring you some water and you two can catch up."

"Anthony?" I angrily asked.

"Yea. Your Caribbean friend, Anthony Rice. He's the agent who brought you to me," she explained as she walked out of the room.

Anthony was supposed to be long gone from New Orleans. Why had he dismissed my specific instructions and stayed?

Anthony walked through the door carrying a bottle of water in his hand with his nervous face wearing a half smile.

"What the hell are you doing here?" I angrily asked him.

Anthony's half smile disappeared into nervous energy as he hastily unscrewed the plastic top from the bottle and placed the water on the lampstand. "I'm sorry Achim. I was just doing my job," he explained almost shaking. "I knew you would get mad about this."

"Your job was to take your damn money and get the hell away from New Orleans. Those are real hard orders to screw up Anthony," I barked shaking my head! "You put all of us at risk by staying here."

"I left Achim. I really did leave. I left New Orleans just like you told me too."

"I promise, I did exactly what you asked." "Problem is, once I got to New Mexico and opened the envelope, the instructions inside told me to come back to New Orleans."

"What!" I shouted.

"The instructions told me to return to New Orleans and go to the Lowe's Hotel downtown," Anthony continued. "I did exactly what I was told to do Achim. I'm sorry. I'm just following orders."

It was Mr. Darryl; it couldn't be anyone else but him. For some reason, he must have rearranged Anthony's orders to bring him back to New Orleans, totally against my own wishes. Anthony had been Johnny on the spot to rescue me, most likely because Mr. Darryl had him following me.

"Tell me the truth. Were you following me Anthony?"

Anthony bit his lower lip and softly shook his head before looking up into my eyes. "No Achim. I wasn't following you." I could tell from his expression that he didn't want to talk about it anymore. Anthony had graduated. He now had his own secrets that he was obligated to hide.

"Anthony, were you following Jessica? Where is she and is she alive?"

"Yeah. She's still alive," Anthony pointedly answered.

"Why the hell were you following her?"

"He wasn't following her either," a voice declared from outside the room.

I immediately noticed Mr. Darryl's gold walking cane and his sharply creased three-piece suit as he entered the bedroom. As he limped his way to my bed, Mr. Darryl took off his black Fedora hat and gently tossed it at my feet. The sweet smell of his powerful cologne dominated my senses as he neared me.

"Anthony was following orders, Achim. It looks like he'll be working here in New Orleans for good."

"I wanted to send him to Oakland, just as you and I discussed, but it seems like I have been overruled. Someone believes Anthony's better off here with you."

"So, someone above you kept Anthony here and endangered my whole operation?"

"Mr. Darryl, does Robert Charles realize that if NOPD found Anthony and questioned him about the murder of Ryan Foster...."

231

"Son, I understand the damn danger!" Mr. Darryl yelled, interrupting me. "How about you, Achim! Do you give a damn about the danger?"

Mr. Darryl's eyes were ablaze with anger as he stared down at me, almost like he was a spirit hovering above me in my bed, ready to condemn me to hell. It was then that I knew he had found out about me and Jessica Baker. There was no need for any specific words to be said between us. He knew I had gotten emotionally involved with Jessica and in the process, I had compromised our mission and Robert Charles. That was a big no-no in our line of work. The bonds of my mutual trust with Mr. Darryl had been broken. I felt a single tear roll down the side of my face. For me, this whole thing had become a big mess.

"I asked you this before we embarked on this mission Achim. Back then you told me you didn't know about this woman."

"I'm going to ask you this again Achim, and I want a completely honest answer…. if you still can give me one."

"Is Jessica Baker Okay…. or is she not?" Mr. Darryl pointedly asked.

Mr. Darryl's stare pierced my soul. I knew what he meant. Was Jessica Baker innocent or was she a black tool in this white madness? My heart wanted to believe she wasn't part of the madness. Yet, I had to logically consider if she had been. Had she fooled me? Was the whole kidnapping merely a staged event to fool Robert Charles into some sort of mistake? A staged event to pull us out from the shadows and into the light. Was Jessica's professed love for me, simply a ploy to lure Robert Charles into a trap? All the realities of this situation had to be well considered. This was a black woman that had been in a romantic relationship with a dangerous white man. Daniel Fitzpatrick, a white man who was the leader of a deadly White Supremacist organization. How could I safely assume that Jessica had not been weaponized against me?

From the look on Mr. Darryl's face, I knew those were his inner thoughts. Unlike me, Mr. Darryl wasn't confused by this cloudy emotion called love. For him, this was simply warfare. This was all combat for Mr. Darryl. Nothing was off limits or outside of the realm of possibility. For centuries, the White Supremacists played dirty. They had always played dirty ever since they forced the first African to board their ships bound for the concentration camps in the New World. Now, I had to decide because my heart was at war. Would the spirit of war within me prevail or would my spirit of love triumph?

"I believe Detective Baker is innocent in all this Mr. Darryl," I stated. "Yes, she's a cop. Yes, she made a mistake and slept with this white Race Soldier, but she didn't know who Daniel Fitzpatrick truly was."

"I'm willing to forgive her for that, even if you aren't."

"Are you willing to stand on what your heart believes?" Mr. Darryl inquired. "How do you really know who or what Detective Baker is?"

"There is no way for me to know. I can't know for certain," I quickly rebutted. "No one can know anything for certain in this world."

"What I do know is that I love her."

"And if I'm wrong about Jessica. I'm willing to accept the consequences."

In frustration, Mr. Darryl snatched his hat from my bed. "You have lost your damn mind son," he blasted, venting his anger. Mr. Darryl turned and looked over at Anthony, who was clearly uncomfortable witnessing our conversation. After a silent second of staring at him, Mr. Darryl's voice boomed throughout the room.

"Does this make any damn sense to you young blood?" Mr. Darryl rhetorically asked Anthony.

"This negro has fallen in love with a treasonous black woman that was screwing the leader of a White Supremacist terrorist group."

"A black female cop that was sleeping around with a white cop."

Mr. Darryl and I watched as Anthony awkwardly shrugged his shoulders as he stared up at the ceiling, scared to utter a word or engage himself in our discussion.

"I know this all sounds crazy to you", I jumped in.

"But I believe in her. Jessica Baker is a good woman."

"So now that she done slept with you and made you feel all special…. She's a good woman now? Come on Achim, you of all people can't be this naïve."

"Call it whatever you like Mr. Darryl."

"For years you have trusted my judgment and we have done a lot of amazing things together. For years you have believed in me and we both have made Robert Charles proud. Now I need you to believe in me one more time."

"Yes, this woman was in love with a White Supremacist. Yes, she is a cop but there is more to this than a lost black woman. She was lost but I was able to find her, and she in turn was able to find herself."

"Isn't that what Robert Charles is all about?" I sincerely asked. "Why are we out here doing all this damn fighting if we have no one worthy to save?"

"I love this black woman. I love her," I declared.

"The White Supremacists have taken a lot of things away from me. They took away my family. They took away my career. They took away all my money, but they won't take my love away from me. I won't allow it."

I raised myself and sat up in the bed. Jessica was still out there in danger, and I was done debating. As I began to move, my muscles felt weak and sore. I powered myself through the light headedness as I rose to my feet. My first few steps were exhausting and painful, but I had to block it out. Jessica needed me and deep inside, I knew I needed her.

"We can't let you leave here Achim," Anthony whispered to me as he caught my stumbling body. "You're in no condition to leave, let alone go out looking for trouble."

"Trouble came looking for me Anthony, and I'll be damned if I hide away from it."

Anthony sat me back down on the bed and handed me the bottle of water. Forcing me to drink it. "You're fucking crazy," Mr. Darryl lamented while shaking his head in disgust.

"You're going to walk into an obvious ambush and risk Robert Charles, all because of this treasonous black bitch."

"No!" I shouted back at him. "I'm going to do the damn job Robert Charles hired me to do."

"I'm doing the mission Robert Charles was formed to do in the first place. Save the black family."

"If I'm stupid for going to do this, so be it."

"By your standards, none of us are even remotely redeemable or even worthy of Robert Charles's sacrifice. Not me, not you, no black person would be. Not even that damn drug addict Eric Davis. Yet, I've killed a black person to try and free him from prison. I have done what the hell needed to be done for this mission Mr. Darryl. I killed Kevin Longstreet and I didn't bat an eye."

"If I can go all out to save Eric Davis, then I can go all out to save Jessica Baker. The line between love and war doesn't exist, there both the same. Do you understand what I'm sayin….there both the same. No difference."

I motioned for Anthony to bring me my pants and shoes. Mr. Darryl stood and watched me get dressed in silence before walking over towards a window. My decision had been made and he knew it. For me, Robert Charles was more than just a covert Black Empowerment organization. We were not here just to kill White Supremacists or expose those racists who hide themselves behind their power and wealth. This was all about black love. This was our power in this ever-weakening world. The power of war to eliminate those whose selfish behavior harmed the preciousness of the entire group, combined with the loving power to rescue those confused souls who had honestly wandered down the wrong path, it's the very essence of God's will. The awesome powers bestowed upon us to discern between right and wrong in a messy and confused world that is totally controlled by White Supremacy. A battle between the righteous good, versus the forces of evil. A war of the hearts.

"Do you know where they took Jessica?" I asked Anthony.

Anthony looked at me with a confused gaze before pointing his eyes towards Mr. Darryl, while shrugging his shoulders at me not knowing exactly what to say. I was his mentor and Anthony's senior in the organization, but Mr. Darryl was our boss. As a new agent, Anthony was undoubtedly still finding his way into Robert Charles's heart. If I were in his position, I likely would have done the same thing.

"Go ahead and tell him Anthony," Mr. Darryl ordered. "Tell him where they have hidden her."

"If Achim wants to go save her. That's his own damn business."

I looked over at Anthony and he began to spill the beans. "They are holding her at a dive bar over in Westwego," Anthony described. "Earlier you asked me who I was following, well, someone ordered me to follow Daniel. Both Daniel Fitzpatrick and the black lady Captain that snatched up Detective Baker were still at the dive bar when I left an hour ago."

The news sunk in like a ton of bricks. My intuition told me I knew exactly where Daniel had taken her, but my desire to disbelieve the information demanded that I get the verbal confirmation. "This dive bar wouldn't happen to be named Andy's, would it?" I asked Anthony.

"Well…. Yeah," Anthony admitted. "Detective Baker is at Andy's Tavern."

"That's why you shouldn't go Achim," Mr. Darryl chimed in while staring out the window. "It would be best for all of us if you left this one alone. This is an obvious ambush. Infighting within NOPD is not our damn problem."

I understood Mr. Darryl's point. Even if Jessica wasn't in on all the police misconduct, it still wouldn't matter. Andy's Tavern was merely a front business for the Freedom of White Life White Supremacist organization. The bar itself was where they held their meetings, conducted their business deals, inducted new members and planned their terrorist operations. FOWL members from all over the state of Louisiana would flock to Andy's for quarterly meetings and rallies. It was quite literally a hub of Anti-Black activity.

"Mr. Darryl is right Achim," Anthony began. "Daniel Fitzpatrick has been hidden away inside that building for over a week now."

"There is no telling what kind of traps you will encounter if you just run up in there."

"Do you have any idea why the black Captain is involved in this?" I interrupted.

"The Captain is Detective Baker's boss. She is the District Captain and she didn't obtain that rank without burning a few bridges," Mr. Darryl admitted.

"Her name is Wolf. Gwendolyn Wolf," Mr. Darryl explained with moist eyes.

The remorseful look on Mr. Darryl's face was telling. Mr. Darryl knew this woman. This NOPD Captain was Mr. Darryl's long-lost Gwendolyn. The love of his life that Robert Charles had denied him so many years ago. The woman he was supposed to spend the rest of his life with.

"Gwendolyn is not an ally. In fact, she is to be considered a mortal enemy," he went on to explain.

"Gwendolyn is black but sadly, when push came to shove, she chose the other side. She thought she had better ideas then us. Gwendolyn believed she had a better way to change things for black people," Mr. Darryl described. "Her goal was to try and destroy white supremacy from within, by integrating herself into white society."

"As time has proven her theories profoundly wrong, Gwendolyn has only grown more stubborn in her distaste for

Black Empowerment. Her pride has caused her to be unable to admit that the years she spent chasing this ghost of white acceptance, have been a total waste."

"For decades now. Gwendolyn Wolf has lived a life of lies. Lies constructed solely to protect her ego from her own black reality."

"Sometimes living out those lies is much easier then recognizing the cold hard truth gentlemen," Mr. Darryl concluded.

"Is this your infamous Gwendolyn, Mr. Darryl?" I finally asked. "The long-lost love that you never had?"

"Yes, she is Achim."

"She was the woman I was supposed to marry."

"But we had a major difference in what we both wanted to do with our lives."

"She wanted to change the system from the inside, while I on the other hand, wanted to destroy the system from the outside. In the process of doing it her way, the system does what it always does to any black person who thinks like Gwendolyn."

"It morphed her from a change agent, into a black tool. A black tool that White Supremacy uses to protect itself. She's too far gone to realize her own futility because she's too focused on things that don't directly address systemic racism. Gwendolyn is stuck in the rabbit hole of integration."

"So, is that why you don't want me to go after Jessica?" I followed up. "You still love Gwendolyn, don't you?"

"I'm not concerned about Gwendolyn. I'm more worried about you, son. Gwendolyn and I have both made our poor decisions in this life. I just don't want you following in our footsteps."

"Mr. Darryl, Bill Devers mentioned something about a deal before I killed him. Did Robert Charles try to make a deal with FOWL?" I asked.

Mr. Darryl walked up to me and looked me directly in the eyes. His expression was far from unflinching and his demeanor was demonstrative. "No Achim, Robert Charles did not try to make any deal with FOWL," he answered. Mr. Darryl slowly backed away from me and started walking out of the bedroom before pausing and turning around. "I do still love her Achim," he began. "But I can't allow my love for her to cloud my judgment any longer."

"I just hope that you can learn that lesson a bit earlier than I have. Learn from me before you make the same mistake that I made."

Mr. Darryl limped out of the bedroom and I turned my attention to Anthony. "You can leave too if you aren't cool with any of this," I began. "There's no use to you hanging around unless your orders are to follow me."

"I do have orders, but that's not why I'm staying Achim," Anthony explained. "I'm not letting you go to Andy's Tavern and do this by yourself. You have always looked out for me and I owe you a lot. I can't just stand back and watch you do this alone."

With that statement, Anthony had won my respect. He didn't have to risk his life for any of this. Going to Andy's was going to be a shit show. The place was sure to be crawling with violent White Supremacists. I wouldn't have blamed Anthony if he had decided not to help and just followed me, keeping his distance while watching me struggle to save Jessica. Yet, he had volunteered to put it all on the line with me because he respected me. He was a rider.

I nodded my head at Anthony, and he helped me sit back down on the bed. My muscles were still sore, and I felt very faint. I dug deep to summon all my strength. There was no other option except to ignore my pain and exhaustion.

As I drank another bottle of cold water to hydrate myself, I saw Rita walk into the room. She wore blue latex gloves and carried a long syringe that looked to be filled with a yellowish-brown liquid. "I hear you are leaving me Achim," she said with a smile as she approached my bed.

"Before I let you leave, I need to give you this quick shot," she proclaimed. "This shot will help take the edge off and give you a nice burst of energy."

"I'm no dummy ma'am. You aren't about to inject me with a damn thing," I shot back. "I know how Mr. Darryl works. You inject me with that shit, and I wake up two days later in a hotel room in Texas."

Rita rolled her eyes at me while wearing a confident smile. She placed her hand on my shoulder and gently began to rub me. "If you knew how Mr. Darryl does things, you would know that you would still be asleep right now. He wouldn't have allowed you to wake up in the first-place mister."

"I'm not here to give you this shot under orders from Mr. Darryl. I'm here to help you Achim."

"I wasn't trying to spy on you guys, but I heard ya'll in here arguing. It caught my attention and I couldn't help but to listen."

"When I heard the name Gwendolyn Wolf, that told me everything," Rita said with a telling grin.

"You know her?" I asked.

"Oh yeah. I know Gwendolyn. I've known that woman for decades now. We still see each other from time to time at social gatherings around the city."

"So, you both are friends?" I inquired.

"Lord no," Rita blasted back. "We aren't friends. We just keep some of the same company that's all. Mardi Gras crews, sorority functions and church events. Stuff like that. We see each other and it's always cordial. Nothing more than your typical southern hospitality."

"I've been a friend of Robert Charles for a while now. I started doing this when I was in college, so I've seen a lot of this all play out over the decades" Rita explained.

"Hell, I was one of the first friends of Robert Charles to meet Mr. Darryl when he came down here from Memphis. I knew Mr. Darryl and Gwendolyn Wolf before they started fooling around with each other," Rita described as she used an alcohol swab to clean the skin on my arm.

"Mr. Darryl was a strong black man, but for some reason, Gwendolyn was his weakness. You see, for Gwendolyn, Mr. Darryl was just a little bit of fun. He was a nice-looking fellow who dressed sharp and looked handsome. Mr. Darryl had a few dollars in his pockets and wasn't a complete bumbling idiot. He was smart and a decent looking guy and she enjoyed his company, but not enough to want to marry him. Gwendolyn was too ambitious for that."

"Mr. Darryl on the other hand, adored the ground Gwendolyn walked on, I mean he was infatuated with her. All the movers and shakers in the city knew Gwendolyn. She was quite popular."

"For some reason, Mr. Darryl was convinced that he needed to marry this woman. I never understood why he fell for her so hard. Gwendolyn was certainly nice looking back in those days, but she was also a bit strange by our standards back then."

"What do you mean by strange?" I followed up curiously.

Rita looked me straight in my eyes and giggled to herself. She was enjoying this conversation and I could tell. Rita grabbed me by my arm and tied a long rubber band around my elbow. I felt my fingers began to tingle as she tightened the knot. After several seconds of looking, she finally found a large juicy vein and playfully poked at it with her index finger. "That's the one right there boy. I can't miss that vein." Rita grabbed the syringe and pulled the cap off.

"Gwendolyn is bi-sexual Achim," Rita finally admitted with a grin. "She was a married woman that ran around cheating on her husband with all kinds of people. Hell, everybody knew it back then. We just minded our own business, not like today where a person's sexuality has to be public knowledge."

"She was married to a hot shot black lawyer that moved here from Miami. Gwendolyn and her husband had some grand plan to secure political power in the black community. In truth, they were mostly just looking out for themselves, but they made a good team, especially around the rich white folks down here."

"Because of that...we didn't bother them."

"So, we didn't bother them?" I questioned. "By not bothering them, you really mean Robert Charles saw it fit to leave them alone."

Rita gave me a stoic look before squeezing an air bubble out of her syringe. She wasn't going to entertain my question, but I understood the logic behind her statement. For some reason, Robert Charles had given Gwendolyn Wolf and her husband an easy pass.

"Gwendolyn and Mr. Darryl fooled around on the low, for years," Rita continued.

"Word on the street is that Gwendolyn's husband finally caught wind of her extra-marital relationships and was planning to divorce Gwendolyn because of it. Her husband knew that Mr. Darryl was a member of Robert Charles and that scared him."

"Gwendolyn's husband had earned a small fortune winning several lawsuits against the city," Rita explained. "Apparently, he thought Gwendolyn was scheming to double cross him. So, he quit his job, took all of his money and sold all his property before leaving New Orleans to go to D.C."

Rita took the syringe and gently pushed it into my vein before squeezing its potion inside of me. She pulled it out and cleaned the blood from my arm before taping a cotton swab over the puncture.

"There you go Achim. That ought to help your muscles rebound faster. It's a little cocktail cooked up by a black doctor who is a friend of Robert Charles. You will feel like Superman for about 12 hours, but after that you gonna need to rest for a few days," she explained before winking her eye at me.

"What happened to Gwendolyn and her husband?" I inquired. "Did they divorce?"

"No, they didn't divorce. Gwendolyn fooled him into coming back to New Orleans and fixing the marriage."

"Gwendolyn and Mr. Darryl still messed around with each other though. He had been assigned to keep an eye on the couple, so Mr. Darryl never truly disappeared."

"Mr. Darryl fell in love with his source," I murmured to myself.

"Yea he sure did," Rita proclaimed. "After a year or so, Gwendolyn's husband found out she was still up to her old habits, so he planned to leave again."

"One month before filing for divorce, Gwendolyn's husband was found dead in his car, outside of a gay night club."

"Legally, he died of an overdose, but word on the street is Mr. Darryl took care of him for Gwendolyn by slipping a few pills in his drink. No one will ever know what was really going on in that case. Mr. Darryl wasn't the only person who wanted that man dead."

"Mr. Darryl thought with her husband gone, Gwendolyn would live happily ever after with him."

"Well, that wasn't the case," Rita detailed. "Gwendolyn stopped seeing Mr. Darryl and she stopped sleeping with him. Almost immediately, Gwendolyn openly started dating .... a white lady. No one saw that coming."

"A white lady?" I asked.

"Yea. She took her dead husband's money and ditched Mr. Darryl."

"Wow!" I let out in shock.

"Who is the white lady?"

Rita flashed another gentle smile at me before picking up the used syringe and carefully placing the cap back on top of it. She had me in the palm of her hands and she knew it. Her story sounded too unreal for me to believe; too thin to be reality. Yet, in life, the truth is always thin, and reality is always unbelievable.

"Let's just say the white girl is not a friend of Robert Charles," Rita said with a giggle.

"We all knew Gwendolyn fooled around with women from time to time. We just never thought she would fool around with....that woman."

"We don't know much about this white woman, besides the fact that she comes from a wealthy lineage and her family is very liberal. In fact, her family is responsible for funding a lot of the gentrification we have experienced here in New Orleans."

"That's got to be it," I said clapping my hands. "It was gentrification. Gwendolyn is in this for the money. That's why she is helping these bastards."

"Maybe. Maybe not," Rita responded. "I'm not sure we will ever truly know why Gwendolyn Wolf is doing what she is doing. All of this is just sad and it's hurting our people and dividing Robert Charles."

Rita pulled a business card out of her pocket and placed it in my hand. I read her title and name, then noticed she had scribbled a personal message on the back of it. Before I could finish reading it, she tapped me on my shoulder.

"If you start feeling bad again, just give me a call and I'll come fix you up," Rita told me with a smile. "You take care now Achim. Go get Jessica. She needs you."

After disconnecting my IV's and heart monitors, Rita turned around and walked out of the bedroom. I got myself dressed and followed Anthony out to his car. As I began walking, I felt the effects of Rita's injection start to course through my body.

The pain from my wounds were barely noticeable and I felt my energy level increase with every step forward. Anthony opened his trunk and showed me the armory he had stashed away within it. I looked down at an assortment of shotguns, rifles, handguns and sharp machetes.

"Please pick whatever weapons you're going to need Achim," Anthony allowed. "What's mine is yours. Take as many as you want."

Reaching down into the trunk, I grabbed two handguns and several preloaded magazines. After stuffing one of the handguns underneath my beltline, I took the other and gave it to Anthony, along with a spare magazine. "We won't be needing any of your damn rifles today. This battle is going to be up close and personal my friend."

Before Anthony could close the trunk, I reached in and grabbed a long silver blade with a thick wooden handle. I examined the blade to reassure its sharpness and potential. It was perfect. As the smile burst across my face, I noticed Anthony looking at me with a curious stare.

"Well, you can't get much more personal then chopping up someone to death," Anthony opined while nervously shaking his head and grabbing a shotgun. "I'll stick with the guns. You can have the knives."

Anthony hid away his shotgun in the backseat underneath a long raincoat and jumped behind the wheel. He drove the car outside of the gated property and we hit the highway towards the Westbank of New Orleans. I noticed that the streets of the city were busy with activity. NOPD had set up roadblocks and I could see large groups of black people roaming the streets while holding up signs, many of them chanting loudly and pumping their fists. As Anthony drove in silence, I turned on the radio and found out that black protestors were once again in action.

"The protests are back," I stated looking at Anthony.

"Yeah," he replied. "Word got out that a black woman was abducted by a white man and a black man had been shot. Now the community is angry as hell and protesting again."

We drove our way through the bottleneck traffic near downtown and made it over the Mississippi River Bridge, to the Westbank. An expressway on the Westbank took us to Westwego, and Anthony exited off the expressway into a mostly white subdivision near Andy's Tavern.

"What's the plan?" Anthony asked me as he stopped at a stop sign.

"There is no plan. This is an ambush, remember."

My answer concerned Anthony. His car sat still at the intersection, as he refused to move it forward. "Achim, what the hell are we doing man?" He shouted nervously.

"You don't have a plan for this?"

"No, I don't, and you shouldn't worry about that," I replied. "They are expecting me. One black guy, not two of us."

"What I need you to do is to sit back and just wait outside."

"Wait for my signal, then come through the backdoor blazing when its time," I explained. "Take no prisoners."

"What will the signal be?" Anthony asked.

"You will know the signal when you hear it."

Anthony drove the car several blocks before slowing and making a slow right turn into a piece of property with a large parking lot surrounding a single-story building. It was Andy's Tavern. I could really feel the energy and excitement pumping through me now. It was that time again, a time to kill. I took my handgun out and chambered a round. Reaching into my pocket, I pulled out my cell phone and scrolled through my phone apps until I found the right one. I needed to be prepared to record everything inside.

"Not many people here today," Anthony noted as he pulled into a parking space.

"Is the car you were ordered to follow still here?" I asked.

"Yeah, it's right there," Anthony observed while motioning towards it. "That's the car Captain Wolf and Daniel used to kidnap Jessica."

"Alright. Well stay out here and wait for my signal."

"If the police roll up, just drive off without me. No need to worry about me. I'll be okay."

I exited the car with my loaded handgun and sharp blade in hand. Walking up to the front door of Andy's, I looked inside and noticed that the lights in the place were dim. One white redneck sat at the bar, while a white female bartender stood idle looking up at the large flat screen above a mountain of liquor bottles, nothing looked out of the ordinary. Opening the door, I walked into the cool air-conditioned space and pointed my gun at the bartender. As she turned to me, I saw a look of terror streak across her face when she realized what I was doing.

"Hands in the air bitch!" I yelled.

"You too Larry the Cable Guy," I screamed at the redneck! Both complied with my demand, shooting their hands high in the sky in terror.

"Where is Detective Jessica Baker?" I asked the bartender.

The bartender gave me a confused looked that was riddled with fear and anxiety. She began to shake her head, as her face became red with fear. "I have no idea who that is," she blurted out with a shaken voice.

"There are only three people here," she explained. "If you want the money. I'll go to the cash register and give it to you. Just don't shoot anybody."

"Where is the third person?" I asked.

"I'm over here," a voice said.

I turned and looked towards the back corner and saw an older black lady seated at a table by herself. In between her fingers, she held a lit cigarette. For a brief second, I watched in startled shock as this lady blew a cloud of smoke out of her mouth. I pointed my gun at her and motioned for her to put her hands in the air.

"Let me see your hands in the air too then, since you want to hang out in a place like this," I instructed. "I think we met yesterday, didn't we?"

"You are the infamous Gwendolyn Wolf, aren't you?"

"Yes, I am." She replied with a smile. "Can I assume that Mr. Darryl sent you here to kill me?"

"No one sent me here," I answered as I walked towards her. "I'm here for Jessica Baker."

"Now let's see those hands in the air Madam Officer," I ordered.

"I'm not armed and I'm not putting my hands in the air like I'm some fuckin criminal," she declared with a bit of aggravation. "Jessica isn't here, and neither is Daniel, so you're wasting your time if you came here for her."

"Mr. Darryl should probably be more interested in what these two are up to right now, instead of coming here and trying to kill little ole me."

"But since you're finally here Mr. Jeffers, it's probably a good idea that we finally have a frank discussion." Captain Wolf stated as she flashed a large brown folder in the air.

"I know all about you Achim. I have been waiting a very long time to finally meet you and tell you a few secrets. From one Robert Charles hitman, to another."

Chapter Ten

From a distance, we both watched as the two men strolled out of the two-story house and walked up to the trunk of the car. The shorter of the men popped open the trunk before lifting it up and pointing inside. The taller black man reached into the trunk, pulling out two guns and a long knife. "That must be the bleach killer right there. That must be him, Captain Wolf was right," Daniel whispered from the passenger seat.

"That fuckin asshole," Daniel whispered to himself. "I should kill his ass right now."

I felt Daniel push his gun up into my armpits as I held onto the steering wheel. I could see the anger and fear in his eyes.

Daniel no longer resembled the man I once adored. He was out of control and his temper was volatile. He was now someone else I had never known, or maybe this was who he had always been. Maybe I had failed to see him for who he truly was. Everything that had once protected Daniel was gone, and he was a man that had nothing to lose. I felt my own fear consume me in the moment as his gun pointed at me, especially when he drove the guns cold barrel into my warm armpit.

"Alright Jessica. We'll wait until they leave, then we make our move in, just like I told you. Understand," Daniel instructed.

I nodded my head in the affirmative and then took a deep breath to calm my nerves. The two men loaded themselves into the car and slowly drove out of the driveway. Once they had finally departed, it would be time for Daniel to spring his trap. When the car was out of our view, I noticed Daniel peering at the large two-story home. He examined it studiously as if he were a hunter looking for a fatal weakness, in order to exploit his prey. I sat quietly waiting for instructions, too scared to move or say a word. After about twenty minutes, Daniel must have gained his courage as he leaned in close to me.

"Drive into the driveway and park next to the front door," Daniel barked as he once again shoved his gun into my armpit. "Let's go! Move!"

The car rolled off the black street and onto the clean light grey concrete of the home's wide driveway. Bittersweet memories of my childhood came to me when I looked at the perfectly landscaped lawn with its gorgeous assortment of flowers. I pulled up next to the front door and put the car into park. Then Daniel reached over and killed the engine, before taking the keys out of the ignition.

"Now get out slowly and walk to the front door. No tricks or I'll shoot you dead in your back."

After removing my seatbelt, I opened my door and eased out of the car. I knew Daniel was serious and I was in no position to resist his demands. As I began walking towards the front door, I felt Daniel's looming presence behind me. I could hear his light footsteps against the walkway. Even though I could not see it, I knew his concealed gun was trained on me. He was stalking me. Waiting for just the right moment to pounce and eliminate me from his world.

"Ring the doorbell," Daniel whispered as we arrived at the front entrance.

Reaching towards the shining white button near the doorknob, I pressed the button and immediately heard a muffled bell ringing from within the house. Seconds later, the unmistakable sound of slow footsteps walking towards the front door could be heard. Then the door opened, and I saw her familiar face. The enjoyable childhood memories of spending time with her flooded my consciousness.

"Oh my God!" She said with a motherly smile and a cracking voice. "Hey Jessica, are you alright baby?"

In an instant, she looked over my shoulder and saw Daniel. The look on her face changed from blessed relief, to foreboding terror. I wasn't alone and now she knew it. She backed away from the door with her hand over her mouth. I felt Daniel's gun up against the small of my back as he launched me forward through the doorway.

"Into the house now," he barked as I stumbled over the door frame and fell on the hard tile flooring.

In an instant, I looked up and saw Daniel violently strike Aunt Rita on her head with his gun. The blow sent her plummeting to the floor, as blood flew from her mouth and nose. Aunt Rita was knocked out cold and laid motionless with her eyes closed. Daniel slammed the door shut and grabbed me from the floor.

"Get the fuck up," he whispered as he rose me to my feet. "Now. Where is he?"

Daniel stood behind me and put his gun to the back of my head. He pushed me forward through the hallway, guiding me as I walked in front of him like a bullet shield. As we crept forward, the unmistakable sound of Teddy Pendergrass's "Love T.K.O." could be heard coming from the living room. He pushed me into the large living room, with its marble black floor and fine Persian rugs. Out of the corner of my eye, I noticed an old man sitting on a long leather couch with a chrome colored coffee table in front of him. In his hand was a small glass with several large ice cubes, swimming in a pool of brown liquor. It was then that I smelled his cologne and saw his gold-plated walking cane.

"Daddy!" I screamed out. I immediately felt the force of Daniel grabbing me by my neck and pushing me down to my knees. "Shut the fuck up Jessica," Daniel ordered.

"My little girl," my father calmly responded. "I love you sweety. I'm so damn sorry this all went down this way."

My father took a sip of his drink, then placed the sweaty cup on the coffee table in front of him before grabbing a remote control and muting the music. He looked up at Daniel and without hesitation, he began to speak to him. "Officer Fitzpatrick, after all of these years that we've worked together, you decide to turn on me."

"Killing me and my daughter won't spare your life. It's too late. Debbie and Gwendolyn have screwed both of us."

The words from my father's mouth left me stunned, and in a state of disbelief. My father knew Daniel and had participated in his criminal activities. Daniel had known who my father was. That's likely what attracted Daniel to me in the first place. He had been using me for more than just sex.

"No, your screwed Percy Darryl," Daniel responded. "With the help of your little daughter right here, you, Robert Charles niggers killed three of ours. There is no real loyalty in this battle, only revenge and control. You know that Percy."

My father shook his head, while attempting to hide his disgust within a frustrated laugh. "How much did Debbie pay Gwendolyn to betray us both?" He coolly began. "And now she's turned you against me."

"You should ask Gwendolyn why I need to die and not her. You're pointing your gun at the wrong enemy. None of those killings was any of my doing."

"Enough!" Daniel screamed with a stone face. "Gwendolyn doesn't work for Robert Charles, you do. It was your job to keep Robert Charles out of our business and you failed. Now you have to pay."

"That's not where I failed Daniel," my father stated looking into my eyes.

"Plus, your claim that Gwendolyn isn't a member of Robert Charles isn't true. She most definitely is one of us."

Daniel laughed out loud. His laugh created a spooky echo throughout the large room. He was agitated and I could see that his frustration was beginning to boil over.

"You're full of shit," Daniel began.

"Debbie wouldn't marry a member of Robert Charles! Try another lie asshole."

From my knees, I looked up into Daniel's blazing eyes. Despite my inner fears, I had to respond. I had to tell my truth. If I indeed, was going to die today, nothing would be left unsaid.

"My father wouldn't lie about that Daniel," I began. "If he is telling you this, it's for a reason. I believe him."

Daniel let out a low angry sigh and cocked back to swing the barrel of his gun towards my skull. My body tensed as I anticipated his coming retribution. I closed my eyes waiting for the punishment, but as the precious seconds crawled by it never came. Instead, I heard my father's booming voice.

"Don't hit her!" He screamed. "She's not who you want. I'm who you came here for. Robert Charles is who you have a grudge with, not my daughter."

"Plus, hurting either of us won't resolve anything for you."

My father grabbed his gold cane and slowly rose to his feet. With his free hand, he motioned down towards the coffee table beneath him. He pointed at a long brown cigar sitting alone in a black marble ashtray.

"May I smoke my cigar?" He asked Daniel with a slight grin. "I'm sure you aren't going to deny a feeble old man a few final pleasures."

"If you haven't already heard, the Governor will be granting clemency to Eric Davis here in a few days. So, our mission for the Davis family is finished."

Daniel began to panic, pointing his gun at my father and aiming at his head. Undeterred, my father slowly reached down and picked up both the cigar and a silver lighter. With a poker-faced grin, he put the butt of the cigar in his mouth and sparked a flame.

"You see Daniel," he began as a white cloud of smoke left his mouth. "I'm not some dangerous black assassin. I'm just an old black man that needs a few puffs to ease my mind."

"Gwendolyn is indeed a member of Robert Charles. I know because I recruited her. She's one of our assassin's. Who do you think murdered her late husband Daniel? Contrary to popular belief, it wasn't me who killed the man. Debbie and Gwendolyn double crossed me, just as they are doing to you right now Daniel."

"I destroyed my marriage, abandoned my daughter and let down the few siblings that still trusted me. All because I pursued Gwendolyn and did my best to protect her in all of this mess. I fell in love with her and did everything I could to protect her from herself."

My father looked down at me with moist eyes, and a hardened expression as a haze of white smoke floated above his head. The memories of my mother crying in her bed alone, resurfaced in my mind. It was then I realized that my father had left us for Captain Wolf. She was the other woman that I had always wondered about as a child.

"So, you're trying to tell me you were fucking Captain Wolf?" Daniel said mockingly. "You're full of lies boy."

"If I wasn't sleeping with her," my father began. "We all wouldn't be here, and Debbie wouldn't have pulled all the strings for these murders to occur."

"Gwendolyn's late husband was a business partner of Debbie's parents. They all represented the interests of several large energy corporations that operated in Louisiana."

"Debbie's parents used Gwendolyn's black husband to steal land from descendants of slaves who had owned the land since Reconstruction."

"Most of the stolen land was located in bayou's that sat atop huge reservoirs of untapped oil and natural gas."

"Gwendolyn's husband hoodwinked black landowners into signing over their property rights to his law firm. The law firm then leased the land out to energy corporations. Once the rightful landowners were tricked, they were forcibly removed from their ancestral homes, which allowed big oil and gas to come in and control the land outright."

"Debbie's parents and Gwendolyn's husband all got rich and made out like bandits, but there was one problem," my father added.

"When Debbie's parents were too elderly to continue working, Debbie took over their business to find that Gwendolyn's husband would assume full ownership of all the stolen land when her parents died. Debbie couldn't allow that to happen or she'd lose everything."

"To make sure she didn't lose her meal ticket, Debbie targeted Gwendolyn's husband by cozying up to Gwendolyn and starting a sexual relationship."

"That's when Robert Charles got involved," Mr. Darryl explained. "The black landowners whose land was taken from up under them, reached out to Robert Charles for help getting it back."

"I was sent to work the case and eventually, I contacted Gwendolyn. She told me that she wanted to end her marriage but had no way out. Over time, Gwendolyn and I began a business and romantic relationship with each other."

"Once I fell in love with Gwendolyn, a lot of things changed for me," he admitted.

"The landowners never got their property back, Gwendolyn's husband mysteriously died, and Debbie somehow got the woman I adored."

My father eased himself down on the couch below him and placed his lit cigar in the ashtray. His eyes projected a somber, yet jovial state as a light grin adorned his face. Slowly, my father crossed his legs and leaned his walking cane up against the coffee table in front of him.

"Daniel…. I knew Gwendolyn Wolf would trick you into coming here after me," he admitted. "Hell, I was expecting you to be here."

"She has to do this. There is no better way for Debbie to make sure Gwendolyn and I, are punished for the years we have been seeing each other."

"The decades that we both hid away our love and lied to the world, all for our own selfish reasons. It's been a total waste."

Daniel lowered his gun slightly and peered down at my father, who wore a stoic expression. On the table sat two small clear shot glasses with several cubes of melting ice inside. Next to the shot glasses was a half full bottle of brown cognac. My father reached down and poured cognac into the two glasses, before waving Daniel over to have a drink with him.

"I figured maybe we could talk some business and avoid this whole mass murder thing Gwendolyn sent you here for. I'm hoping me and you could make a deal, man to man."

"I didn't come here for your money buddy," Daniel began. "I'm here for revenge. The same type of revenge you and your spooks carried out against Ryan, Josh and Bill Devers."

"Your black money won't buy your way out of this nigger."

"You're wrong Daniel," I interrupted. "My father isn't trying to buy his way out of this."

"He's trying to buy you a way out of all this mess he's created. He's trying to save your life."

Daniel glanced down at me with a shit eating grin on his face. I could tell that my point had missed him. Suddenly, I felt a hammering blow strike my stomach, almost like someone had hit me with a baseball bat. I collapsed further to the floor. Falling from my knees, to plummeting flat on my back. Above me stood Daniel with his foot digging into my stomach.

"Enough of your lip you bitch," he screamed.

"Nobody is buying any of your fathers shit today. The only thing that will be bought is coffins for all you Robert Charles fuckers."

"Don't hurt her," my father boldly responded. "You hurt my daughter, and the deal is off, and we all die."

In an instant, Daniel once again pointed his gun towards my father. I could feel Daniel increasing the pressure of his foot into my stomach, as he aimed in. "Damnit old man!" He yelled. "I told your dumb black ass there will be no deals made."

"Daniel, there needs to be a deal if you want to live you white fool!" My father yelled back.

"Do you actually trust your boss Gwendolyn? Do you know who she really is Daniel?" He started in.

Daniel stood still as a blank stare dominated his face. He didn't reply to the question and the room grew uncomfortably silent. For the first time during this encounter, Daniel seemed unsure of himself. I quietly watched from the cold hard floor, as my father seized his moment.

"Do you know why she encouraged you to come here to kill me? Did you even ask yourself that question?"

"Did you ask Gwendolyn how she knew I would be here today? At this particular house?" He asked before taking a big puff of his cigar.

It was mesmerizing to watch my father work his magic. He had both Daniel and I enchanted with his every word. We both hung on his every expression and movement. He had control of the room now, he knew a secret that neither of us knew. I could feel Daniel gently ease his foot off my stomach. His face began to turn red and his eyes began to moisten. Then, in the sudden panic of realization, he jumped backwards, leaving me to lay on the floor to my own devices.

"Daniel," my father called out with a wide smile. "How did you not suspect that Gwendolyn use to be a member of Robert Charles? How did you miss that Debbie is the person behind the murders of your white partners?"

"Debbie no longer needs us, and now she has gone about the business of getting rid of old tools that she has no use for."

"No!" Daniel let out in a screeching voice. "You're full of shit boy!"

"Gwendolyn and Debbie want me dead," my father interrupted. "They want us both dead. We are of no use to them anymore."

"So, you can kill me today, but they will surely see that you are killed as well. You will be removed to wash away any proof of all the things we have both done in their name."

"If you kill us, there is no place you can run to. Hell, knowing Gwendolyn, she's probably outside waiting on you right now. Debbie and Gwendolyn are ruthless Daniel. I'm guaranteeing that they kill you before you ever see a day in court. Everything we've done will be swept under the rug."

"Freedom of White Life has a lot of likeminded friends in high places, you nigger," Daniel shot back in an angry voice. "We own New Orleans. We own Louisiana. We even own Captain Gwendolyn Wolf. She can't touch me!"

"True indeed," my father replied with a smile. "You guys own all of that, but how do you know that your likeminded racist friends haven't sold you up the river already?"

"Look at you Daniel. You're a wanted man and on the run. You know too much and they are going to kill you."

"This isn't just about race Daniel. It's about race and power."

"You my friend, are about to become a white sacrifice at the altar of Debbie's power. You are about to become the white fall guy. The infamous lone wolf."

"Since Robert Charles has exposed you. Now you're a big-time liability for your racist comrades. After all that you've done for Debbie Wolf and her family. All the years of loyalty you gave them. These bastards are going to pin these murders on you and leave you for dead."

"Gwendolyn is just taking care of Debbie's dirty work for her…. Like any good black coon would do. Just like you bastards used Kevin Longstreet, your white pals are using Gwendolyn to erase you. It's all a cycle."

"But if you don't kill us. If you instead take my money and allow me to hide you away, there is a chance that we all will live through this Daniel."

"As much as Robert Charles wants you dead for the crimes that you have committed against the black community, having you alive benefits us."

"Your presence offers a level of discomfort for my adversaries. I value that discomfort Daniel and I'm willing to pay for it."

"I am willing to protect you. Plus, I'm the only option you've got left."

"No!" Daniel shouted. "No way am I working with you damned people!"

Daniel began to back up, walking backwards towards the hallway as if he were about to make a run for it. Before entering the hallway, Daniel looked over his shoulder and suddenly stopped dead in his tracks. He went motionless as though paralyzed and too scared to move any further.

"Your partner, Bill Devers turned down this very same offer from me," my father chimed in. "He came to me pleading before he was killed. He knew your higher ups were looking to wash their hands of all the dirt we've done."

"Bill was going to sell you and Gwendolyn out. He correctly read the writing on the wall. He knew someone had to be the fall guy in all of this and he didn't want it to be him. At least not while he was alive anyway."

"But Bill dragged his feet and made a few demands I just couldn't accommodate.... I suspect his loyalty to your White Supremacist movement tugged at his little heart. So, Robert Charles continued as scheduled and there was nothing, I could do to stop it."

"And because Robert Charles did.... Bill Devers is dead."

"You don't have to make the same mistakes Daniel. You can be smarter than Bill Devers. Smarter than Gwendolyn Wolf. Smarter than Debbie Wolf."

"You can actually do the right thing for once and save your own life in the process."

Tears began to roll down Daniel's face and his gun slipped out of his hand. A loud clap rang out as the gun bounced on the marble floor. Daniel was stuck, too stunned to move or react to my father's words. The weight of the revelations he had just heard could literally be seen falling upon him. He was an abandoned soldier with no army to reinforce him or back him up. Daniel's shocked expression told me he had come to the realization that he had no one he could truly trust. My father took another puff of his cigar. The strong odor of its smoke pulsed through the room as the lit end of the cigar brightened to a hot orange with his powerful pull. While slowly exhaling, he calmly reclaimed his seat on the couch and crossed his legs, which exposed his perfectly shined black shoes and his expensive silk socks.

"Time is of the essence. We don't have all day for you to make a decision Daniel," he lamented as traces of white cigar smoke followed his every word.

"You need to decide right now."

Daniel's face turned flushed red and he zeroed in on my sitting father. I felt myself beginning to tremble as I tried to make myself speak. Gathering the words to plead with Daniel to see the logic in my father's offer and spare himself from a fate we all knew he was destined to meet. Part of me still cared for Daniel. A part of me wanted to believe that behind all his lies, selfishness and hatred, stood a person who could be redeemed.

"Daniel you have a family. You have children. Is all of this worth hurting them?"

"I'll never take any deal from you people," Daniel passionately began. "I am at war with you damn people. Either all of you black bastards die, or we all die."

"If I got to die to protect my family. So be it!"

"I will never surrender. I will never stop fighting you. I may die, but you will never conquer us. We will live forever and as long as we live, you people will be sure to suffer!"

Following Daniel's words, the unmistakable sound of a single gunshot echoed from the dark hallway. Daniel's body crumpled and fell to the floor. I saw his blood pouring from the back of his head as he laid still, motionless. His blood painted his perfectly straight brown hair, into a bright reddish ugly color. Daniel's eyes were still open, as his mouth struggled to suck in life giving air.

"Daniel!" I instinctively yelled, as I ran to his collapsed body.

Kneeling, I was able to see the extent of Daniel's mortal wound. I knew it wouldn't be long. A small stream of blood gushed from his nose as Daniel labored to breathe. I heard the familiar sounds of a body fighting for life. Then his eyes began to fade, and it finally came. Death had arrived for Daniel. For him, his hateful struggle was over and his monstrous grip on my heart vanished with his last moments of existence.

I felt the touch of a familiar hand grip my shoulder. I looked up and saw Achim Jeffers staring down at me with eyes filled with emotion.

"Step away from that bastard Jessica," he whispered. "I know you have a good heart. All this crazy shit and confusion is over. You're with me from now on."

I rose to my feet and collapsed into Achim's arms. He held me tight, driving me into his hard chest. For the first time in a long time, everything made sense. This was divine providence. Achim had come to rescue me from myself. I had gotten myself lost in this silent war. He loved me enough to seek me out and trust that I could be saved. He was a black man that valued me when I saw no value in him. He stayed with me when I tried my best to run away from him. I had been a black woman looking all over for better, only to find my better, in who I really am as a black woman. My tears changed from tears of grief to tears of thankfulness. Tears of love. Tears of undivided loyalty.

"It's okay baby," Achim whispered. "We are going to be alright; I promise. We are going to be just fine."

My father stood up from the sofa and helped my Aunt Rita sit down next to him as she held a bloody white towel to her mangled face. With tenderness, my father rubbed her back and gave her a kiss on her forehead.

"You'll be alright," he said. "We'll get you taken care of."

"You never could take care of your women Percy Darryl," a female voice said from the hallway.

Captain Wolf emerged from the dark hallway. In her hand she carried a black handgun, while she boldly walked into the living room with a confident swagger. In a fit of anger, I pushed myself free from Achim's arms and grabbed Daniel's gun from the floor.

"Captain put your gun down now or I'll lay you down like the dog you are!" I screamed with authority.

Captain Wolf looked over at me, giving me a dismissive snicker before bursting out in a full out laugh. "Darryl, you better get your damn daughter and tell her to calm her nerves," Captain Wolf declared. "Jessica is still confused. I tried to get her onboard with the program, but she's just like her mother. She is a lost cause."

"Jessica," my father said to me. "Lower the gun baby doll. Gwendolyn isn't about to do nothing to us. I got this."

Achim stepped towards me, grabbing the gun from my hands before restraining me with a tight hug. "Baby we're okay. She's not worth it Jessica. Neither of them are worth it," he whispered as he wiped the tears from my face.

"I'm sorry it had to come to this Percy Darryl," Captain Wolf said to my father. "I really am, but we don't have a choice. It's a shame it all must end like this. We had this beautiful thing going, but you and Debbie had to ruin it."

"Your still as selfish and power hungry as the day I first met you. We may be getting older, but some things between us will never change Gwendolyn," he sarcastically responded.

"They sure don't Darryl," she interrupted. "You and your little buddies decide to come after me, so I'm looking out for myself. Next time, don't send your daughter to do your dirty work."

My father laughed and stood up from the sofa before walking towards Captain Wolf. "What makes you think it was you we were after, Gwendolyn?" My father asked.

"You're small fries. You're just the white woman's Negro help. I am not concerned about you. I know who pulls your strings remember, and it's her that I want. It was her that created this mess in the first place."

Captain Wolf took several steps towards my father. She reached her hand up towards his face and affectionately rubbed his chin. My father didn't flinch nor pull back. It was almost like they both had shared history. A history that was intimately familiar.

"Are you still angry at me because of her Darryl?"

"You never understood that it was you I really loved all this time."

"You were always so sexy when you got jealous," Captain Wolf relayed with a deep gaze.

"I used to love it, now I realize that your jealousy was just a cancer for the both of us. This thing we had could never last because you would never allow it."

"Let's be honest. None of this was really about racism for us. We didn't give a damn about stolen property, gentrification, the Davis family or all these murders. This has always been you against her. Little ole Percy Darryl against the control freak Debbie Wolf."

"Oh yes," Captain Wolf explained as she stared into his eyes. "I told your protégé, Achim, everything. He knows everything about us now. He knows all about our past."

"Well," my father began. "It's good that Achim knows the truth about us. It will do him well to learn from my mistakes with you. I fell in love with you and you ruined me. For that, I have no one to blame but myself."

My father walked towards me and gave me a kiss on the cheek before looking up at Achim. "You are truly ready son."

"You made the right decisions today. You are ready for leadership in Robert Charles."

"Where I fell short, you will far exceed me as a black man."

"You knew when to choose black love over the mission. That's the kind of wisdom both Gwendolyn and I somehow lost along the way."

Tears began to flow down my father's brown face. It was the first time I had ever seen him cry. Even during my mother's months of chemotherapy and at her funeral, I had never once seen him shed a tear. I wrapped my arms around my dad, attempting to console him in his moment of regretful reflection. Forgiving him for the many empty nights he delivered to me and my mother.

"I'm retiring Gwendolyn," he announced. "I've given enough of my life to Robert Charles. I'm done being the black secret agent. You and Debbie have tortured me enough."

"Achim," my father murmured as he wiped the tears from his eyes. "I hope that you don't think any less of me, given what you have found out about me son."

"Mr. Darryl," Achim stated. "I'm disappointed as hell."

"I believed in you."

"I dedicated my life to fighting White Supremacy. I've done things in the name of justice that I will have to live with forever."

"I risked my life for what I believed in."

"Now to find out that you are working for the other side. Working for the very people I have dedicated my life to fighting…. it sickens me."

"You and Gwendolyn, the both of you are meant for each other."

Achim looked over at Rita and nodded his head at her. "Thank you, Rita. You can come with us. We are about to leave. Our work here is complete."

Achim grabbed my arm, leading me and Rita down the hallway towards the front door. "Let's get outta here Jessica," Achim ordered as we walked to a car parked at the end of the driveway.

As the front door shut behind us, I heard a loud gunshot ring out from within the house. I looked over my shoulder debating if I should return inside, as concern about the well-being of my father flooded into my spirit.

"No Jessica," Achim ordered. "Let them sort out their own problem, we have to go."

Aunt Rita put her arms around me and tenderly whispered into my ear. "Come on Jessica," she began. "Your mother made me promise to take care of you before she died, and that's what I'm going to do."

Inside the car sat a young-looking black man, nervously sweating in the front passenger seat. As we neared the car he reached down and pushed a button, unlocking the car doors for us. Achim eased me and Aunt Rita into the back seat before taking his spot behind the wheel. "Alright let's roll," Achim proclaimed with urgency as he started the car.

"How are you Jessica? I'm Anthony," the young black man stated with an accent, as he turned around in his seat to shake my hand.

Achim backed the car into the street and drove us away from the house. I could sense from the somber look on his face that my father's betrayal had hurt Achim deeply. From the back seat, I reached forward and placed my hand on his shoulder to offer him a little bit of comfort. As the car glided down the street, Achim glanced back at me and gave me a head nod before asking me a question.

"Jessica, when did you finally figure out that I worked for your father?" He asked.

"I started to suspect you worked for Robert Charles when we went on that seafood date in the Bywater," I began. "It was really clever of you to have our date at the same place Daniel would have his family outing."

"I understood the message you were trying to send, loud and clear."

"I'm glad you caught that hint," Achim replied with a grin.

"Listen, I'm sorry I had to conceal who I was from you," he continued. "I had a job to do and I believed that the job was important for our people."

"That said, this doesn't change how I feel about you Jessica. My feelings for you made this all very hard for me. I hope that you can understand that I love you and that my feelings for you are real."

"Yes, I do understand," I replied. "There are certain things you can fake, then there are certain things that can't be faked. I could tell that you were real, that your love was real."

"I trust you Achim and I felt your love."

Achim reached back towards me and embraced my hand. With a tight squeeze, he looked into my eyes with a sincere stare before returning his attention to the road ahead. It was almost like Achim had finally decided to return the knowing hand squeeze I had given him, weeks ago. My Aunt Rita let out a loud sigh before clapping her hands together. On her face was a wide beautiful smile that overpowered the ugly sight of her busted lip.

"Where Percy Darryl and Gwendolyn Wolf failed, you two will succeed," she began. "Mainly because your love for each other is real and not conflicted."

"I'm proud of you both. Robert Charles is proud of you. You two are what Robert Charles is all about. The love you share for each other will win this war for Robert Charles and Black America."

I was shocked. Aunt Rita had invoked the name Robert Charles. The look in her eyes as the name left her lips had a sense of reverence to it. I had never heard her say the name before, but simply the way she said it, signaled to me that my Aunt had something more to tell me.

"What do you know about Robert Charles Aunt Rita?" I asked. "Are you a member too?"

Once again, I felt the hand of Achim reach back from the driver's seat and touch my knee. This time, in between his fingers he held a business card with my Aunt's name printed on it.

"Here Jessica, read the back of the card," he explained. "Read it and everything will make sense to you."

I flipped over my Aunt's business card and noticed the small words scribbled in blue ink. They read: "Robert Charles will not authorize the elimination of Gwendolyn Wolf or Percy Darryl. Save Jessica Baker, and both of you sever ties with Gwendolyn Wolf and Percy Darryl permanently."

"No, I'm not a member," my Aunt replied. "But I will let you in on a little secret."

"I am one of the thirteen executives of Robert Charles."

"Not even your father knows that his little sister, was actually his big boss," Aunt Rita said with a smile.

"During my junior year in college, I and a few of my classmates befriended the descendants of a black man from Mississippi that was lynched in New Orleans on July 27, 1900."

"The vivid story they told us about Robert Charles's death and his extraordinary accolades was intoxicating for all of us. I will never forget that day, and how the story of his bravery made me feel," my Aunt explained.

"Soon after meeting his family, I was invited into the Robert Charles secret society. They needed nurses and other black professionals to round out their organization and they recruited me heavily. Personally, for me, it wasn't a hard sell. I eagerly joined and soon found myself holding a lifelong executive position."

"Around the same time, your father got himself into a bit of trouble in Memphis," she continued. "He had been arrested several times and some white folks up there nearly killed him. That's why your father walks with a cane. Your grandmother worried herself to death about Percy, so I decided to find a way to bring my brother home and keep him alive."

"Eventually, I sent a few friends of Robert Charles up to Memphis to recruit him," she explained as she smiled at me.

"He would never have come back home if he knew that his little sister had sent for him. Percy was too proud for that, but your mother was able to convince your father to start a new life with Robert Charles."

"Not long after he arrived in Baton Rouge, Percy and your mother got married."

"Percy adjusted well to life as a Robert Charles hitman, and was our best field operator."

"So, when distraught black landowners came to Robert Charles detailing incidents of stolen land and a nefarious law firm, we naturally assigned your father to the case."

"Your father was ordered to infiltrate the law firm that conned black people out of their land, by contacting and recruiting Gwendolyn into Robert Charles. We had no interest in killing Gwendolyn or her husband. They were both black and we were more concerned about the motives of Debbie and her parents."

"We understood that it was only a matter of time before Debbie and her parents would rid themselves of their black business partners once all the stolen land had been acquired. That's what racists do to their black tools and Gwendolyn's husband had entered into a state of danger that he unfortunately failed to realize."

"Little did we know that Debbie had already contrived with Gwendolyn to kill her husband, and along came your father to give them the perfect cover to do so."

"Your father and Gwendolyn began a romantic relationship shortly after he contacted her. Somewhere along the way, your father was made to believe that if he eliminated Gwendolyn's husband, both he and Gwendolyn could make off with all the money from the stolen land."

"All of this happened right after you were born Jessica."

Aunt Rita paused to put herself together, using her bloody towel to wipe away tears. It was almost like she was forced to relive her brother's painful betrayal all over again. In the front seats, I could see Achim and Anthony shaking their heads in silent frustration as they looked out of the window.

"After Gwendolyn's husband was killed," she continued. "Percy realized that he had been fooled."

"Gwendolyn never intended to elope with Percy, instead she and Debbie moved in with each other and lived in luxury. That drove your father crazy and only fueled his desire to continue chasing after her. That of course, further ruined the relationship between your mother and your father."

"Your father was a defeated man and he wore his defeat badly. Coming home to you and your mother only reminded him of what he truly was and what he could never be."

"For years, your father continued to sleep with Gwendolyn, even after her and Debbie became legal partners," Aunt Rita described.

"That's how Percy got himself involved in the Eric Davis mess. He kept hanging on to Gwendolyn and Debbie used him to intensify the gentrification of black neighborhoods in New Orleans."

"When did you begin to suspect that Mr. Darryl was helping our enemies?" Achim broke in.

A long pause fell over the car as Achim drove us towards the Westbank. Aunt Rita turned her head towards the window next to her and looked out over the Mississippi River's muddy water. After several seconds, my Aunt turned back towards me and looked into my eyes.

"I suspected your dad was working with FOWL after I lost the state senate race to Rodney Davis," she admitted. "The loss was painful for us, as it was our attempt to bring Robert Charles out of the shadows and start to gain a political foothold."

"Somehow, Rodney knew everything about my campaign. Almost like he had somebody on the inside."

"I suspected Percy was feeding Rodney information, so I kept him out of the loop. Once I started doing that, my campaign numbers improved."

"But it was too late, we lost to Rodney Davis," my Aunt said with disdain. "A man whose political fortunes were bank rolled by Debbie Wolf."

"Wow Ms. Rita," Anthony let out in shock. "State Senator Rodney Davis is funded by Debbie Wolf?"

"Yes," she replied. "Debbie controlled Rodney Davis, up until the moment he went off script and started tossing around the idea of an Anti-Gentrification Bill."

"Robert Charles found that the NOPD had formed a special task force to combat crime in the black community. Like always, these special task forces that the NOPD stands up, are completely littered with racist. Many of them are members of FOWL and other assorted White Supremacist groups. They claimed the goal of this task force was to lower the crime rate in certain wards of the city, but they just ended up increasing crime in those areas."

"Officers Daniel Fitzpatrick and Bill Devers were the two lead detectives of the task force. A task force that Gwendolyn and Debbie Wolf used to flood the streets with drugs and terrorized the black residents to the point that they sold their homes to investors, at dirt cheap prices. The whole operation was lucrative for FOWL and Debbie. Hell, even Jessica's father made money off of it."

"So, when Rodney Davis decided to stand on his own two feet and shine a light on gentrification efforts in New Orleans, he pissed off his white paymaster and Debbie Wolf conceived a plot to send him a message. FOWL setting up his nephew Eric Davis was his warning to tread lightly or be destroyed."

"What about the murders of Thomas and Jeffery Roberts?" I asked. "I found mountains of records that show the task force monitoring them. Why were Bill and Daniel targeting the two brothers?"

Aunt Rita paused again, this time her eyes were fixed to mine and her gaze grew cold and detached. I could almost feel her considering whether to tell me the truth. Something had hurt my Aunt Rita and she was reliving it all in her mind. Then I heard the voice of Achim ring out and provide me the answer.

"Jessica," he began. "The Roberts brothers were members of Robert Charles. They were ordered down here from Chicago, to detail the illegal activities of the task force."

"They reported directly to your father. Unfortunately, Mr. Darryl betrayed them and gave FOWL the scoop on the two brothers in an attempt to protect Gwendolyn. They never had a chance," Achim explained while holding up a beaten brown folder. "The Roberts brothers were targeted by NOPD. When the time was right, Debbie approved their murders and the four white FOWL bastards pinned their deaths on Eric Davis for good measure."

"She took care of two birds with one stone. Effectively neutering Robert Charles while putting a leash on Rodney Davis," Achim conveyed.

"So, killing all these White Supremacists was some sort of revenge Achim?" I asked.

"No," Aunt Rita interjected. "Not exactly."

"A few years ago, Rodney Davis approached lawyers who represented us and asked Robert Charles for assistance. He said he wanted to get his nephew out of prison and clear his name, but we knew that wasn't the real reason he came to us."

"Rodney was preparing to run for Congress and there is no better publicity than a comeback story, wrapped in redemption. For Rodney Davis, the NOPD would play the role of Goliath to his David."

"He came to our lawyers with fingerprint evidence that tied FOWL members Josh McRoberts and Ryan Foster to the Roberts brother's crime scene. We reviewed it and found it to be credible."

"Rodney begged us to help him," she detailed. "He offered to pay us handsomely for our services."

"We knew Rodney Davis was trying to run for Congress and that this publicity stunt would land him on the front pages of the newspapers again. We also knew that Debbie was still filling his campaign coffers. It was clear to see that she had sent Rodney to us, but we were unsure why Debbie was turning on her White Supremacist partners in crime, to advance the political career of a bootlicking black politician."

"Then it dawned on me what she was doing," Aunt Rita continued. "Debbie was cutting her losses and moving on."

"At this point, the historically Black neighborhoods in New Orleans had been totally gentrified. There was no need to have FOWL members selling drugs and creating crime in white neighborhoods. White America already has a huge opioid problem. If you believe in promoting White Supremacy, then selling cheap heroine to white hipsters isn't going to help you."

"But FOWL didn't see it that way," Achim broke in.

"As an organization, they made tons of profits from running crime in the black neighborhoods and they were hard pressed to stop making money just because liberal white folks were showing up to buy their dope. Daniel and Bill stopped selling drugs and robbing black people, but they allowed Ryan and Josh to continue on with those practices," Achim explained.

"Debbie and Gwendolyn needed to find a way to stop them. FOWL's drug trafficking was negatively affecting property value in newly gentrified white neighborhoods. FOWL's drug profits were hurting Debbie's bottom line."

Now it all made sense. I remembered the night Daniel and I were at the Kevin Longstreet murder scene. Captain Wolf was initially concerned about a mole within the NOPD that had leaked vital details about Kevin Longstreet being an informant. Given all that had been revealed to me, I was now certain that Captain Wolf was in fact the mole. The day I was sexually assaulted, Captain Wolf had threatened me. Sending me the not so veiled threat that if I connected the murders of Kevin Longstreet and Ryan Foster to the NOPD, she would expose my affair with Daniel. Now, I knew why she had done that. It wasn't about some ideal of police loyalty; it was about power.

As Achim exited off the expressway and drove us into the small town of Harvey, Louisiana, I could not help but to wonder why Debbie had decided not to use my father to kill the FOWL members.

"Why didn't Debbie or Gwendolyn just tell my father to kill the FOWL members?" I asked my Aunt. "Why go through all the trouble and have Rodney Davis contact Robert Charles?"

"Because Debbie was finally cleansing herself of your father too," Aunt Rita added.

"Yes, Achim is correct. This was most certainly business for Debbie Wolf, but it was also so much more. This was personal for her. Debbie had played the long game and now it was time to cash in her chips and eliminate your father."

"For years, your father and Gwendolyn had been sleeping around with each other, while Debbie watched in silence. No matter how much Debbie tried to separate the two of them, their love for each other always brought them back together. Debbie finally came to realize that no matter how hard she tried; she could never quell a black woman's desire to be with a black man."

"That drove her crazy. Debbie could control almost everything about Gwendolyn's life, except the love that was in her heart," my Aunt opined.

"Now that Percy was no longer needed, Debbie wanted to eliminate him for good, and in her mind, there was no better instrument to do away with your father than Robert Charles itself."

"Was Debbie trying to eliminate two birds with one stone again?" Anthony asked as Achim pulled into a raggedly looking storage facility.

"Yes," Achim answered. "Except this time, she miscalculated badly."

"Debbie believed when we found out that Mr. Darryl had betrayed us and worked with FOWL, we would murder him for his betrayal. She believed that we were as cold blooded as she was."

"She was not just wrong about that, she was naïve," Achim stated confidently.

"Robert Charles was also playing the long game with Debbie," Achim relayed.

"Per the orders of your Aunt Rita," he continued. "We had no intentions of killing Gwendolyn and Mr. Darryl.

"Debbie Wolf was our focus all along, and now we have all we need to take her down for good," he stated as he pointed at a storage unit.

Achim parked in front of the storage unit entrance and reached into his pocket to pull out a set of keys. "Come on Anthony, let's go grab a few things," he ordered.

Achim and Anthony left the car and lifted open the storage unit door. Aunt Rita and I watched as both men rummaged around until they found a small cardboard box before walking back to the car.

"What do you have in there Achim?" My Aunt asked.

With a smile on his face, Achim cranked up the car before opening the box and allowing us to peer inside. "In this box, I have God's justice" he began with a chuckle.

"Jessica, your friend Bill Devers didn't trust women, and that included Debbie Wolf. It seems he liked to keep records of everything to protect himself."

"Before I killed him, he told me that Mr. Darryl had attempted to make a deal with him. I suspect Mr. Darryl and Gwendolyn knew he had records and wanted to use the records against Debbie for themselves. There is no honor amongst thieves, especially when thieves are secretly in love with each other."

"Anthony was able to get me a copy of his house keys, so before I killed Bill, I took the opportunity to sneak into his home and grab a few things."

"This box contains incriminating evidence of Bill Devers communicating with Debbie and Gwendolyn Wolf about houses she needed to buy. Houses that were owned by black families. Black owned houses that would eventually be raided by the NOPD or targeted by FOWL to be robbed."

"All of the targeted houses were sold below market value. Once Debbie's corporation bought and remodeled them, many of them were resold at ten times the price they were originally purchased. Debbie and FOWL made a ton of money and no one was the wiser. Black families lost everything and were given pennies on the dollar as far as value."

"Now, it's time we correct that injustice," Achim passionately stated.

"Ms. Rita, our plan will be to support the election of Rodney Davis to Congress. When he is elected, Anthony will pay Debbie a visit on behalf of Robert Charles and issue her and Rodney a few demands."

"Policy demands, property demands and of course monetary demands."

"So, we own her now," Aunt Rita said with a laugh.

"Yes, Aunt Rita, we do. We have power. Either she meets our demands, or we destroy her like we did Daniel Fitzpatrick and Bill Devers," Achim added.

"What about my father and Gwendolyn?" I asked.

"What about them," Achim dismissively answered. "They will be fine."

"As much as she may have wanted Mr. Darryl dead, Debbie won't try to kill him anymore because Debbie will soon find out that she still needs Mr. Darryl, more then she thinks. She will soon be more worried about Gwendolyn divorcing her for Mr. Darryl and taking half of everything she has."

Achim grabbed his cellphone and opened a recording app before pressing the play button. The phone blasted the shaken voice of Captain Gwendolyn Wolf detailing how a jealous Debbie Wolf had threatened to kill her if she continued to sleep with Percy Darryl. Gwendolyn explained that Debbie Wolf was physically abusive and gave accounts on how Debbie would emotionally torture Gwendolyn if she failed to obey her. Achim pressed the pause button and looked back at Aunt Rita with a smile.

"After my long conversation with Gwendolyn Wolf today, I suspect that Debbie will have a change of heart. Who the hell knows how their deadly love triangle will come to an end," Achim elaborated?

It all made sense now. Debbie had counted on using Captain Wolf's greed and thirst for power to her advantage, as she had done before. This time it backfired. My father and Captain Wolf had both made a world of mistakes and betrayed Robert Charles. Both were insatiably selfish. They had used their blackness for themselves and ignored the community. Yet, they both seemed to have found a way to help turn the tables on Debbie Wolf. As the car grew silent, I looked over at my now smiling Aunt Rita and I intuitively knew it was all because of her. Robert Charles had somehow gotten to them. Maybe they chose their love for each other over their greed, or maybe it was as simple as them choosing to live instead of being killed by Achim. Either way, my smiling Aunt remained quiet about the truth, surely enjoying her victory alone in her own world as she gazed out of the car window.

"Debbie Wolf is literally trapped," Aunt Rita stated out of nowhere with a giggle. "After all these years of Debbie being one step ahead of us, Robert Charles has finally turned the tables on her racist ass."

Achim drove us back to New Orleans and we arrived at a towering hotel near the Mississippi River. He pulled the car up to the front entrance and parked near the valet stand. A black gentleman in uniform slowly walked up to the driver side and Achim lowered the window.

"Reservation for Achim Jeffers?" He instructed. "Penthouse Suite."

The valet instantly snapped to attention and opened the door for Achim. "Mr. Jeffers, yes sir. We will take good care of you tonight," the valet dutifully remarked. Achim popped the trunk before stepping out of the car and opening my door.

"You're with me beautiful," he stated, looking straight into my eyes. "I've got something special planned for you tonight. Anthony and Ms. Rita are leaving us here."

Achim offered his hand and helped me out of my seat. The Bellmen approached us and Achim leaned over and whispered to him. Anthony slid behind the wheel and cranked up the car as the Bellman unloaded several items out of the trunk.

"I love you Jessica," Aunt Rita said with tears in her eyes. "Your mother would be so happy for you right now. I wish she was here to see this."

I leaned back into the car and hugged her. We both held each other and shared tears in the heartfelt moment. Never had I been so thankful to have Aunt Rita in my life. I remember the childhood feelings I had as my father left me with her that day. The emotions of abandonment and confusion that I felt as my father tried to convince me that this was the best thing for me. Now, I understood God's why, and felt his blessings.

I closed the passenger door and we both watched Anthony and Ms. Rita drive off. Achim grabbed my hand and led me to the hotel lobby. As soon as Achim and I walked through the large glass doors, I immediately felt the ice-cold air swarm all over me inside the lobby. Achim knowingly wrapped his arms around me as the bellmen jetted in front of us to find an open elevator. After a few frantic seconds, the nervous bellmen found one and pressed the button.

"Sorry for the inconvenience Mr. Jeffers," he blurted out.

"No problem young man. Just chill. We're good," Achim reassured him.

The elevator doors opened, and the Bellman ushered us inside before hitting the button for the top floor. Long seconds passed as the elevator rocketed upwards toward our destination. Finally, our ride to the heavens came to a sudden stop and the doors split open. Achim led the way as we all walked to the front door of the suite with its gold-plated door handle. He unlocked the door and with a cute smile he held it open for me.

"Ladies first," he stated.

I walked in and saw the beautiful red rose pedals that were littered near the doorway. The room was scented with a sweet fragrance, and on the dining room table sat a large gift wrapped with a powder blue bow. The décor of the room was gorgeous, and the panoramic view of the Mississippi River was awe inspiring.

"Go ahead," Achim encouraged. "Go open your present."

I walked over to the table and tore open the box. Inside was my NOPD badge, two airline tickets to Cartagena, and a letter that was signed by my Aunt. The letter read: There is a reason I wanted you to be a cop Jessica. Don't give up on your dream. Where Gwendolyn failed, you will succeed for us. Your job will be waiting on you when you return from your vacation. Robert Charles needs to have you in the belly of the beast because you are one of us. You and Achim enjoy the Presidential Suite together. Robert Charles is indebted to you both forever, as is the Black Community. By the way, your apartment wasn't ransacked, I just had a few friends pack away some of your things for you. I took the liberty of packing two bags for you so you and Achim can enjoy this week with each other. If you need the rest of your stuff, just give me a call and I'll have it delivered to your suite. Love Aunt Rita.

The bellman pushed his buggy inside the suite and unloaded four luggage bags. Achim gave him a hundred bucks and the young bellmen's face exploded with an enthusiastic yet grateful smile.

"Mr. Jeffers, there is a bottle of natural apple juice and a fifth of Jack in the fridge just like you asked. Would you like me to mix a drink for you sir?"

Achim looked at the young man dead in his eyes and smiled. "No, that's quite alright. I can fix that myself. I've gotten pretty good at making that drink."

The bellmen walked out of the room and closed the door behind him, leaving Achim and I alone in the Presidential Suite. Achim walked up to me with a wide smile and embraced me with a tight hug before giving me a soft kiss on the forehead.

"Come with me, I want to share something special with you.", He said as he grabbed my hand.

Achim led me towards the large panel windows, where he stood behind me and held me close. The view was amazing. Before us was the beautiful city of New Orleans. We silently watched as the Mississippi River flowed southwards, savoring the moment as we shared it with each other. Scores of cars and people filled the streets and walkways below us. All while I watched from above, almost like I was a Goddess.

"It was right here, at this exact spot, that I knew that I was in love with you Jessica." Achim explained. "I couldn't enjoy this type of beauty without you here next to me."

Feeling overwhelmed with emotion, I leaned up towards his lips and we began to kiss. For at least one night, there would be no war for the both of us. Just black love.

Author & President of Spirit of 1811 Publishing LLC

Josiah J. Starr established Spirit of 1811 Publishing in 2019 in order to promote an agenda of empowerment within the Black Community through black owned and controlled media. He is a staunch proponent of black ownership and economic empowerment. Born to a military family in Erlangon Germany, Josiah was well traveled as a young child before ultimately settling down in the small town of Homer, Louisiana. Upon graduating High School, Josiah earned an athletic scholarship and attended Southern University in Shreveport for two years. After moving to Baton Rouge he earned a Bachelor of Arts Degree from Southern A&M University. After college, Josiah served in the United States Coast Guard as a Commissioned Officer. In the Coast Guard stationed aboard several USCG cutters and served in Bahrain, Kuwait and Iraqi during Operation Enduring Freedom.

After his military service Josiah decided to continue to follow his passion for traveling the world's oceans and earned his Merchant Mariner's license. He currently operates vessels in the Bering Sea, Gulf of Alaska, Pacific Ocean, Caribbean and Gulf of Mexico. Josiah is the husband to the lovely Brittani Starr and the father of his young son Azariah J. Starr. Josiah is the son of John Henry and Naomi Starr and the brother of Johnnie, Marcus, Jeremiah and Jedidiah Starr.

Follow Spirit of 1811 Publishing on Instagram, Facebook, Twitter and TikTok. Visit our website at www.spiritof1811publishing.com and sign up for books specials, newsletter updates and exclusive offers.

Author's "Playlist" while writing
War of the Heart

- "War of the Hearts", Sade, Promises
- "Your Love is King", Sade. Promises
- "Still Dreaming", Nas Featuring Kanye West, Hip Hop Is Dead
- "If I", Foxy Brown, Ill na..na
- "Where Ya Heart At", Mobb Deep, Murda Muzik
- "No Thing On Me (Cocaine Song)", Curtis Mayfield, Superfly
- "The World Is A Ghetto", War
- "Black Moses", Meek Mill & Pusha T, Birth Of A Nation Soundtrack
- "Love T.K.O", Teddy Pendergrass
- "Giving You All My Love", Carl Thomas, Emotional
- "The Soundtrack", The Game, 1992
- "Ghetto In The Sky", Master P, Only God Can Judge Me
- "City Lights" Mink Slide
- "Corazon Poetico"
- "Come Live With Me Angel", Marvin Gaye, I Want You
- "Band Practice", 9th Wonder, The Wonder Years
- "LetMeRideSoul!!!!!", 9th Wonder, Tutankhamen
- "Undying Love", Nas, I Am
- "Ghetto Life", Master P, MP Da Last Don
- "Bring It On", Jay-Z, Reasonable Doubt
- "On Top Of The World", 8Ball & MJG, On Top Of The World
- "In The Line Of Duty", 8Ball & MJG, On Top Of The World
- "Comin Up", 8Ball & MJG, On Top Of The World
- "Use Me Up", UGK, Too Hard To Swallow
- "Touched", UGK, Ridin Dirty
- "Tha Blues", Lil Wayne, Lights Out
- "G.O.D Part III", Mobb Deep, Hell On Earth
- "Back In The Day", Erykah Badu, Worldwide Underground
- "Losin Weight" Cam'ron Featuring Prodigy, S.D.E
- "Do You Wanna Chill", Michael Watts, Texas Ballers (Screwed/Chopped)
- "Kiss of Life", Sade, Love Deluxe
- "Wish I Didn't Miss You", Angie Stone, Mahogany Soul
- "Where There Is Love", Patrice Rushen

- "Pink Cookies In A Plastic Bag (Remix)", LL Cool J
- "Mama Say", Spectac & 9th Wonder
- "Neon" Dam Fuck
- "We On" Gemstones Featuring Lupe Fiasco
- "Gonna Be Alright", P.K.O., Tha Good, Tha Bad, Tha Mafia
- "You Can't Stop The Reign" Shaq Ft. The Notorious B.I.G (Screwed/Chopped)
- "Its For You", Shanice
- "Us Placers", Lupe Fiasco
- "Welcome To New New York", Cam'ron
- "Can't Forget About You", Nas
- "Verbal Intercourse", Raekwon Ft. Nas
- "2nd Childhood", Nas, Stillmatic
- "The Message", Nas, It Was Written
- "It Ain't Hard To Tell", Nas Illmatic
- "Mama Knows", The Game ft. Nelly Furtado
- "Why My Homie", Silkk The Shocker, The Shocker
- "Ain't Gonna See Tomorrow", Mystikal, Let's Get Ready
- "The Light", David Banner & 9th Wonder, Death of a Pop Star
- "True To The Game", Ice Cube, Death Certificate

CPSIA information can be obtained
at www.ICGtesting.com
Printed in the USA
LVHW052116220221
679631LV00005B/236